"I will public[…] I have chosen my bride.

"You need only make up some reason as to why you cannot wed with me—perhaps you don't love me, after all?"

"Of course I don't love you!" Claire protested. What a ludicrous notion! How could she love a man she didn't even know? "I've only met you twice!" she pointed out reasonably.

"Three times," Ian corrected her. "And that's enough to establish at least an attraction, don't you think so?"

Claire gasped softly. "I am *not* the least bit attracted to you, I assure you!"

"Are you not?" he asked.

Claire's heart did a telltale flip against her breast. She was horribly afraid he might feel it, as well. "Not at all!" she lied.

He grinned wickedly, as though somehow he knew differently. "Pity," he said. "Because I'm *quite* attracted to you…!"

* * *

The Impostor Prince

Harlequin® Historical #818—September 2006

Praise for Tanya Anne Crosby

"With remarkable insight and soul-stirring emotions, Ms. Crosby…gives readers an enthralling glimpse into the human heart."
—*Romantic Times BOOKclub* on *The MacKinnon's Bride*

"With her talent for spinning engrossing yarns and painting vivid characters and setting, Ms. Crosby will again capture your heart."
—*Romantic Times BOOKclub* on *Perfect in My Sight*

TANYA ANNE CROSBY

The Impostor Prince

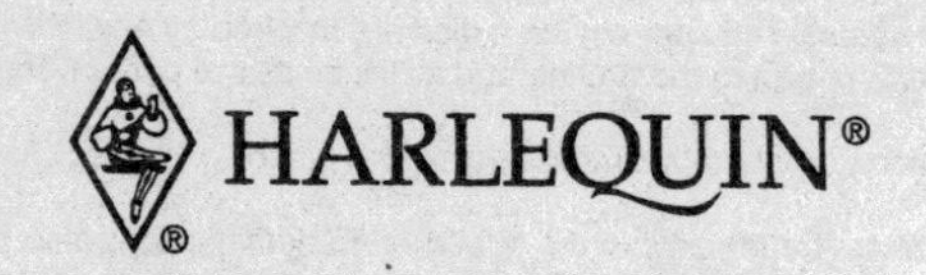

TORONTO • NEW YORK • LONDON
AMSTERDAM • PARIS • SYDNEY • HAMBURG
STOCKHOLM • ATHENS • TOKYO • MILAN • MADRID
PRAGUE • WARSAW • BUDAPEST • AUCKLAND

ISBN-13: 978-0-373-29418-3
ISBN-10: 0-373-29418-2

THE IMPOSTOR PRINCE

This edition published by arrangement with Harlequin Books S.A.

www.eHarlequin.com

Printed in U.S.A.

Available from Harlequin® Historical and
TANYA ANNE CROSBY

The Impostor's Kiss #683
The Impostor Prince #818

The Impostor Prince features characters you will have already met in

The Impostor's Kiss.

DON'T MISS THESE OTHER NOVELS AVAILABLE NOW:

#815 MISTAKEN MISTRESS
Margaret McPhee

#816 ABDUCTED AT THE ALTAR
Charlene Sands

#817 THE GLADIATOR'S HONOR
Michelle Styles

Prologue

Northern Scotland, 1831

Ready to strike when the leader gave the word, seven men watched from their perches within the trees as the unfamiliar vehicle approached—for the third time.

They needed this loot, but something about the closed carriage left the leader ill at ease. Though unmarked, it was far too luxurious to leave itself so vulnerable.

Either the occupant was foolish or lost…or the carriage was bait to catch a thief.

Ian MacEwen cupped his hand over his mouth to call out a signal, but indecision froze his lips. Twice before he'd let it pass, but the carriage's presence was like a frosted pitcher of ale set before a thirsting man. It didn't matter that it might be laced with poison; its sparkling contents were tempting beyond reason.

"His direction's as bad as me Minny's haggis," remarked one of his men.

"A week ago, I'd 'a given the use of my cock for that haggis," commented another, almost too quietly to be heard.

But everyone heard.

No one answered.

What did one say to a man who'd lost his youngest daughter to a battle against hunger? Almost three years old, Ana had been her name—sweet and shy, with little red curls and a button nose. Everyone understood why Rusty Broun was here tonight. He had three more little birds waiting at home with their mouths open wide and their bellies as empty as Glen Abbey's coffers.

"Trust me," Ian said to his men.

And he knew they would.

They followed him blindly, consumed with hope. Good men, all of them. They'd leave this place if they could, but where would they go? To London to feed off sewer scraps? Who would take them in with their wives and their bairns?

No, he had to do something. But what?

Silence was his answer, a ponderous, weighted silence that trampled heavily over bracken and snapped twigs below.

Anticipation was as thick as the lowering fog.

As yet, they hadn't killed for their loot, but tonight...they might be forced to wield their weapons if the approaching vehicle was a trap.

Someone could die.

How many more children would die without their aid? The image of little Ana's suffering face spurred his decision once and for all. He called out the signal for his men to strike.

Let consequences fall where they may.

"Kiak-kiak-keiek-keiek!"

Within the instant, the carriage was beneath them.

Ian was the first to descend.

Drawing the black hooded mask down over his face, he landed cleanly upon the rooftop. Before the driver could shout, he had his blade at the Asian's throat. Rusty Broun came down behind him, motioning for Ian to move below into the carriage. His blade replaced Ian's at the driver's throat. The rest of his men dropped to the ground, surrounding the vehicle, barring its path through the woods. Forced to slow down, the carriage careened sharply. Ian nearly lost his grip, but swung back and managed to open the door.

Stunned by what he saw inside, he dropped to the ground, staring stupidly at the occupant.

All thought of highway robbery vanished.

It was like staring into a looking glass.

His hesitation cost him a jab in the jaw.

Ignoring the bone-splitting pain, he sprang into action and flung himself into the carriage, hurling the stranger backward and knocking the blade from his hand. The knife flew upward, smacked the rooftop and ricocheted downward, skimming the man's head, drawing blood.

The carriage bolted into movement.

Ian struggled, pinning his opponent to the floorboard, slamming his head down. He tried to tell the man to stop so that he could remove his mask and reveal himself, but the man fought like a lion.

Frustrated, Ian slammed his head down into the man's face. "Stop!" he commanded.

Finally, the stranger ceased struggling long enough to allow Ian to reach up and snatch the hood from his face.

For an interminable moment, he stared down into uncannily familiar eyes.

Bloody hell—the man could have been his twin.

It just wasn't possible. "Who are you?" Ian demanded, confused.

"Who are you?" the man countered. Without warning, he bucked, renewing his struggles. Ian had little choice but to head-butt the fool again, but the devil hang him if he'd meant to butt so hard.

The man's eyes rolled back into his head and he ceased struggling at once, going limp. Ian checked for a pulse and exhaled in relief when he found it strong. There wasn't much time before the man regained consciousness.

Blast it all, what was he supposed to do now?

Certain it was no coincidence that they shared the same face, he snatched off his hood and jerked the man up to quickly remove his coat, waistcoat and shirt. He switched shirts with the man while the carriage thundered over uneven terrain, drew his own hood over the man's head, then shrugged into the man's coat, leaving the waistcoat for later. He opened the door and yelled for the driver to stop.

The man complied at once, and Ian dragged the former occupant of the carriage out onto the grass and laid him down.

"You are not dead yet, *denka-sama,*" an unfamiliar voice remarked, unmistakable relief in his tone.

Ian peered up at the driver. Somehow, the little bugger had managed to escape Rusty's blade.

Ian didn't respond immediately.

The shouts of his men were coming nearer now.

They would find the man, he was certain, and whether the stranger revealed himself, or not, Rusty would know what to do with him.

"Let us return home, *denka-sama?*" the foreigner asked. "We should never have come here."

Home.

That's where the answers to Ian's questions lay waiting to be discovered. Somehow he knew it. Still, he stared down at the hooded stranger, undecided.

"He is alive?" the driver asked.

"Alive as you and me."

"Then let us go quickly!" the driver persisted. "No good can come of this now!"

"Over there!" he heard Rusty Broun shout in the distance.

His men gave a frenzied battle cry, and he knew they'd been discovered.

"Go!" Ian ordered the man, bounding into the carriage.

At once, the driver whipped the horses into motion.

He didn't even give a backward glance as they sped away. There would be no turning back.

Instinctively, Ian knew the answers to Glen Abbey's troubles lay at the end of their destination.

Chapter One

One week later

The door to the pawnbroker's stood slightly ajar, beckoning the wary. A swinging wooden sign read: Money Advanced On Jewels, Wearing Apparel And Every Description Of Property.

The large display window held but a meager sampling of the wares offered within. Today's teasers included a distinguished-looking portrait of someone's grandfather with a pipe dangling from his lips, a few prayer books, a mismatched set of spoons displayed fan-style and a multitude of brooches.

Claire Wentworth stood outside the little shop, clutching the heavy wooden box that contained her grandmother's fine silverware. Hesitating before going inside, she stared into the display window, examining an old brooch. The brooch, too, had belonged to her grandmother, along with one of the prayer books stacked atop a pyramid-style display. Claire hadn't been able to redeem them, and now the items sat awaiting a new owner.

It couldn't be helped.

Her brother was all she had left in this world. No amount of money or possessions could compensate for his death. The silverware could be replaced, she decided. Whatever memories they inspired were hers to keep, despite their loss.

But there was only one Ben.

Resolved, she took a deep breath and pushed open the whitewashed door, stepping into the now all-too-familiar shop. As the sign promised, inside were all manner of wares: furnishings, tapestries, snuffboxes, jewelry, blankets, an assortment of dusty hats, clothing and just about anything else one might imagine, including a heavy old sword that must have been wielded by somebody's noble ancestor in some ancient battle. Its hilt was worn to the wood and the blade bore the scars of many blows—someone's history sold for the price of a week's rent. The thought of it sickened Claire, but such was life and there was no use bemoaning her circumstances.

No prayer or rueful wish could change the facts: Their father's death had left them in debt. Ben had intended to honor those debts, but he'd chosen to do so by gambling away the remainder of the estate and he'd ended up in far worse trouble than debtor's prison.

Now, it was up to Claire to rectify the situation.

Making her way toward the privacy closets, she passed through the common shop, choosing the compartment second to the end. (The last one was, apparently, occupied because the door was closed.) Once inside, she bolted the door, feeling safer even though she knew that was an illusion. With a sigh, she heaved the silverware box onto the counter to await the clerk.

At least four gas lamps lit the dust-filled shop, but none of their dusky light reached the privacy closets, which were open only to the counter. The goods offered here were cast in shadow, along with the faces of their owners. Either the occupants were ashamed of their circumstances or they were thieves peddling ill-gotten wares.

The clerk was occupied with someone in the last stall. That door had been closed, or Claire would have chosen it instead. The occupant of the darkest little closet was weeping softly. Fortunately, the clerk on duty seemed the most compassionate of the three—Claire recognized his voice—and he spoke to the girl gently.

"What name shall I write?"

The girl paused. Claire imagined she swallowed before answering. The first time Claire had ventured in here, she'd been unable to find her voice.

"Sarah…Sarah Jones."

Claire didn't recognize the name. But then, she hadn't used her true name, either.

Once released into the shop's inventory, Claire's possessions would be lost forever. Even if she could manage to raise the funds, she wouldn't raise them in time to redeem her belongings, of that much she was quite certain.

"Your own property?" the clerk interrogated.

It was an obligatory question, but Claire doubted it

was a true concern for the shop owner. She'd noted the shady sorts who frequented the shop, and not once had a clerk requested proof of ownership from Claire. For all the clerk knew, Claire might have stolen the items from an employer.

The girl's reply was soft. "Yes, of course."

"Three shillings," the clerk offered.

Claire wondered what the girl was selling.

The girl gasped, clearly affronted. "But, sir! This is fine—"

"Three and six," the clerk snapped, and Claire recognized the finality in his tone.

"Please...take a look at the stitching," the girl argued. "The gown was purchased from one of London's finest—"

"*My* patrons won't pay more," the clerk interrupted, unimpressed. "Three and six—take it or leave it."

Silence.

He wouldn't offer more. Claire had sold the man enough by now to recognize when negotiations were over. He would stand silently, his face an emotionless mask, waiting for the decision to be made.

"Very well," the girl relented, sounding defeated. "Three and six."

As though he had expected her decision, Claire heard the clerk count out the coins at once. The compartment door opened and closed and the girl's footfalls hurried away. Claire waited patiently, knowing her position in this gloomy place. Here, the shopkeeper ruled and the genteel were no more respected than the downtrodden.

Fortunately, she didn't have long to wait. The clerk

appeared at once, his graying hair hanging over thick, dirty glasses. He brushed his greasy bangs aside and gave her a nod, recognizing her. And well he should; he owned nearly half her possessions by now. With a heavy heart, Claire lifted the latch of the box, then the lid, revealing the precious contents.

"Splendid!" he exclaimed, dispensing with formalities. He gave her an assessing glance. "And you're quite certain you wish to part with it?"

Claire shrugged.

She wasn't certain about anything except that she was in a terrible pinch.

He seemed to think about it a moment, and then offered, "Eight guineas."

Claire's gaze snapped upward. "Eight guineas!" she repeated, aghast.

Whatever pleasure the clerk had expressed at seeing her offering now vanished behind his mask.

Claire arched a brow, knowing better than to bait him, but she couldn't help herself. She had at least a shred of pride left. "Surely you mean eight guineas *just* for the box, sirrah!" The box alone was worth far more, as the lid was inlaid with ivory.

The man smiled, amused, though he shouldn't have been. Claire was hardly in the frame of mind to be entertaining.

"Nah. I'm overstocked on silverware as it is—be rid of the lot. Eight guineas it is."

Claire tried to reason with him. "But these are pure silver!" she explained, laying a hand protectively over her grandmother's heirlooms.

His mask didn't crack.

Claire used the clerk's own bargaining tactic against him. She remained silent, waiting for him to speak, realizing that the first to open his mouth would be the one to lose.

It didn't work quite as well as she'd hoped.

"Bah!" the clerk exclaimed. "Silver isn't worth as much as it once was. Nine guineas is my final offer."

Claire narrowed her eyes at him. "Nine guineas wouldn't buy me a hat and a blessed pair of shoes!" she informed him tautly, slamming down the lid. A lady didn't use vulgarities, she knew, but she couldn't help herself. "No thank you, sir!" she said with as much aplomb as she could muster and, with some effort, lifted the box from the counter, fully prepared to lug it the entire distance home. For that insulting price, she'd take the silver to her grave! Nine guineas wouldn't put a dent in the remaining one hundred-fifty thousand pounds she owed for Ben's ransom.

"Be seein' you," the clerk said a little smugly.

Claire was so furious she didn't even bid him farewell. Seething, she marched through the common shop and right out the door, tears of frustration pricking at her lids.

What was she supposed to do now?

She was down to her last possessions and still she hadn't raised nearly enough money to cover Ben's debts. To some, two hundred thousand pounds might not seem like much, but she had scarce more than fifty thousand now after selling nearly *everything* she owned. The remaining one hundred and fifty thousand pounds seemed quite impossible.

Lord, but it was a dreary day—as dreary as her mood.

Cursing the mist, Claire started home, preoccupied with her thoughts. As she reached the corner of Drury Lane, sensing a presence at her back, she turned to find a stranger about twenty paces behind her, his focus settled unmistakably upon her box. Looking sinister in his dark overcoat and wide-rimmed hat, he strode with terrifying purpose toward her. Alarmed, Claire quickened her pace.

Could he be one of Ben's captors, following her to make certain she complied with their demands?

More likely, it was just some petty thief.

She tried to remember whether she had spied the man in the pawnbroker's shop, but there had been no else one inside she could recall except the weeping girl and the clerk.

Had the man followed her *to* the shop and waited outside while she took her business inside?

No, Claire didn't think so. She hadn't noticed him before now, and as suspicious as she was becoming, she doubted she would have missed him.

Her heart skipped a beat.

He could have already been inside the pawnbroker's shop—perhaps in one of the privacy closets. He would have been able to overhear everything she had been saying. Nine guineas might not be motivation enough for her to sell her grandmother's fine silver, but she was quite certain a thief wouldn't care about its real or sentimental value. If he could get the nine guineas from the pawnbroker, that would certainly be motivation enough.

Or had the pawnbroker set the man upon her? She trusted no one these days. It behooved her to remain wary.

The mist turned to rain. She could almost hear the man's footfalls behind her, but she was afraid to turn around. Her breath caught painfully in her lungs as she hurried through the crowd.

Please God—don't let him be after me! she prayed silently, and thought perhaps the sound of his footfalls ebbed. It was difficult to tell with the rain pattering down on her head. Her hair must be a horrid mess by now—her curls were stuck to her face.

Calm down, Claire, she commanded herself. *Think clearly.*

Maybe he wasn't following her after all? Maybe it was just her imagination? She was beginning to see conspirators on every corner.

She cursed Ben's infernal gambling habits and said a quick prayer that he was well—wherever he might be. She hadn't actually spoken to him since the morning he'd gone missing. She had only his captor's word that he was alive and well.

She had considered hiring a private investigator, but how would she pay the man? And even if they were able to find Ben and free him, there would be no guarantee the criminals wouldn't come after him again. He would still owe them the money, after all.

Rain pelted her and she spit a few strands of hair away from her lips. Lord, she should have kept at least one good hat. Weaving through the mob, she ducked beneath umbrellas, clutching the box of silver to her breast as she looked about for a hansom. To her dismay, there were none to be found.

At the moment, she heartily regretted not taking the

one remaining phaeton, despite the fact that it was nearly in shambles and that she'd never handled one. It was a long way to Grosvenor Square and certainly too far to have to dodge footpads in the pouring rain. For all the fine talk about the new Metropolitan Police force, where was a bobby when you needed one?

Chapter Two

The journey to London should have taken longer, but they'd flown through town after town, stopping only when exhaustion demanded it.

After staring at the blue-velvet interior of the coach for a week, Ian was anxious for a bed, a bath and a fresh change of clothing—in just that order.

They were in London, at last, and despite his weariness, a sense of anticipation enveloped him. The answers he sought were near at hand.

He peered out the window at the passing throng of people and a sea of black umbrellas. If the sun had ever truly made an appearance in this dingy town, it was fleeing now, retreating swiftly behind soot-covered buildings as the black, unmarked carriage emerged into the city.

He'd been to London only once, as a youth of seventeen, but it hadn't changed much in the eleven years since. The streets were still littered with people and the Thames was as rank as ever. Even at a distance, he could smell its unmistakable stink. It was a mystery to Ian what drew people to this squalid city. Already, he craved the fresh Scottish air and the rolling hillside of Glen Abbey. He wasn't made for city life and didn't plan to be here long—no longer than it would take to settle his bloody affairs.

Sinking back into the seat, he drew out the letter he'd discovered in his newly acquired coat pocket and read it again, carefully, digesting the information.

My dearest Fiona,

Obviously, it was a letter to his mother. But the writer must have known her intimately to address the letter so informally.

Please accept my sympathies on the loss of your father.

Evidently, it was written sometime after his grandfather's death.

He was an honorable man, the letter professed. Those who admired him—myself included—will feel his absence deeply.

As he stared at the yellowing parchment, Ian felt a momentary pang of loss that he'd never known his grandsire. There was hardly a soul who had met him who didn't have a kind word to speak of him.

How well had the author of the letter known him?

He paused to consider the man to whom the carriage and coat belonged. They shared a kinship, Ian was certain. It could hardly be a coincidence they looked so remarkably alike.

He felt a prick of guilt for his treatment of the man, but just a prick. He shrugged it away, resolved that he was doing the right thing. *Merrick* would have his life returned to him soon enough. Until then, Ian intended to make use of every means available to reveal the truth.

Raking a hand through his hair, he continued reading the letter. The remainder was somewhat more cryptic, referring to events in the vaguest manner, leaving one to merely guess at the meaning.

By now, you will have realized my intentions.

Precisely, what intentions were those?

For your own good and for that of my son, I cannot, at present, justify releasing it to you, lest you fall prey in your aggrieved state to some cold-hearted opportunist.

This particular passage disturbed Ian more than any other. His mother had told him that his father was murdered just before his birth. Who, then, was this son the man referred to?

An image of *Merrick* accosted him.

Could it be…?

He shook his head, unable to wrap his brain around the shocking possibility.

And yet, who was this man who felt compelled to protect his mother from some *cold-hearted opportunist?*

And what was *it* he couldn't justify releasing into her possession?

Glen Abbey Manor?

It would explain much, though how would this man have gained possession of the estate to begin with, when it had belonged to the MacEwens for nearly five centuries?

The rest of the letter was reduced to rants, as though written in some altered state of mind—perhaps the man had been inebriated.

Only one more passage stood out amidst the rest. It was scribbled on the back of the letter, almost as an afterthought: The sound of a kiss is not so loud as a cannon, but its echo lasts much longer. I suffer a ringing in my ears that will not cease to torment me.

It was signed, simply, *J.*

J. had evidently never dispatched the letter.

Had *Merrick* intended, after all these years, to deliver it to his mother?

Why now?

The answer seemed obvious enough, though Ian wasn't prepared to accept it. That he could have had a brother all these years and not known—perhaps even a father. That his mother could have lied to him. That she would have abandoned one of her infants…

It was enough to sour his mood all over again—if the bone-seeping mist hadn't already managed to do so.

Refolding the letter, he slipped it back into his coat pocket, then withdrew the gold-and-silver calling card-case from the waistcoat pocket, removing a single card to inspect it for nearly the hundredth time. The initials J.M.W. were engraved upon the case itself. The calling card read: J. Merrick Welbourne III, HRH, the Crown Prince of Meridian.

J. after his father, most certainly, as the card intimated a third generation of descent. So J. the son was carrying a letter written by J. the father, and the intended recipient was Ian's mother. Furthermore, J. the son held the title of HRH, the Crown *Prince* of Meridian, which would make J. the father…king of Meridian?

Ian settled back into the seat to contemplate the overwhelming evidence. As outlandish as it all seemed, there was one thing that just couldn't be denied—the remarkable resemblance between Ian and Merrick.

Ian's entire life seemed suddenly a web of lies.

What *was* true was that his mother had kept secrets from him, and that those secrets had affected the lives of every person in Glen Abbey.

Ian was wholly disheartened by the knowledge.

They were nearing their destination—Ian could feel the driver's relief in the renewed vigor of his driving. He had kept to himself the entire journey, answering questions only when forced to, but he was beginning to feel the driver suspected something. It was on the tip of his tongue to tell the man to slow down, but as the thought crossed his mind, a woman's scream curdled his blood.

At once, the coach lurched, careening to one side as the driver struggled to stop. Ian bounced into the window and then into the facing seat as the carriage came to an abrupt halt. He was out of the rig as quickly as he could regain his bearings. The sight that greeted him on the street made his heart falter.

His worst fear was confirmed. They'd hit a woman;

she lay sprawled facedown in the middle of the road. For a frightful moment, she didn't stir.

Ian sprinted to her side, kneeling to inspect her.

Her long ebony hair fell haphazardly from pins to cover most of her pallid cheek. Her wooden box had tumbled from her grasp and had settled in two pieces not more than a foot from her head, spilling silverware into the street like a river of fine silver.

He didn't see blood—that much was heartening—but she'd yet to move. Then she groaned, and he blew a sigh of relief.

The driver hurried to his side. "We did not hit her!" he swore.

Ian cast the man a censuring glare. Of course they'd hit her, blast it all! Wasn't her limp body proof enough?

The chatter of voices rose as curious onlookers surrounded them.

It took Claire a befuddled instant to realize she lay kissing the gravel on Drury Lane.

She moaned, more out of embarrassment than in pain, and struggled to her knees to find she had an uninvited audience.

How utterly humiliating!

One man in particular was kneeling at her side, gawking down at her. A prick of annoyance sidled through her at the sight of him. She realized he meant to help, but his regard only filled her cheeks with heat.

He was unnervingly handsome, with his sun-kissed blond hair and magnificent cheekbones. Claire tried not to notice the color of his eyes.

This moment was certainly not the time to admire

pale blue eyes, even if they were the most remarkable blue she'd ever encountered.

"Thank God you're not injured!" the man exclaimed.

His voice sent an unexpected quiver through her.

It was the chill of the rain, she assured herself.

The fall must have addled her brain. God help her, she'd never entertained such disturbing thoughts in all her life.

She wished he would look away, so intense was his scrutiny.

Shaken as much by the man's attention as by the fall, she inspected her scuffed hands. Then, remembering the footpad who'd been shadowing her, she hurriedly scanned the gathering throng.

She didn't at once spy the footpad, but neither did she care to wait around for him reappear. She began to gather up her grandmother's silver, agitated by her sudden lack of good sense.

The driver of the carriage rambled on, absolving himself of any fault for her injuries. "She ran in front of the carriage," he explained to his master. "We did not hit her, *denka*—she fell!"

Claire cast the driver a reproachful glance.

How dare he settle the blame solely upon her! She hadn't been watching where she was going, that much was certainly true, but he might have driven more thoughtfully, considering that this *was* London and the streets *were* riddled with women and children—even if some of those children were nearly as dangerous as the adults.

She shook a spoon at him. "You, sir, were traveling

much too fast for these conditions!" she accused him. She reached out to seize the bottom half of her box and turned it over, slamming it down upon the street as she cast the driver a baleful glare.

His eyes slanted sadly.

Claire ignored the prick of guilt she felt.

Her box was a wreck, her silver scattered to the four corners, and he had the audacity to look crestfallen by her censure. She wasn't about to ease his conscience so quickly.

"Any child might have run in front of your carriage, and how might you have felt then?" she added.

"Hardly any worse than he already does," his employer said, coming to the driver's defense.

Claire hurriedly gathered up the remaining silverware, grateful for the distraction of her anger to refocus her thoughts. She tossed the pieces into the broken box, annoyed that both men were still staring, neither of them helping.

Neither was anyone else, for that matter. The crowd was thickening around them, heads cocked like parakeets as they gawked down at her while she gathered her belongings from the street.

"How rude!" she exclaimed.

How morbid, to stop and simply stare. She wanted to tell them all to move on and to mind their own sordid affairs, but she knew it would be a waste of her breath.

She directed her anger at the driver, because his gaze was not nearly so unsettling as his employer's. "At any rate, it seems to me, sirrah, that if you felt the least bit badly about running me down, you might be a little more inclined to help me pick up my belongings!"

Both men seemed to realize she was the only one cleaning up the gleaming mess they'd made of the street.

By now, carriages were backed up clear to the corner theater.

"Forgive me...allow me to help," the employer offered.

His driver at once fell to his knees, gathering up her silverware, most certainly scratching the finish as he scooped them into a pile before him. She wanted to tell him to be careful, but in truth, she wanted him to hurry. What did scratches on silver matter when lives were at stake?

The crowd that had gathered began to disperse, apparently bored with the lack of blood and gore. Claire searched the remaining faces for the man who'd been pursuing her.

"Hurry!" she demanded, though not unkindly. "I must be going! It's much too late!"

"A lady shouldn't be walking the streets at this hour anyway," the employer had the audacity to say.

Surely, he hadn't meant it the way it sounded, but Claire took offense anyway. She glared at him. "I beg your pardon! I am hardly *walking the streets,* sirrah."

He blinked, probably realizing what he'd implied. "I meant to say that it isn't safe for a woman to be out and about at this hour," he explained.

As if she hadn't already realized that. "I was on my way home until you waylaid me."

Claire ignored the rain smacking her in the face. She didn't bother to wipe away the droplets. Her hair was doubtless a sad wreck—if not from the fall, then from the rain.

She wished they would both just go to bloody Jericho!

The blond man couldn't begin to realize her present chaos of mind.

The sun was quickly waning and she did, indeed, have a long way to go if she couldn't locate a hansom.

Lord, what if she couldn't? She almost groaned aloud at the thought. What if the streets grew dark before she could make her way to safety? Panic took a firm foothold in her stomach.

Calm down, she commanded herself.

The footpad had surely fled by now. Anyway, he hadn't been following her, she tried to convince herself.

"If you'll allow us the pleasure of your company," the employer said, "we would love to offer you a ride home."

Claire tossed a pitifully bent fork into the mangled box. A ride home with perfect strangers was the very last thing she required at the moment. For all she knew, that's how her brother had disappeared. "I can find my own way, thank you."

And then she spied the man who'd followed her from the pawnbroker's. He stood inside a little shop across the street, staring out the window, waiting.

Claire's heart flipped.

Lord! He *was* following her.

"Well, then...please accept our humble apologies, madam. I suppose we'll be on our way."

Claire snatched up the last of her silver and lifted the box, thrusting it at the employer. "Be a gentleman," she commanded him. "Carry my box to the carriage." Then, without a word, fearing they would change their minds, she stood and hurried to their vehicle.

Chapter Three

Ian watched her march to the rig and let herself in.

Evidently, she considered him the lesser evil.

The thought brought a wry smile to his lips. There were many folks who would disagree.

He glanced over his shoulder, trying to determine what it was she'd spied that had changed her mind so suddenly.

No one stood out.

Ryo, too, seemed a little befuddled. He scratched his head and they shared a look of confusion before Ian motioned for Ryo to return to the driver's seat.

The instant Ian mounted the rig, his saucy little passenger snatched the silverware box from his hands and settled it atop her lap.

"Grosvenor Square, thank you very much," she snapped, and then sat primly before him, doing her damnedest to ignore him, her lovely face a mask—all but the stark green eyes that betrayed her fear.

Ian willed her to look at him.

She refused, denying him even the slightest glimpse into those jade-colored eyes.

Her skin was flawless, save for the fresh scrape on her chin, and he felt aggrieved that he'd had a hand in marring her otherwise perfect complexion.

He eyed the silverware box balanced precariously on her knees, silver protruding despite her efforts to conceal it, and wondered to whom it belonged.

Stolen goods?

It wasn't unheard-of, a female canter, but she didn't strike him as one. And he should know a thief when he saw one.

So who was the little she-dragon trying so hard to ignore him?

One needn't be a London native to know the address she had given him was prime. But why would a woman of her apparent stature walk about London completely unattended with a box full of silverware in tow?

Were the silver a new purchase, the box would have been delivered by the dealer. No upstanding merchant would allow a gentlewoman to risk herself so stupidly.

He studied her while she continued to snub him. Her dark gray gown was neatly pressed, though the cut and material would hardly turn the heads of most women of means. It was as modest as the dresses his mother's nurse often wore, and God knows Chloe couldn't afford extravagant purchases on the meager salary Glen Abbey Manor afforded her.

So, then, was his reluctant passenger merely someone's abigail?

Whatever the case, the lovely little poser was the most intriguing female he'd ever laid eyes upon.

Though he knew better, Ian couldn't keep himself from baiting her. "Most *reputable* merchants deliver their wares," he suggested, and waited for her to respond.

She caught his meaning at once, smart little bird.

Her gaze snapped up, eyes flashing with a brilliance an emerald would envy. Her scraped chin lifted. "Are you implying, sirrah, that I would do business disreputably?"

Like a cornered fox, she was quick to defend herself.

Ian assessed her, taking advantage of the directness of her stare. Her green eyes were striking, with glittering gold flecks that caught the outside light.

Mesmerizing.

Under his scrutiny, her cheeks stained a deeper rose, but she didn't kowtow to him; nor did she seem moved to explain her possessions, even when he narrowed his eyes. Instead, she straightened her spine, bringing his attention to the lovely shape of her breasts. They strained against the bodice of her gown and he couldn't help but note the pebbling of her nipples.

An unexpected surge of desire bolted through him, the sensation so keen it made him shudder.

She was waiting for him to respond, he realized, and it took him another befuddled instant to remember what it was they were speaking of.

Acutely aware of his unwanted arousal, Ian forced his attention to her face. It was the first time in his life that he'd ever felt discomfited by his reaction to a woman. And certainly, it was the first time since he had been just a lad that he had blushed over it.

"I…wasn't…suggesting anything," he lied, and shifted in his seat to hide his indecent evidence. Devil hang him if it didn't suddenly feel as though he'd erected the Tower of London in his trousers.

She lifted a lovely brow, seeming oblivious to his predicament. "Oh, but I believe you were!" she countered. "And I assure you that it was quite rude."

Like a good lady, her eyes never wandered south of his face.

But, heaven save him, that mouth was thoroughly kissable, managing to further distract him despite his resolve.

Damnation. Ian willed her focus to remain steady upon his face. In fact, he dared not blink, lest he lose her attention.

He smiled uncomfortably. "I meant to say only that it isn't safe for a lovely lady to be carrying such a valuable package. It's quite remiss of your…merchant…to send you home without proper escort."

She ignored his veiled compliment. "What you meant to say is hardly what you implied. It would appear, my lord, that you require an education in the art of social discourse. Furthermore," she added, "why I happen to be carrying *any* package—valuable or not—is hardly any of your concern!"

But her temper did him the greatest of favors. His erection diminished at once.

Bloody shrew.

It was clear from the fire in her eyes that she wasn't quite through with him.

"First, you run me down," she pointed out with cool disdain, "then you impugn my character. What next?"

Her lucid green eyes flashed as she tapped her box. "Will you now rob me?" she asked, clearly quite certain of his answer.

Ian choked back startled laughter.

She hadn't a clue how close she was to the truth of his nature. That box would likely feed and clothe a family of four for a lifetime.

Both her brows lifted as she prompted, "Well? Shall I hand over my silverware now and save us both the trouble?"

If only his victims were all so accommodating.

So many quips might have tumbled from his lips just then, if this had been any other time and she had been any other woman. But he was too weary to voice them.

She made no move to hand him the box, he noticed with some amusement. Instead, she drew it closer, looking for the entire world as though she would shred him to tatters if he so much as made an advance toward her.

He half expected her to demand that he halt the carriage at once, no matter what his response.

Despite his reputation with the ladies, it had been some time since a woman had turned his head, much less warmed his bed. But, bloody hell, no woman had ever made him blush then burn, only to dash him so coldly.

He studied her stiff posture and wondered if she were a virgin. It was hardly a proper notion to entertain, but then, he'd long ago divested himself of pretensions. One could not engage in highway robbery, after all—no matter how noble the motive—and walk away a perfect gentleman.

Still, he could be quite charming, he'd been told. So he affected his most disarming tone, hoping for a truce, at least.

He extended his hand, realizing it was presumptuous but needing to know if her skin was as electric as the air surrounding her. "Madam, it seems I am perpetually apologizing."

She eyed his hand as though it were a viper.

Ian persisted. "Let us begin anew, Miss…"

She said nothing, merely glowered at him, and continued hugging her box.

"How is it that your friends address you?" he was bold enough to ask.

Her hand remained planted upon her battered box and she tipped him a smug glance. "If you were a friend, then you would know, wouldn't you, sirrah?" She followed that announcement with an haute little nod.

Whatever response Ian had expected from her, it certainly wasn't that one.

He lifted his brows, withdrawing his proffered hand. Clearly, she hadn't the least interest in furthering their acquaintance.

Damn it all to hell.

Apparently, only Ian perceived any attraction between them. She was as frosty as a Scotsman's arse in winter.

He tried to remember—and couldn't—the last time a woman had so thoroughly rebuffed him.

Considering her refusal to share her name, he didn't bother to introduce himself; it was a moot point, anyway. He wasn't who he was pretending to be. And he wouldn't be in London long enough to make new *friends,* even though the vixen sitting before him was the most annoying, beautiful fishwife he'd ever encountered. He didn't need complications. He was here to find answers, not to fill his bed.

He smiled curtly, resigned to their mutual discord. She returned an equally false smile—one that indicated she was out of patience with him—then turned to stare out the carriage window.

They continued in silence until they neared Grosvenor Square.

Ian recognized the stately mansions lining the street. His passenger leaned forward, as though prepared to leap out the door the instant the carriage stopped. He couldn't blame her. The tension between them now was thicker than a lowland fog.

Still, he had to accept some measure of responsibility for his actions. He *had* nearly run her down and he *had,* in fact, questioned her honor.

Reaching into his coat pocket, he withdrew a handkerchief, offering it to her. No matter that he thought her a shrew, he couldn't let her face her employer with a bloodied, dirtied face.

Like a white flag of surrender, the hanky caught her attention.

She lifted those deep green eyes, narrowing them at the offering. "Do I appear to be weeping?" she asked, making no move to take it.

Ian arched a brow at her.

She lifted her chin higher. "Simply because I am a woman does not mean that I must sob at the first sign of distress. I am quite all right, thank you very much."

Although he tried to keep his amusement at bay, the curve returned to Ian's lips. "Your chin is bleeding," he said, and tried not to feel smug at the immediate change in her expression.

Her eyes widened. "Oh!" She snatched the handkerchief from his hand and said, sounding just a little chagrined, "Thank you. I didn't realize."

The look she gave him was, for the briefest second, entirely too vulnerable. For the first time in his life, Ian hadn't an inkling how to respond.

The carriage came to a halt, and just as quickly as the look had appeared, it vanished. She snatched up her box and shoved open the door before Ryo or Ian could assist her.

"Thank you!" she said, stepping down to the street. "No need to see me to the door." She slammed the carriage door as he rose to follow her.

Had he moved forward a single inch more, it would have earned him a broken nose. As it was, she left him staring eye-to-eye with blue velvet.

As the carriage lurched forward, the interior seemed emptier than it had before.

Outside, thunder flared and rain began to pelt the rooftop.

Or maybe it had been storming all along, because it occurred to him in that instant that, in her presence, he hadn't been aware of anything but her.

Chapter Four

Clutching the battered box of silver, Claire waited until the carriage was gone and then hurried to her front door, closing it quickly against the rain and the prying eyes of neighbors.

From outside, the Grosvenor Square residence might appear as venerable as ever, but inside it was little more than an empty shell. Room by room, Highbury Hall had been stripped of its dignity—pictures removed from the walls, vases and furnishings diminished.

Only the drawing room remained intact, a facade for the benefit of guests Claire no longer received. She would be too ashamed for anyone to witness the decline of their home since their father's death. Their good name was sure to follow.

No one greeted her at the door as she entered the once-grand foyer. Many of the servants had abandoned them. Jasper, bless his ancient soul, had remained, despite the fact that she couldn't pay him. The old steward and his wife had been with the family as long as Claire could recall, but even Jasper and Mrs. Tandy couldn't revive the spirit of their dying abode.

Claire made her way to the dining room and set the box of silverware on the table, patting it once, lovingly, before turning and leaving it to collect dust.

In the drawing room, she slumped into her father's favorite chair, easing into the familiar mold his body had etched into its worn fabric.

She took comfort in the sweet scent of his pipe that lingered, even after so many months. It was hardly ladylike to forget her posture, but she didn't care—not today.

"Did everything go as planned, madam?"

Claire peered up to find Jasper standing in the doorway. She shook her head.

"I am sorry, madam."

"Have we any news?" Claire asked, though she dreaded the answer.

"No, madam. It has been quiet today."

It was always quiet.

No more male laughter rang through the halls.

No more giggling maids.

Claire sighed.

Well, no news was good news, she supposed. At least, it wasn't bad news.

Jasper came into the room, retrieved a folded blanket from the settee and brought it to her, settling it over her lap. "You'll catch a cold," he admonished her.

Claire took comfort in his solicitude but didn't move or acknowledge his complaint. She had truly never felt so bone weary.

"I don't know what we'll do," she worried aloud.

Jasper didn't reply. He'd never been one to dwell on negativity and there was certainly little positive to say. He retrieved *The Times* from the desk across the room and returned, offering it to her. Claire took it and he patted her shoulder.

"I shall have Mrs. Tandy fetch you some tea," he offered.

It still amused Claire that he spoke of his wife so formally.

She wanted to tell him not to bother. Both Jasper and his sweet wife worked hard enough as it was and it was late. And yet, she would, indeed, love a spot of tea. "Thank you," she relented.

He left her to peruse the paper.

Though it was an empty-headed thing to do, Claire ignored the front-page headlines, unable to bear the thought of adding more discord to her life. She turned to the society page and rolled her eyes at the frivolous headlines plastered there.

Lord Burton had eloped with Emma Percy, a mere merchant's daughter. Everyone was up in arms about it. Claire could think of far worse things, such as losing a father, then a brother.

Her eyes stung as she recalled the tears in her father's eyes during his final moments. He hadn't wished to die so soon, but he'd known it was his time and he'd held her hand tightly as he'd said his goodbyes. Even some four months later, some nights as she drifted to sleep, the memory of his final breaths haunted her. There had been nothing peaceful about his parting. Riddled with pain, his every breath had been labored and his last had frozen in an openmouthed gasp.

She pushed the images away, searching the paper for something frivolous.

She found her distraction in another headline.

HRH, the Crown Prince of Meridian had gone missing after his much-celebrated arrival in London. Speculation had it that his royal father expected him to find a suitable bride and he, apparently, had no wish to do so. And, much in the fashion of any spoiled, cornered monarch, he'd run away from London.

What a pity.

She rolled her eyes. Why should anyone care about some ungrateful prince from some inconsequential province?

Claire had never met him, but she recalled the hullabaloo after his first visit to London some three years past. Her good friend Alexandra, who'd been invited to a royal soiree in the prince's honor, had told Claire the prince had seemed arrogant and bored with everyone but himself. Alexandra had said he was rude, rebuffing all attempts at polite conversation. In fact, Alexandra had had a terrible crush on him until she'd suffered the misfortune of sharing a dance with the man. Forced upon her by Lexie's mother, Lady Huntington, he'd treated Alexandra to a painful ten minutes of unrelenting silence and then had deposited her without a word at her mother's side. Embarrassed, Alexandra had wept for two days after.

Disgusted, Claire tossed the paper aside, ignoring the voice in her head that cautioned her to retrieve it before the ink could mar the fine ivory cloth of the settee.

God's truth, she couldn't care less who was doing what to whom. Didn't anyone have anything better to worry about?

God bless Emma Percy; may she be blissfully happy every last day of her life! And Mr. Runaway Prince would come home as soon as his royal papa snipped his purse strings.

In the meantime, how was Claire supposed to raise the remaining banknotes to ensure her brother's safe return?

Jasper returned suddenly…without the tea.

In his right hand, he held a small parcel. He stood in the doorway, his color ashen, a look of horror on his face.

Mrs. Tandy came to look over his shoulder.

Claire sat upright, her skin prickling with fear. "What is it, Jasper?"

For an instant, the steward seemed unable to speak. He lifted up a trembling hand, offering Claire the package. But he seemed hesitant to come forward.

"Forgive me, madam. I—I would have spared you…b-but I fear it's important."

Claire bounded to her feet, her heart tripping as she approached the steward. Without a word, she took the jewel box from his hand and lifted the lid.

She swooned at the sight of its contents.

Even before the carriage had come to a halt, it seemed half of London swarmed them.

In all Ian's life, he had never had so many lackeys nipping at his heels.

Ryo did not alight from the vehicle. The older man sat watching while servants greeted Ian, then ushered him inside, spit-shining his boots and brushing off his coattails while they babbled on about missed appointments with faceless names.

One servant, apparently about to swipe Ian's boot with his sleeve, paused and peered up at him curiously. They were Ian's best pair of boots, but they were worn and dusty from too many days on too many roads. No amount of spit-shining would bring back their original luster. He hadn't had the luxury of time to trade shoes with Merrick. He'd left Merrick wearing his own pants and boots and had absconded with his jacket and just about everything else.

Ian gave Ryo a single, backward glance as he was dragged away, wondering how much the driver knew. Something about the look in the Asian's eyes gave him pause.

Inside, the house was like nothing Ian had ever encountered—a far cry from Glen Abbey's ancient, neglected appearance. From the street, the Berkeley Square residence had appeared much the same as any other London manor. However, one step within revealed a decor that bordered on the ostentatious. Mediterranean in flavor, it gave the impression of embarrassing wealth.

Whereas Glen Abbey's windows wore faded, brittle draperies, here the gold-velvet coverings were rich and fresh. Not a speck of dust marred the portraits or furnishings, which were constructed mainly of gold-painted wood. The foyer itself was enormous, with a massive, domed ceiling bearing angelic images that brought to mind a painting Ian had once seen of the Vatican's *Cappella Sistina.*

An enormous claw-foot table graced one side of the entry; upon it sat a golden chalice he imagined could be a replica of the Holy Grail. It was ornately carved with twisting grapevines embedded with jewels in place of grapes. If they were, in fact, real, each separate gem would feed a township for a year.

Alongside the chalice sat a mother-of-pearl lined dish that was overflowing with calling cards. Above the table hung a massive, gold-framed portrait with the image of a man who looked uncannily like Ian, though much older, with graying sideburns and crow's feet about the eyes.

The sight of it gave Ian a momentary startle.

He paused before it, oblivious to the chattering of servants surrounding him.

It was like gazing at his own face eroded by time.

The man's head was bare, but though his hairstyle was thoroughly modern, he wore a baroque-style, gilded blue coat that appeared to belong in some bygone era.

"Sir?"

Ian looked down at the older man who stood at his side and tried to clear the fog from his brain.

"Your Highness?" the man prodded, his voice tinged with concern. "Are you quite all right?"

Ian blinked.

Not quite.

But he didn't confess it. The less he said, the less he must worry about concealing his accent.

He nodded, biting his tongue. There were so many questions he wanted to ask. All in due time.

Ian gazed back at the portrait, wondering who the

man was. Sire? Grandsire? There could be no doubt they shared the same blood.

"I never get over the resemblance myself," commented the servant at his side, obviously resigned to Ian's moment of sentimentality. "Though I must say, His Majesty resembles him so much more."

Ian nodded, clenching his jaw. It was becoming more and more apparent that his entire life had been a bloody sham. Your Highness? His Majesty? What the blazes? The title had been embossed upon Merrick's *carte de visite,* but Ian hadn't believed it. It seemed incredibly absurd to think Ian had spent his entire life scraping for copper while his flesh and blood dined on pheasant and fine wines.

The portrait hanging before him called his mother a liar. The blue eyes of its subject seemed to be smirking at him, taunting him with long-kept secrets, secrets he was determined to discover.

And God save everyone who'd had a hand in deceiving him—his mother included—because there was going to be hell to pay.

"Sir," the man prodded again, "I don't mean to hurry you, but His Majesty wishes an audience in one hour. Perhaps we should refresh ourselves?"

Ian cocked a brow and looked down at the servant, amused by his choice of words. "*We* should refresh ourselves?" he asked.

Did the man plan to crawl into Ian's bath along with him?

The man fidgeted under Ian's scrutiny. "Yes, sir."

"Very well, then...*we* wouldn't wish to keep *His Majesty* waiting," Ian relented, taking pity on the man.

He started once more down the hall. "Lead the way," he directed the servant, walking slowly so the man could overtake him.

But the man also slowed his gait to keep at Ian's heels. Damn, what was he—a wretched dog?

By now, their multitude of followers had fallen away, dispersed to the four corners of the gargantuan house, leaving only two sets of footfalls to echo along the hall.

Ian stopped, gave the man an impatient wave and said again, more firmly, "Lead the way." He hadn't a clue where to go in this bloody museum.

The servant nodded and scurried ahead of him. All the way down the hall, the man continued to look back uncomfortably over his shoulder.

As they made their way through a maze of corridors and stairwells, all dotted with closed doors, Ian examined the portraits he passed along the way—all similar faces with similar expressions. None seemed the least contented with their lot in life.

Halting before an open door, the servant turned him to the wall, clasping his hands behind him in a military fashion. "Here we are, Your Highness! I shall have your bath drawn at once," he promised, without looking again at Ian. "Welcome home, sir."

Welcome home.

To a place he'd never set eyes upon.

What a damned hum.

"Thank you—" Ian hesitated, uncertain what name to call the servant.

"Harold," the man supplied, still without looking at him.

"Sorry," Ian said automatically. Where he was raised,

men respected other men—including one's servants—by learning their names.

"Not to worry, sir," Harold replied, meeting Ian's gaze briefly. "I hardly expected you to recall; it has been three years, after all, and you've hundreds in your employ."

Hundreds.

Glen Abbey had merely a handful of employees.

Though he hadn't a clue why, his thoughts returned to the girl from Grosvenor Square. Did her employers treat her well? Did her mistress know her name?

Ian wished she'd shared it. Now, she was destined to remain a nameless face in a memory bound never to fade. Regret would have lowered his mood, if it could have gone any lower.

"Right," Ian said, and gave the man a rueful smile that went unnoticed.

He stepped into the room assigned to him and the door closed behind him, allowing him the first moments of privacy he'd had in a week.

Like the rest of the house, this room was big, but the style was indefinable—not Mediterranean, precisely, not Arabic, nor Oriental, but some odd mixture of every culture.

The iron-and-wooden bed was like something out of an Arabian tale, with fine, pale blue fabric draped over it from a wrought iron-wheel suspended from the ceiling. The muted midnight-blue satin spread stretched upon the bed was unmarred by even a single crease.

Oversized blue- and black-satin pillows gilded with Far Eastern symbols were littered across an uncarpeted, dark-wood floor, lending the room a sense of calculated chaos.

The draperies, too, were pale blue and sheer, flowing into the room like a billowing moonlit mist.

On the far side of the room sat a dark-wood table that was too low for chairs. Gathered at its center were half-a-dozen fat candles of various heights and widths—a luxury to his people. And surrounding the short, stocky table were more pillows in shades of blue and black; these were plain, without the gilded symbols.

Two sets of double doors led from the room; one set at his back, another to his left. He made his way across the room and opened one set, revealing a closet in which every nook and cranny was filled with hanging black, blue and white garments. It wholly embarrassed the single, freestanding wardrobe that occupied Ian's room in Glen Abbey.

In fact, this was not a bedroom at all, he decided. It was an apartment. And when he thought of all the bellies that could have been satisfied for the cost of a single item within it, it made his belly churn.

Unbidden, the memory of Rusty Broun's little Ana accosted him. The child would have been three years old the week after her death. Her face, gaunt with hunger, would bedevil him for the rest of his days. It was for her, as much as for anyone, that he had come seeking answers—for Rusty's sweet Ana, and for all of Glen Abbey's wee innocents who depended on Glen Abbey Manor for support.

He turned his back on the luxurious fabrics hanging in Merrick's closet and went to the bed, settling down on it as he glanced about the room.

How could any man surround himself with so much rubbish when babies were literally starving to death?

Ian experienced an unholy stab of guilt merely standing in the midst of it all.

He collapsed on the bed, wondering how Merrick could lie amidst the cool satin sheets and not feel…

Devil hang him, but it did feel good, he thought, as he dragged himself backward and stretched out on the massive piece of furniture. Hell, his feet didn't even reach the edge, and he was taller than most men.

He shook his head in disgust over his lapse in character, but guilt fell at the heels of exhaustion. God save his rotten soul, but it couldn't hurt to wallow in a wee bit o' comfort for just a bit.

He was fagged to bloody death.

As he sprawled in the silky bed, closing his eyes, Ian thought not of little Ana, nor of Glen Abbey, nor even of his mockery of a life, but of a green-eyed beauty with disheveled hair and a wit as sharp as his grandfather's claymore…and lips that looked to be as soft as the satin caressing his cheek.

What he wouldn't give to have a taste of that mouth.

He drifted toward sleep imagining his mystery woman in the most wicked of positions, her mouth coaxing him to climax.

So what the blazes if she wouldn't even give him her name? His thoughts were his own and she couldn't very well slap him in his dreams.

Chapter Five

No longer was the preservation of honor a luxury to be considered. The contents of the box—a severed finger and a threatening note—necessitated that even the lowliest of solutions must be weighed.

Until now, Claire had not resorted to begging, but today she would add that particularly distasteful endeavor to her growing list of embarrassments.

To that end, her greatest opportunity lay with Lord Huntington, Alexandra's father. Though he was known to be a frugal man, he was kind at heart, and if anyone might feel compelled to help her, it would be he. He had, after all, known her most of her life.

At any rate, she didn't know anyone else well enough to solicit money from them. It was Ben who was everybody's friend. Claire had always been content to remain in his shadow. She'd never been particularly fond of, or very good at, idle conversation. And though she had many acquaintances, her circle of true friends was quite small.

In fact, it numbered the grand sum of one.

Hoping her best friend wouldn't wake this morning while she was visiting with her father, Claire awaited Lord Huntington in his office, gnawing anxiously at her thumbnail as she inspected the heads of exotic animals hanging about the room.

Lions bared their teeth at her. Small, doglike creatures seemed to be cackling down at her. Great, deerlike beasts, taller than Claire, turned their noses up at her disapprovingly.

In all the years she'd known Lexie, she'd never entered her father's office. Lord Huntington was most often abroad, managing his business affairs from behind the telescope of a hunting rifle. When in residence, though, he'd always had a kind word for Claire and for Ben.

Ben, in fact, had turned to Lord Huntington for financial advice after their father's death, and Lord Huntington had, in the beginning, taken Ben under his wing. Claire only knew this because she'd overheard a discussion between the two concerning debts and assets when they'd joined Lexie and her father for dinner one evening.

"Sorry to have kept you," Lord Huntington said as he entered his office.

Claire bounded to her feet, sucking in a breath to calm her ravaged nerves. "My lord!" she exclaimed. "Please, no need to apologize."

"Sit down, my dear," Lord Huntington directed her as he approached the desk. He flicked his hand when she didn't at once sit.

Claire plummeted into the chair, though her stomach seemed disinclined to follow.

"I do realize you're busy, my lord," she offered, wanting him to understand how truly grateful she was even for a moment of his time. "You know I would never intrude unless the matter were urgent."

Lord Huntington took a seat behind the enormous cherry-wood desk that dominated his office. He leaned forward, resting his elbows on the surface. He was a rather handsome man, despite his advanced age, and his smile reminded her of her father's. He clasped his hands together and set his chin on two steepled fingers, waiting for her to speak.

Claire suddenly couldn't find her voice. She opened her mouth, but words became difficult.

He lowered his fingers and dropped his chin to rest on his joined hands, his look concerned now. "What is it you need, dear girl?"

Claire was grateful for his directness.

Averting her eyes for an instant, she said a silent prayer that her father would forgive her for this moment of utter disgrace. Then she met Lord Huntington's gaze, secure in the knowledge that her father would never accept his only son's demise over the salvation of his family estate or his name.

"I—It's Ben," she stammered. "My lord, please don't speak a word of this to anyone—not even Lexie—but Ben…he's…gone missing."

Lord Huntington sat up straight in his chair, dropping his hands to the desk. "What do you mean, 'gone missing'?"

Tears pricked at Claire's eyes. "Well, someone has kidnapped him and is holding him for ransom. And I am expected to raise two hundred thousand pounds—one hundred fifty more—or they tell me…" Her eyes misted. "They say they will kill him."

Huntington slapped on the desk. "What?"

"I'm afraid it's true, my lord," Claire assured him. "In fact, last night, they sent a particularly gruesome gift as a testament to their sincerity."

Choking back more tears, Claire disclosed everything—her father's debts (of which he was already aware), Ben's gambling (of which he was not), Ben's disappearance and the box that had been delivered to Jasper last evening.

Lord Huntington pursed his lips. She wondered if he didn't believe her.

"I have heard of this sort of thing before," he said finally. "But, my dear, there is no need to panic as yet. They will not harm your brother as long as they know you are willing to deal with them. I have a friend with the Met," he began.

"No!" Claire exclaimed. "They said no *bobbies!*"

He cocked his head.

"They are watching. A strange man followed me from the—" She stopped, not quite able to share the indignity of having to sell her most-treasured family possessions. "Someone is following me. Were it not for the incompetence of this lunatic driver last evening and his arrogant…"

The image of the man's employer came into her head and momentarily dazed her. The memory of that smile—startling white teeth and crooked, mocking lips—accosted her.

Claire blinked, forgetting for the briefest instant what she was saying. She fingered the scrape on her chin.

"Were it not for this driver?" Lord Huntington prompted her.

"Well, I might not have arrived safely home," she finished a little breathlessly, embarrassed by her moment of absentmindedness.

Lord Huntington didn't bother to question her about the particulars of the accident, nor did he comment on her scratched chin. She must have concealed it well enough, she reasoned, and dropped her hand into her lap.

There was an interminable silence.

"So, then, what is it you need from me?" he finally asked.

Gone was the fatherly aura. His visage was suddenly more like that of the pawnbroker's, like that of a man considering his own affairs.

In truth, Claire had hoped he would offer something without being asked.

"I thought…perhaps…that you might let us…*borrow* the money …"

Huntington lifted a brow. "Borrow?"

"Yes, my lord. I am quite certain Ben would relinquish Highbury Hall to you upon his safe return."

She refused to consider the unthinkable—that he might not return. But if Ben should die, Claire would inherit the house and she would honor her agreement.

"You could sell the house," she persuaded him, "or keep it. It's worth at least one hundred thousand pounds, and I am quite certain it is worth far more. I was told that Lady Kensington recently remodeled their home for the sum of seventy-three thousand."

"Nash's services do not come cheaply," Lord Huntington allowed, speaking of the architect who had been hired to do the task.

"Yes. But their home is scarce the size of Highbury Hall. And they merely remodeled. The property itself is worth much, much more."

Lord Huntington sat back in his chair and eyed her. "And what would prevent Ben from reneging once he is released by his captors?"

Claire leaned forward, hoping, praying for his agreement. "I could sign a note," she offered.

Lord Huntington said nothing for a moment and then shook his head. "No, that just wouldn't do. Forgive me for speaking frankly, my dear, but your signature isn't worth the paper it's written upon. Not to disparage you, but your brother could very well renege and no one would so much as slap his hand for doing so."

It was true that she hadn't the least bit of control over her father's estate. She was a woman, after all. Claire's hopes were dashed as quickly as they had been raised. Her shoulders slumped. "But, my lord, Ben wouldn't!"

"You cannot know that," Lord Huntington countered. "He might very well claim I took advantage of your...predicament. And perhaps it would be true," he admitted. "Certainly, many would believe it."

"But, my lord, *I* am offering," Claire pointed out. "*You* are *not* taking advantage!"

"No, I'm sorry," Huntington replied.

He wasn't going to help; it was obvious by the tone of his voice and the stubborn set of his shoulders.

Claire couldn't entirely blame him.

"However…"

Claire's head snapped up.

"I have always thought you a lovely girl," he suggested.

"Thank you," Claire said, blinking.

"You must know that Lexie's mother and I have been estranged for some time."

Claire's gasp was almost inaudible. She was suddenly afraid of what he would say next.

"In fact, as you know, she has taken up residence at our country estate."

Claire swallowed.

"Let us not mince words, Claire. If you would, perhaps, be interested in an arrangement, I might consider the loan, after all."

Claire's mouth opened to reply. Then she closed it again.

She'd never expected such a scandalous proposition.

She stared at Lord Huntington, horrified by the possibility that she might have, at some point, given him the wrong impression. He had never intimated that he was romantically interested in her.

He was her father's good friend. Her best friend's father.

"In fact," he continued. "I might even be persuaded to make the loan a gift."

Claire shook her head. "My lord—"

"You needn't answer just now," he said, and opened

a drawer. He removed a card. "Take some time. Think about it. And if my offer does not suit you, I know a man who may be able to assist you in locating your brother."

He snatched his pen from the inkwell and scratched something on the card.

"Thank you," Claire said numbly. She stood, her mind reeling. "I'm so sorry for having burdened you."

Her stomach turned.

He handed her the card. "Keep in mind that Ben is a grown man," he said. "And whatever befalls him is of his own doing."

"Yes...thank you," Claire repeated. "Please...give my love to Lexie when she awakens."

"Of course, my dear."

Claire didn't wait for him to see her out.

She hurried to collect her belongings and practically ran out the door, clutching the card in her hand.

It wasn't until she reached the street that she dared even to examine it. On one side of the calling card was Lord Huntington's full name and address. Scribbled on the other side was the name and the address of one Wes Cameron, Private Investigator.

She shuddered, uncertain whether it was Lord Huntington's offer or the name and address he'd offered her that caused it.

Tears pricked at her eyes as she walked down the street toward Highbury Hall.

They were neighbors, for God's sake!

She had supped with his entire family!

She had considered Lady Huntington a second mother in the absence of her own, and Claire and Lexie had practically grown up together, spending summers at each other's country estates.

The idea of lying with Lord Huntington—and more—was worse than unthinkable—it was utterly distasteful. It would be tantamount to carrying on with her own father.

First thing in the morning, she would seek out Wes Cameron. It was the only acceptable solution.

Chapter Six

The following morning, Ian awoke fully dressed sprawled atop a strange bed.

Disoriented by the unfamiliar environs, he tried to regain his bearings.

London.

Berkeley Square.

He was lying on an enormous bed, pretending to be someone else, with no one seemingly the wiser.

And thanks to complete exhaustion, he'd had the first sound night's sleep he'd enjoyed in nearly six months.

He lay still a moment, determining how best to proceed and wondering how Merrick fared in Glen Abbey. Had he revealed himself as yet? Or did he, too, have cause to hold his tongue?

Only time would tell.

One thing was certain—the man was bound to have had one hell of a headache after Ian's head butt. Only Angus McPherson had a harder head than Ian.

Morning light streamed in through draperies that had, apparently, never been drawn. The sun's rays cut a gilded path across the room, illuminating the figure of a man seated cross-legged on the bare floor at the far end of the apartment.

The unexpected presence gave Ian a start.

It took him a groggy instant to realize it was only Ryo, who sat facing the bed, his eyes closed. He remained still, his palms resting on his thighs. Was he praying? Meditating?

In either case, what the devil was he doing in Merrick's bedroom?

"You are awake, *denka,*" the little man said, though he hadn't bothered to open his eyes.

Ian dragged a hand across his whiskers. "Bloody hell! It's damned fortunate for me that you weren't bent on my demise," he groused. "I never even heard you enter the room."

The foreigner opened his eyes, tilting Ian an undecipherable glance. "A man at peace has little to fear. But he who seeks revenge should remember to dig two graves," he said cryptically.

A warning?

Ryo sat unmoving, his passive posture scarcely any threat. Ian studied him, wondering what role he played in Merrick's life. It was quickly becoming apparent he was something more than a driver.

A bodyguard, perhaps?

But the notion nearly made Ian laugh out loud. Ryo was hardly of a stature to protect himself, much less anyone else. And yet, he *had* somehow managed to evade Rusty Broun.

"You have much to do today," the little man announced, ceasing with the riddles and disregarding Ian's scrutiny. "Your father wishes an audience. He was much displeased that you did not seek him at once upon your return."

So bloody what.

Let the bastard wait.

Considering how best to evade everyone for the remainder of the day, and Ryo in particular, Ian dragged himself to the edge of the bed to remove his boots.

Ryo was right about one thing: Ian did have much to do today. However, none of it had a bloody thing to do with Ryo's, Merrick's or his father's agenda.

"I must first speak with you regarding a matter of some importance," Ryo said.

Ian grimaced. He wasn't entirely certain he wished to hear what the man had to say. He stood and turned his back to Ryo, pretending to occupy himself with his morning ministrations.

Someone, presumably Ryo, had arranged a fresh set of clothing upon the valet at the foot of the bed. Ian examined the shirt he was wearing, unbuttoned the wrinkled garment, removed it and tossed it upon the bed, glad for the change of clothes.

So, he determined, Ryo was a driver, a bodyguard, a secretary and a valet. What else?

"I have a tale I wish to share, if you will allow it."

"Go on," Ian allowed, though reluctantly.

"In my country," Ryo began without further invitation, "there is the tale of a man whose horse escaped him and wandered into the territory of the northern tribes."

Whatever he'd expected the man to share, it certainly wasn't a blessed bedtime story. He cast Ryo a questioning glance.

Ryo ignored it, continuing with his tale. "Everyone consoled this man, except his father, who said, 'Perhaps this will turn out to be a blessing.'"

Unbidden, Ian's thoughts wandered to the girl from Grosvenor Square.

It was doubtful he would ever see her again, so why did he persist in thinking of her?

He'd dreamed of her this morning. Thank heavens he hadn't pleasured himself in Ryo's presence. He didn't embarrass easily, but a little privacy was certainly in order. It seemed a man couldn't even relieve himself in this place without a bloody audience.

"After a time," Ryo persisted, "the man's horse returned with a mare. And everyone congratulated him, except the father, who said, 'Perhaps this will soon turn out to be a curse.'"

Ian fastened his trousers, willing away the evidence of his unwanted arousal. Damn, he apparently needed only think of the woman to lose control over his body's reaction.

"Is there a point to this fairy tale?" Ian snapped.

"Well, since this man now had two horses," Ryo went on, ignoring Ian's question, "his young son became fond of riding and eventually broke his leg by falling from his horse. Everyone consoled him, except his father, who said, 'Perhaps this will soon turn out to be a blessing.'"

Ian finished dressing and sat on the bed, waiting for the end of Ryo's nonsensical tale.

"So what's the moral of the story?" he asked.

"One year later, the northern tribes invaded. All able-bodied men took up arms and nine out of ten men died. But the man's young son did not join the fight because he was crippled, and so, both the son and his father survived."

Ryo sat quietly, staring back at him.

He seemed to be looking for some reaction to his story, Ian thought, though what he was searching for, Ian hadn't a bloody clue. "That's it?" he asked.

Ryo nodded.

Bloody hell.

Ian had never been one to mince words. If he'd been discovered, let the man say so instead of speaking in riddles. "Is there something you're trying to say?"

Ryo heaved a sigh, then finally spoke clearly, "Only time will tell whether the journey to Glen Abbey will be, not merely your father's misfortune, but yours as well, *denka*."

He leveled Ian a look that spoke volumes, and Ian realized that Ryo knew more than he was willing to reveal—much more.

The driver added, "Last night I was summoned to give my report. I revealed nothing."

"Why?"

He narrowed his eyes at Ian, reaching up to stroke his short beard, as though in contemplation. And then he returned to his riddles. "It is said that three things cannot long be hidden: the sun, the moon and the truth." He sighed. "The wine of fate has been poured. Now, everyone must drink."

Claire swallowed her pride and revealed her destination. It was far more palatable than Huntington's offer.

How could she ever face Lexie again after her father's indecent proposal? How could she ever bear to show her face to the world if she were to commit such a disgraceful act?

"Madam!" Jasper argued with her. "Surely Lord Huntington could not mean for you to go there?"

Claire ignored his protest. "I haven't any choice," she told him.

And truly, she didn't.

She most certainly didn't need the distress of an argument this morning. Jasper had never dared question her before her father's death and before Ben's disappearance. She forgave it now only because she understood he felt a certain obligation as the only remaining male in the household. She tried to exercise patience—she truly did—despite the fact that his solicitousness rankled her in her present state of mind. But she was quite certain he would never say such things to Ben, were Ben in her position. And God forbid that he should ever have parted his lips to second-guess her father.

"I cannot fathom how Lord Huntington could think to direct you to such an unhealthy address. Not only is that place unseemly, it is unheard of—"

"Really, Jasper," she interrupted. "You have nothing

to be concerned about." She lifted a brow. "As you can plainly see, I am in disguise."

The steward scrunched his nose as he examined her dress. "As *what,* madam?"

Claire thought it rather apparent. "As an honest but poor working woman," she replied reasonably, and gestured down at the plain brown, threadbare dress and weathered black boots she'd discovered in the servants' quarters.

"But, madam, surely you do not wish to be confused with the working women of that quarter?"

Claire had to think about his question an instant, and then her eyes widened as she caught his meaning. That wasn't at all her intent! "You don't mean...?"

His cheeks stained red. "Not that!" the steward exclaimed, realizing now that he had insulted her.

That was thrice her honor had been questioned in the past twenty-four hours!

She seized her reticule from the foyer table, then reconsidered the wisdom of carrying a purse with her at all. It certainly didn't do much for her disguise. Poor women didn't carry purses, did they? Frowning, she set it down again.

"You simply don't belong there," Jasper persisted.

Claire refrained from telling him that it wasn't the first time she'd visited the rookeries. Her hands flew to her hips. "What would you have me do instead, Jasper?"

No one would simply hand over the amount of cash she required. She didn't have any favors to call in, and she didn't have much left of value to sell—nothing but her body, and she hardly relished the thought of lying with Lord Huntington.

And it wouldn't do much good to offer anyone else the house. Lord Huntington had made it perfectly clear no one would deal with her simply because she was a woman.

She eyed the reticule, wondering how Cameron would know who she was if she hadn't any proof. Besides, as sad as it might be, she planned to offer him the set of silverware for his services. She picked up the reticule again and opened it, revealing a calling card and a butter knife. She had considered carrying a spoon as an example of what she was offering as payment, but the knife would serve a dual purpose. She withdrew the calling card, tapped it against her chin as she considered it and then shoved it back into the purse. Anyone could print a *carte de visite.*

Ignoring Jasper as he babbled on, she considered her locket as proof instead. She put down the purse and removed the necklace from her neck, then opened the locket and examined the miniature of her mother, reading the inscription although she knew it by rote: *To my darling daughter, Claire.* Tears pricked at her lids and she closed the locket again, shoving it into the purse, not wanting anyone to see it.

The locket would do. She and her mother bore a striking resemblance and the inscription was clearly written to Claire. She would carry the purse, she decided. It was plain enough.

That decided upon once and for all, she turned her attention to her querulous servant. "I appreciate very much that you are concerned," she said, "but please remove yourself from the door at once."

"Madam!" Jasper continued to protest.

"Jasper, this behavior is entirely inappropriate," she advised him. "You are *not* my father. *I* am the mistress of this house and *you* are to do as you are told. Now, please remove yourself."

"Yes, madam," he relented, looking properly chastised, though he still seemed unwilling to budge. "What will you do if someone gives chase?"

The answer was quite obvious, Claire thought. "Run, of course."

The note of alarm in his voice escalated in response to her calm, rational reply. "What if they should try to snatch you?" he persisted.

"I shall scream," she answered without hesitation and with entirely more confidence than she felt.

He was certainly succeeding in his attempt to unnerve her.

"But, my lady, what if they should cover your mouth?"

Claire's brows drew together. "Then, I suppose I will be forced to bite them," she replied, though, in truth, she'd never, before this instant, even considered committing such a crude act upon any human being.

She had not even considered it at five years of age, when Ben had snatched her braids and pulled her, screaming and kicking away from the stables where she'd hidden away to watch the birth of their new foal. Ben had insisted it was unseemly for a girl to watch such a crude act of nature, and threatened to tell their father if she didn't come away from the stable at once. Claire had refused and he had dragged her willy-nilly away.

"But, madam, please…what if they catch you unaware?"

Claire tried to skirt around him in an attempt to reach the door. "Jasper, I am venturing into a very unsavory area. I *assure* you I will *not,* for a single instant, be caught unaware."

The old servant sighed, realizing at last that Claire was unwavering in her decision.

He should have realized sooner.

When her mind was made up, she wasn't likely to change it. How many times had Ben called her stubborn, and how many times had her father merely laughed at the accusation? It might not be her most endearing trait, but her father had often told her, with a hint of admiration, that he felt sorry for any man who thought to take her reins.

"At the very least, allow me to drive you," the servant offered.

Claire shook her head. "No, that won't do. The coach is in shambles," she reminded him. "And besides, you can't see well enough to drive. I shall do well enough on my own, thank you very much!"

It wasn't her habit to point out a man's handicaps, but this might well be a matter of life and death. The last thing Claire needed was to have an old man hobbling after her while she was running for her life. It was enough she was putting herself at risk.

"Very well," Jasper relented. "But if you must go, let

me tell you something about a man's greatest vulnerability."

Despite the fact that there was no one about to hear what he had to say, Jasper leaned forward to whisper in her ear.

Claire felt her face burn as he proceeded to explain where best to strike a man.

She gasped in surprise. It seemed the southern-most region of a man's…territory…could be quite delicate.

When Jasper straightened, color bloomed in the old man's cheeks. He couldn't quite look at her and for that Claire was grateful. "A swift lift of the knee should do it," he said, as he moved away from the door.

"Thank you," Claire replied. "I shall remember that."

"God be with you, madam."

Ian didn't fool himself. Merrick was certain to return, and it was inevitable he would be discovered. Until then, he intended to make good use of the time Ryo had offered him.

Evidently, his brother's curious servant was willing to let Ian drink from the wine of fate, so long as he was willing to dig his own grave if he strayed from the path of truth onto the path of revenge.

The man's silence was yet another validation of Ian's suspicions. Why else would Ryo remain silent, unless he believed that by doing so he was still serving the king's son?

Making his way below stairs, Ian searched the corridors for something—or someone—familiar to guide him. As he passed through the halls, strange faces leered back at him from the portraits hanging on the walls. With lifted brows and arrogant smirks, they seemed to be watching him as he stumbled from room to room.

His gut twisted at the thought of meeting the man whose blood coursed through his veins.

At last, near the foyer, he encountered a familiar face—the servant who'd escorted him last evening to his quarters. The man was dragging a large, rolled carpet from a cavernous room. Apparently, the hall was being prepared for some grand event.

"Good morning, Harold," Ian greeted him.

Surprise registered in the servant's eyes. "Why, thank you, sir!" he replied at once. "Did you sleep well?"

"Indeed," Ian returned.

"I did come to prepare your bath last evening as I said I would, but you were sleeping sound as a babe in the womb and I didn't have the heart to wake you," the servant was quick to explain.

"Thank you," Ian replied, and meant it profoundly.

This morning was soon enough to slice his way through the web of lies.

The servant seemed uncomfortable with their discourse. He peered down at his unwieldy load, avoiding his eyes. "Well, I won't keep you, sir," he said, and started to drag away his burden.

"Just one moment," Ian demanded.

"Yes, sir?"

Ian stood, tongue tangled, trying to determine how best to ask for direction to his father's office without drawing attention to the simple fact that he'd never stepped foot in this accursed mausoleum before last evening.

Damn Ryo. The least the bugger could have done was lead him to his father.

"Your Highness?" the servant prompted, his expression turning sober. "Are you quite alright?"

"Quite," Ian replied, then asked, "Have you seen my father, Harold?"

"Oh, yes!" Harold replied at once. "I believe His Majesty is waiting in his office."

Bloody hell—Ian knew that much. What he didn't know was *where* the office was.

"Yes, well...please go tell him I will be there directly," Ian demanded of the servant.

The good man didn't hesitate. He cast down his load and hurried to do Ian's bidding. "Of course, sir!" he said, and tripped over the roll of carpet before scurrying down the hall.

Ian followed, grateful that the servant was too preoccupied with his important new task to realize he was being trailed. Finally, Harold stopped at a door at the end of a twisting corridor and hesitated before knocking on the doorframe.

Ian brushed past him. "Good morning, Father," he said with false charity, before Harold had the opportunity to announce him. "Thank you, Harold," Ian said, dismissing the servant.

"Yes, sir," Harold said. He scratched his head as he walked away.

Ian looked at the older occupant of the room. His father seemed to shrivel behind the shield of his desk. He quickly opened a drawer and set something inside, then closed the drawer again.

Ian had the feeling he'd interrupted something of import.

"Come in," his father said.

His hand clenching at his side, Ian did as he was told and stepped into the room.

"Close the door," his father directed.

Ian complied, studying the man who'd abandoned him as an infant. There was no question in his mind that they shared the same blood. Looking at him now, he experienced the same shock he'd felt when he'd first stared into Merrick's face.

As he stood there, considering the years of deceit, a battery of emotions assaulted him. Anger rushed in at the forefront, though he couldn't ignore the painful swell of bitterness that surged up from his bowels like a raging tide.

Why had their father accepted one son, evidently showering him with riches and titles, only to reject the other?

Why had Ian and his mother been cast away like so much trash?

What relationship had his parents shared that could possibly justify either of their actions?

And who the bloody hell was the woman he called Mother?

"You caused me quite a scare," his father said.

You caused me a lifetime of despair, Ian countered silently.

The old man sighed and his expression suddenly softened, the worry lines easing from his brow. "I refused to believe you would abandon your duty, Merrick. Rather, I thought you dead—or worse, kidnapped. I even half expected a ransom letter. When it did not come, I hired a private investigator to seek you out. Where in creation did you go?"

Why did you go? Ian wanted to ask him. *What could an infant possibly have done to send you away?*

He relaxed his fist, carefully considering his answer.

Truth sat upon the edge of Ian's tongue, ready to leap off it like a raging lion.

His father waited patiently.

Recalling the letter Merrick had carried in his coat pocket—the letter intended for *their* mother—he said, "I was searching for…a woman."

It was the truth, but not the entire truth.

His father smacked the desk. "Is that what you nearly gave me heart failure over? Dash it all, Merrick! A woman? You needed only wait two measly weeks before every available chit in London would be lying pandering at your feet! Or did you forget that you have agreed this time to choose a bride?"

Ian didn't answer.

Let the man think whatever he may. The letter to his mother—the real reason his brother had *fled* London—would be broached soon enough.

"Sit down!" his father commanded him, evidently disgusted with Ian's lack of response.

Ian didn't budge.

The time for a father's demands were long past.

"Merrick," his father said, his tone softening again. He pleaded with his hands, mistaking Ian's silence.

"Son, I know you don't *wish* to wed, but please don't embarrass me yet again."

Ian held his tongue. He tried to keep his expression devoid of emotion. The fool still had not a clue to whom he was speaking. It fueled his anger.

"Victoria has gone to great lengths to accommodate us."

Who the devil was Victoria? And why should Ian give a bloody damn what lengths she'd gone to, to accommodate Merrick—or the bloody liar Merrick called Father?

"In your honor, Victoria has gathered the most influential of London's families and many of England's loveliest ladies. It is imperative that, this time, you take your responsibility seriously. You must finally choose a bride."

"Imperative for whom?" Ian dared to ask, trying to sound casual. He suspected the only person his father cared about was himself. But what of Merrick's wishes?

"I would have Meridian align itself propitiously, of course. What manner of question is that?" his father asked, the color of his face heightening.

Ian shook his head.

So, Merrick's marriage was to benefit their father…just as he suspected. "Let me be clear. When do you wish me to choose a bride?"

"Tomorrow evening, as agreed upon," his father said defensively. "You are behaving as though you had no part in this decision. We made an agreement, and I will not be swayed. It would behoove us to consider Victoria's protégées. Her favorites will do very well in William's court."

"So you wish me to choose my bride tomorrow evening from among Victoria's protégées?" Ian repeated. "Because they will have the king's ear?"

His father's expression revealed little remorse. "If at all possible, yes, of course."

Ian suddenly didn't envy Merrick's life at all. "It will be that simple? You want me to choose the woman I will spend the rest of my natural life with, and you wish me to choose her during the course of a single evening, amidst a select crop of spoiled chits whose mothers and fathers owe *Victoria* their favors?"

His father's face turned florid, though his voice remained calm. "Merrick, you've had ample time to make up your mind before now. If you recall, this is hardly the first time we've been through this process. Victoria's daughter Drina is merely twelve or the decision would be simple enough and I would make it for you!"

Process?

Merrick's life was a process?

"Three years ago, all of London practically set itself ablaze for you—fireworks, galas—and you treated their daughters with little more than bored disdain. It took years, not to mention great expense, to unruffle feathers. I will not continue to discuss this. I have never asked anything of you but this one thing, and in this request you will obey me."

"Or else what?" Ian baited him. "Or you will disown me?"

His father lifted his chin. "You will leave me little choice."

Old fool, he already had. Long, long ago.

He didn't even realize with whom he was speaking. That's how well he knew his chosen son.

"I would die a brokenhearted man, Merrick. But I *must* be assured Meridian will have a worthy prince to succeed you. And I must look into my grandson's eyes before I die!"

Some unnamed emotion twisted Ian's gut at his father's disclosure, but he was determined to ignore it. What did he care if the old fool was dying? It wasn't Ian's problem. Whether they shared the same blood or not, the man was a complete stranger to him.

"And what if my son should prove unworthy, *Father?* What will you do then?"

Will you abandon him, too?

The old man's brows collided, his expression turning to one of utmost concern. "Merrick, what is this strange tone I hear in your voice?" He seemed genuinely confused and wounded. "I have never known you to be so insolent. Why do you mock me?"

Ian didn't answer. He dared not part his lips lest everything come spewing out.

His father's expression remained troubled as he continued his argument. "At least I offer you the opportunity to *choose* your queen. I was never afforded that luxury myself. My marriage to your mother was preordained, and my father's marriage before mine! It is a tradition I have forsaken at your request, but I have been patient long enough. We are running out of time."

Again, Ian's stomach roiled. His pulse beat against

his temple, sounding far too much like an iron clock ticking in his head.

Time, indeed, was running out.

Soon, he would be discovered.

Was their father dying?

His father said, his tone brooking no argument, "Choose your bride, Merrick, or, by God, I will choose her for you."

"Very well," Ian agreed, forcing himself to answer calmly.

Anger warred with fear and sorrow in his mind.

The anger he understood, but the fear and the sorrow were completely illogical. He didn't know this man. He shouldn't care if he turned up his toes right before his eyes.

"Don't worry," he assured the king. "I fully intend to satisfy my duty…to Meridian."

A motherland he had never set foot upon. He had never even heard its name in all his given years.

To bloody hell with Meridian.

But he *would* choose a bride for Merrick, if only so that he could concentrate on other matters. And if his brother didn't wish to go through with the betrothal, he could bloody well explain to all of London that his father had two sons, not one, and that his brother had chosen his bride for him.

His father relaxed. "I knew you would not disappoint me. You have always been a good son."

Ian's gut turned violently, the sensation twisting through his chest like a viper, striking at the muscle of his heart. It left him wounded and poisoned with rage.

Merrick was the good son, was he?

Devil hang Merrick, too!

What, in God's name, could a helpless infant have done to deserve being designated the bad son?

"You may go now," his father proclaimed. He opened the topmost drawer and removed an ivory card with bold, black lettering. He handed it to Ian. "I would advise you to discontinue Cameron's services at once."

Ian was, for the briefest instant, too overcome to respond.

"He has connections from St. Giles to Bow Street, and even Westminster. The last thing we need now is a scandal."

The man seated before him was a living scandal.

Ian eyed the card with a keen sense of vengeance, ignoring Ryo's warning. The card read: Wes Cameron, Private Investigator. He should bloody well let Cameron do his job and expose *His Majesty* to the masses—except that Ian wanted to be the one to reveal the man. And once he had the proof he required, he would enjoy seeing him squirm.

His mother was another matter. He loved her fiercely, but he wasn't certain he could bear to look her in the face again.

He would deal with that later.

He reached out and snatched the card from his father's hand, then spun away, vaguely aware that a drawer opened and closed as he walked out the door.

In polite society, Wes Cameron's name was whispered, never spoken. When his services were employed, one could be certain the circumstances were dire and the means of resolution would never be questioned. If one were desperate enough to seek his services, one must also be bold enough to seek him out, as his office was located at the edge of civilization—on the fringe of London's rookeries, where thieves were as thick as the city's fog.

Claire was beyond desperate.

After her experience on Drury Lane, however, she made certain to hire a hansom to take her all the way to High Street. It was an extravagance she could scarce afford, but neither could she afford not to spend the money—not if she wished to live to see the sunrise.

Rather than turn into the one-way street, the hansom dropped her at the corner, leaving her just a few yards to walk. She took a deep breath and forced her feet forward, hoping the cabbie would keep to his word and wait for her.

The streets were filled with dirty little children. Claire's heart went out to every one of them, though she knew they were not the innocents they appeared. She'd heard the tales; footpads and cutpurses made their livings here, and many of the younger children stole to pay off their guardians.

A mangy gray dog lunged at her from a doorway as she passed, yapping and snapping at thin air. Claire shrieked and leaped away. She loved animals, but this one clearly did not love her. A face appeared in the window, likely the dog's owner, and Claire cursed him for starving the dog simply to use him as a guard. She'd be certain to keep to the other side of the street on her way back.

Despite her frame of mind, she found Cameron's office easily enough just a few buildings down, though only the address (and not his name) was visible on the door. She knocked first, then pushed open the door. A little bell jingled as it swung open.

Brave man not to lock his door. She had once read that William the Conqueror had purposely left his treasures in plain sight, so certain was he that no one would disturb them. And so fierce was his wrath, no one dared. Such was the impression she had of Cameron.

"Mr. Cameron?" she called.

No answer.

What if she had the wrong address?

Shouldering the door to keep it from closing, she opened her reticule and examined the card Lord Huntington had given her. It read "19 High Street." She peered up at the address on the door. It was plainly marked "19 High Street."

"Mr. Cameron!" she said a little more loudly.

No answer.

Claire frowned.

Please God, don't make me have to come back.

Her nerve nearly failed her, but she entered the building anyway. The office was a single, nondescript room, with nothing on the walls and nothing adorning the solitary desk. In fact, it appeared to be abandoned, but that didn't make the least bit of sense.

"Mr. Cameron?" she persisted.

Again, no reply.

Hoping to discover something about the man she would face, she walked to the desk and opened a drawer. It was filled with papers. She closed it and opened another, discovering a handful of calling cards and a sinister-looking dirk with an ornate ivory handle emblazoned with the letter *C*. It was clearly old and very valuable. She flipped over a card. It read: Wes Cameron, Private Investigator.

She was in the right place but evidently at the wrong time.

Her gaze returned to the dirk, her brows lifting at the confirmation of his character.

She began to reconsider the wisdom in dealing with such a man. But she'd come too far to turn back.

Noticing a door in the back of the room, she went to it and knocked. Again, no answer. She opened the door and peered into a small room filled with boxes and books. Against the wall, half-covered by a large box, a portrait of a man leaned crookedly, as though forgotten. Depicted in military uniform, the subject was handsome, but something about his pale blue eyes was disconcerting; they were like shards of ice, devoid of emotion. The sight of them made her shudder.

Deciding the visit was, after all, a mistake, Claire pulled the door shut and turned to find that she had an audience.

"You!" she exclaimed.

Chapter Seven

Ian was too stupefied to find his tongue.

No matter that she'd taken pains to alter her appearance, he couldn't mistake that face or the green eyes that sparkled with intelligence.

Her manner of dress had deteriorated, but she was definitely the same woman they'd nearly flattened yesterday evening.

Her eyes narrowed at the sight of him. "What are *you* doing here?"

"I could ask the same of you," Ian countered.

Obviously, she wasn't bothering with pretenses today.

His thoughts settled on the silk purse she carried; it was out of place with her threadbare gown. Some unfortunate gentlewoman's possession? Evidently, she was no more than a common thief. Well, they had much in common, he thought.

"What *I* am doing here is not at all your concern!" she answered, lifting her lovely little nose into the air. But as he watched, the color brightened in her cheeks.

Anger at being caught?

Embarrassment?

She walked toward him, evading his gaze, evidently intending to pass by and escape through the door behind him.

"I believe I shall take up my affairs with Mr. Cameron at a later date," she said. "Good day to you, sirrah!"

What affairs would those be, precisely? Ian wondered. Even as he considered the possibilities, his mood soured.

He waited until her hand was on the knob and considered letting her leave without comment—it would doubtless be the better choice—but couldn't keep himself from baiting her. "Couldn't find anything shiny enough to steal?" he asked.

She spun about, as he knew she would, flashing him a wilting glance. "I beg your pardon?"

"I wonder what your Grosvenor Square employer would think of your extracurricular activities?"

She straightened her spine, looking affronted by the question. Her eyes flashed with challenge. "Why don't you go knock on her door and ask her?" she suggested.

"Her?"

Her eyes glittered like multifaceted emeralds. "Yes, imagine that! Now, if you will pardon me."

She swung open the door and departed, leaving him staring at the backside of a closing door for the second time in two days.

Ian smiled.

She was beautiful and fearless—a lethal combination.

And then his smile vanished.

Whether she was a thief or not, he didn't really want her to go, but he hadn't a clue how to detain her.

If she left, he would never see her again, as another chance encounter wasn't likely.

"What is your association with Mr. Cameron?" he asked, opening the door and chasing after her like some smitten schoolboy.

Claire ignored him.

Her legs trembled as she made her way down High Street.

What an infuriating, arrogant, rude scoundrel! She didn't care if he were the King of England; he was nothing more than a brutish lout who clearly had little respect for womankind.

"My association with the man is none of your concern."

Why was *he* here, for that matter?

Was he following her? What were the odds of encountering the same stranger twice in two days? If he hadn't anything to do with her brother's disappearance, then God was surely punishing her for something.

She was so perturbed that she forgot to cross the street to avoid the dog. And she didn't remember until it jumped at her, barely missing her arm and snatching her dangling purse.

Claire screamed.

The dog snarled, pulling at her silk purse in an unholy tug-of-war. She was afraid he would tear it and that she would lose her mother's locket.

"Dirty mangy beast!" she cried, struggling to dislodge her purse from its slobbery muzzle.

Gracious, even the dogs in this part of the city were inclined to thievery.

The animal didn't appear the least bit frightened by

her attempt to intimidate it, but suddenly, the dog released the purse and Claire tumbled backward. Victory at last!

She expected to feel the street against her backside, but the impact never came. Instead, she was caught in a pair of strong, male arms and swept aside as a curricle careened around her. The driver shouted obscenities in her direction.

"What is it with you and carriages?" a male voice asked.

The warmth of his breath against her ear gave her an embarrassing quiver. Claire didn't have to turn to know who mocked her.

She shrugged away and spun to face him. "What is it with you and your need to rescue damsels in distress?" she countered. "Or am I the only fortunate one?"

A tiny smile turned the corner of his lips. "I'm afraid you're the only one."

Claire ignored the trip of her heart.

She didn't want to be attracted to this man. She didn't like him, nor did she trust him.

"Why are you following me?" she demanded as she examined her purse. She grimaced as she noticed the ravaged material.

"I am *not* following you. Miss …"

"I didn't care to share my name yesterday and nothing has changed since then. Thank you for saving me from an untimely demise, yet again, but I'm afraid I must be going now!"

She took one step away from him and the dog snapped at her. Good lord, the man had turned her all about so that she scarce knew where she was standing, much less where she was going. Regaining her bearings, she started toward the corner of High Street and St. Giles, where the cabbie was still waiting.

Suddenly, she noticed the rip in the seam of her purse. An embarrassing whine escaped her as she spun about and scanned the street. Not spying the locket, she opened the purse to make certain it was not lodged within. But it was, indeed, gone.

“Searching for this, lass?” her tormentor inquired, a hint of a brogue apparent in his otherwise too-precise accent.

He was kneeling and petting the dog that had, only moments before, been frothing at the mouth.

Claire scowled at the pair. Animals *usually* adored her.

Her necklace and locket were dangling from the man’s fingers. She approached him, extended her hand and demanded, “Give it to me, please.”

He lifted a brow. “It seems you found something to steal, after all.”

Tears stung Claire’s eyes, but she refused to shed them. She was approaching her breaking point. No human being should have to endure what she had undergone these past weeks. The last thing she needed at this moment was for this man to harass her. She said nothing in response but thrust her hand nearer to his face, begging him without words for the locket.

She didn’t trust herself to speak.

He stood and casually inspected her property, unhooking the latch and studying the tiny portrait as though he had a right to. Then he looked at her, inspecting her as well.

"Incredible likeness...*Claire*."

Claire's eyes threatened to leak against her will. Her lips quivered. "It was a gift from my mother," she felt compelled to explain.

He nodded, spilling the necklace into her palm. And he sighed. "It seems that I am perpetually apologizing to you."

Claire swallowed, grateful that her anger kept her other emotions at bay. "If you were truly a gentleman," she berated him, "you would never have cause for apologies. Thank you very much, sirrah!"

In an effort not to lose her composure, she turned and hurried away, praying she'd never have to set eyes upon the infuriating man again.

Filled with a keen sense of regret, Ian watched her go.

He might have followed, so curious was he about where she might go, but he was forced to return to Cameron's office and wait. He didn't need a bloody investigator nosing about his affairs. If the man happened to discover Merrick's destination, and if he did just a little snooping, he would unearth the truth, and Ian needed more time.

Too much was at stake now.

Too many people depended upon him.

Too many years had gone by to simply appear before his father and say, *Hello, da, it's Ian...the son you didn't want.*

For just an instant, his thoughts returned to Claire, and he smiled as he remembered the way she'd stood up to him. Then, he caught himself and frowned.

He couldn't afford to have his brain riddled with thoughts of beautiful, raven-haired witches. Never in his life had he been so unfocused—or, rather, so entirely focused on something besides his own affairs.

But it wasn't entirely his fault.

The dress she'd worn had nearly unmanned him. As plain and threadbare as it had been, he couldn't recall ever seeing a woman look more stunning. The modest dress accentuated her figure, leaving little to the imagination, as the breeze had sculpted the material to her pert little rear. And those nipples pebbled beneath the thin bodice had left him hard as a stone.

And yet, as much as her body appealed to him, something in her eyes had struck at some long-forgotten corner of his soul.

Was she in trouble?

Was that why she was seeking out Cameron?

Or was it Cameron's companionship she wanted?

He opened the door to Cameron's office, still trying to determine what business Claire might have with the man; the possibilities were endless, and at least half of them were distasteful.

He pushed her out of his thoughts.

No sooner had he settled himself into a chair to wait than Cameron returned. The man seemed a little taken aback by Ian's presence, but he hesitated only briefly in the doorway.

Ian had expected an old bloke; the man who sauntered into the small office was about Ian's age, with the build of a dockhand, the dress and demeanor of a gentleman, and the eyes of a thief—keen and assessing.

Spying recognition in the man's eyes, Ian stood and extended his hand in greeting. "Cameron, I presume?"

"That would be correct," the man answered, coming forward and shaking Ian's hand with a firm grip. "And you are no longer missing, I see."

Ian had had years of practice lying. He didn't flinch at the question. "That would be correct," he said, echoing Cameron's reply. He flashed the man his most genuine grin. "But you may keep the retainer for your troubles."

Cameron returned a half smile and answered without hesitation. "I intend to."

Arrogant bastard, Ian concluded at once, though he might have liked him under different circumstances. Then he chuckled. Bloody hell, it wasn't his money; nor was he likely ever to see any of it. So what did he care?

Cameron averted his gaze as he stepped around Ian and moved behind the desk to settle himself into his chair. "It's not every day someone of your stature ventures into this quarter," Cameron commented. The statement gave Ian a prick of concern.

It would never have occurred to him to send someone else to conduct his business. He had never relied upon others to serve him.

"Not every royal sits on his bum and expects to be waited upon," Ian joked, though, in truth, he didn't know a single royal aside from his father and his brother—and he couldn't claim to really know either of them.

Cameron smiled, but the lack of expression in his eyes remained. "I suppose all's well that ends well," he commented.

"Yes, of course," Ian agreed, deciding that it was his cue to take his leave. He'd be damned if he'd stick around to remain the subject of anyone's scrutiny.

He bade the man goodbye and left the office.

It wasn't very likely Cameron had found Merrick so quickly. Still, the mere possibility was a reminder that Ian didn't have time to linger over damsels in distress, no matter how lovely. He had business to attend to—namely, discovering who the rightful owner of Glen Abbey was and finding out where the estate's money was disappearing to.

It wasn't until he was in his carriage that he realized Cameron had never honored him with Merrick's title.

The man was either more arrogant a bastard than Ian had first determined, or, like Ryo, he knew more than he was willing to reveal. Whichever the case, Ian was certain of only two things: his hours in London were numbered, and his father—self-centered, self-serving, self-righteous bastard that he was—seemed to be the only one who didn't recognize his son.

Chapter Eight

Claire wasn't the sort to give in to fits of the blue devils, but she'd arrived at point nonplus, uncertain what to do or how to proceed.

Deploring the moment of weakness, she turned her face into her pillow and wept, missing her father more now than ever.

She'd come directly home from Cameron's office and gone straight to her room, where she could pretend she was a child again and the world beyond her Grosvenor Square haven was only a place she'd dreamed of exploring. She hadn't even bothered to remove the hideous servant's dress or shoes.

Her father had encouraged his children to do for themselves, but when they'd needed him, he'd always been around.

Now it was just Claire and Ben. And Ben had gotten himself into a terrible mess, and they were cleaned out, and there was nothing left to do but lie across her bed and sob like a helpless babe.

Only she wasn't a child. She was a grown woman, and she *should* be able to *do* something.

She'd reduced herself to begging.

She'd tried to borrow.

All that was left to do now was to sell her body.

Or steal.

And God forgive her, she would rather steal than compromise herself.

As she lay there, she cursed Ben for getting himself into such a bumblebroth. He might have fared better in Fleet Prison. And then, in the next instant, she prayed for him. Her brother was all she had left in this world.

Such thoughts saddened her even further. To distract herself, she turned her mind toward the horrid man she'd encountered in Cameron's office.

It wasn't enough that she was being forced to deal with her brother's disappearance and Lord Huntington's advances; she also had to endure that rakehell's sarcasm and his accusing regard.

Her tears swelled all over again. How dare he use her Christian name? She didn't care if he was the finest-looking man on the face of the earth; he was also the rudest, most arrogant—

A knock sounded at her bedroom door.

It had to be Jasper or Mrs. Tandy. No one else remained. Jasper had informed her while she'd fled up the stairs that Edna, the cook, had regretfully taken her leave, as well. She had two children to feed, after all, and no husband. Claire didn't blame her.

In any case, she didn't care who it was. She didn't wish to see anyone right now. Her eyes felt puffy and she was mortified to be caught behaving like a witless child. "Go away," she demanded, her voice catching on a sob.

She was startled to hear the knob turn and peered up to find Alexandra standing in the doorway.

"Jasper told me you were not receiving, but I insisted. Forgive me."

Claire thrust her face back into the pillow.

Of all people, Alexandra was the last person she wished to see at the moment. Alexandra was her only true confidante, but how could Claire reveal her friend's father's shameful proposal? Claire had never had aspirations to marry, but spending the rest of her life as a kept woman was infinitely worse than even marriage. At least with a marriage contract, she could keep her self-respect.

Alexandra approached the bed, then Claire felt the mattress sink a little as her friend settled on it. "I thought it rather strange you didn't linger to visit with me this morning," Lexie said. "But Papa told me why."

Claire gasped. How could he? She rolled over to face her friend, horrified at the prospect that Alexandra might know her shame.

"Oh, Claire! You shouldn't cry," Alexandra said, entirely without malice. "It makes you look horrid!"

Claire didn't take offense. She knew it was true. Her eyes were surely bloodshot and her nose must be scarlet.

"Don't worry. Ben will turn up. He is far too canny to allow those terrible men to get the best of him."

Claire's lips trembled, recalling last night's delivery. "He'll turn up—but in more than one piece, I'm afraid!"

"Don't even say so!" Alexandra scolded, looking appalled. "You must never give up, Claire! I *know* Papa will help."

Claire said nothing. Lord Huntington had already revealed the nature of his aid.

"He gave me the name of an investigator," she admitted, after a moment.

Alexandra looked at Claire curiously. "Will you seek him out?"

"I already tried. I went all the way to High Street, but he wasn't there."

Alexandra screwed up her face. "I believe that explains those dirty rags you're wearing," she said, gesturing at Claire's dress. "Humph! I cannot believe Papa would send you to such a place."

Claire refrained from telling Lexie about her encounter with her two-time savior. She couldn't bear recounting the odious smirk and horrible accusations. Nor did she care to explain that she'd spent the prior weeks pawning her family's cherished heirlooms, the better part of the morning trying to forget that her best friend's father had propositioned her, and the rest of the day battling devil dogs and avoiding three-foot cutpurses and mad curricles.

No, Alexandra must be spared those dirty details.

It was a wonder they were friends, so disparate were they in nature. Alexandra was a true social butterfly, always attempting to drag Claire into her sparkling world, while Claire was content to remain at home. In truth, Claire half suspected Ben was the primary reason Lexie always sought to include her. The two of them were so much alike, craving attention.

Claire swiped the tears from her eyes with her thumb and sat. "What time is it?" she asked.

"Tea time," Alexandra answered. "In fact, I hope you don't mind, but I took the liberty of asking Jasper to serve us."

Claire shrugged. She really didn't have a taste for tea, or anything else, but Alexandra was welcome to anything she had remaining.

"You really shouldn't lock yourself away like this," Alexandra scolded her. "And that gown! I hope no one saw you dressed that way, Claire. Whatever would they say?" Her brows drew together into a frown. "You're still in mourning, after all."

Claire snatched the pillow and dragged herself backward. Leaning against the headboard, she hugged her pillow.

"The first thing you must do is to remove that horrid dress," Alexandra proclaimed, and stood at once, going to Claire's wardrobe and returning with a clean black gown, as though a simple change of clothing were the answer to all Claire's troubles. Alexandra tossed the dress on the bed and demanded, "Get up!"

Claire obeyed; she didn't have the energy to argue. She turned around so Alexandra could unfasten the gown.

"Ghastly!" Alexandra complained.

Claire couldn't help a tiny smile. She couldn't imagine Lexie resorting to wearing such an offensive garment, not even to save her own life. Although Claire couldn't see Lexie's face, she was certain her friend was crinkling her nose and cursing the fabric as it offended her fingers.

"Whatever were you thinking?" Alexandra asked as she pulled the dress off and tossed it aside, making a noise of disgust as she released it.

Claire grimaced at the nondescript brown pile on the floor.

"Now the shoes!" Lexie snapped, gesturing for Claire to remove them at once.

Claire did so, tossing the poor shoes beside the downtrodden dress. She put on the clean gown, allowed Alexandra to fasten her, and resumed her position on the bed, again hugging her pillow.

"Much better!" Alexandra declared, and joined Claire on the bed. She bounced gently on the edge. "Did you hear the latest *on dit?*" she asked suddenly, affecting a bored tone. Claire did not respond, but Alexandra's enthusiasm for her bit of gossip seemed unaffected by Claire's lack of interest.

"It seems His Royal Highness, the Crown Prince of Meridian, has deigned to return to London at long last." Lexie rolled her eyes, as though she didn't care a whit, but Claire knew better.

"So I read," Claire confessed.

"Really?" Alexandra asked, cocking her head. "Since when do you read the society page?"

Claire shrugged. "I was bored."

Alexandra giggled, then rushed back into her story. "At any rate, it seems the gala is to be held after all. And this time, he shall positively make an offer to someone in attendance. Imagine that! Some girl shall have to endure that horrible bore for the rest of her days!"

"At least it won't be you," Claire consoled her, although it rankled her that Alexandra could bother to discuss such nonsense when Ben's life was at stake.

"True," Alexandra said. "I could *never* stomach his rudeness, though I certainly wouldn't mind being the recipient of those jewels."

Claire's brows lifted, her interest suddenly piqued. "What jewels?"

Alexandra plucked at a loose thread on the bedcover. "I heard it was the only way the Duchess of Kent could be convinced of the prince's sincerity—and you know how much Silly Billy values her counsel. Everyone seeks her approval. She insisted they be presented tomorrow night."

Though Claire didn't much like the duchess, no one could deny that she had great influence. Fortunately, Claire had never caught the woman's eye, so her despotic ways rarely affected her. But there was no doubt in her mind that the duchess knew her name. She knew *everyone's* name. It was quite obvious that her ambition was to sustain her daughter Drina's position of power as heir to the throne. Drina, on the other hand, seemed a good-natured child. Claire had only met her twice, as the Duchess kept her locked away, but she seemed not to have a single ambitious bone in her little body.

"So the jewels will be on display tonight?" Claire asked.

"Yes. And I believe you should attend," Alexandra said. "After all, this is the first time Meridian's crown jewels have been on exhibit, and you're not serving Ben's cause by remaining holed up in this house."

Claire failed to see how mingling at some ball would be to her brother's benefit. And close on the heels of that thought came another. She couldn't help but wonder how well protected the jewels would be. Would they remain encased the entire night? Would there be guards posted?

Not that she would ever have the nerve. But Meridian's royal family would scarce miss a single gem, so wealthy was the country.

Meridian was hailed as a hidden paradise of golden beaches on the edge of the Mediterranean. Bordered by impenetrable mountains on the interior, it was inaccessible except by sea. It had long been the haven of seafaring kings and queens who showered the well-guarded country with riches simply for the privilege of spending a night behind its walls. For centuries, Meridian had been a meeting point for Eastern and Western traders alike. It had made it a policy to shelter every man, whether king, shah, or lowly tradesman—for a price. The country covered no more than two square miles, but was one of the most valuable pieces of real estate in all of Europe.

"Perhaps I will, after all," Claire relented, considering the jewels. A single diamond from the collection would likely solve all her problems. But she just needed a few smaller ones.

If she should happen to touch them, and if one gem should happen to come loose, and if it should happen to fall into her hand…she might not return it.

"Really?"

Claire shrugged. "As you said, what better things have I to do? Sit and wait for Ben to reappear?"

"Oh, yes!" Alexandra exclaimed and clapped her hands. She bounced up from the bed and began to pace, her face flushed. "It will be so much fun! You won't regret it, Claire. I'm certain it will take your mind off *all* your troubles. Oh, Papa will be so pleased."

Claire grimaced at the thought of bearing Lord Huntington's company. But, God willing, the ball might be just the opportunity she needed to ensure her brother's safe return.

Chapter Nine

Returning from Cameron's office, Ian hesitated at the door to his father's house, considering his options.

After seeing Merrick in Scotland, he'd been so bent upon unveiling the truth that he hadn't considered the consequences of his actions; he'd simply reacted. And then, caught up in the ruse, he'd had little choice but to carry it through.

He needed time.

What if Cameron had somehow discovered the truth? What if Ryo had changed his mind and exposed him?

What was the worst they could do to him?

They could arrest him and toss him into gaol, but that wasn't probable. There was no doubt in Ian's mind that Merrick's father was Ian's flesh and blood, as well. Ian was betting he wouldn't risk the scandal.

At any rate, Ian had come too far to simply walk away.

Blast it all. He'd never been afraid of any challenge laid before him. He'd faced angry men across the barrel of a pistol, and had, without a single moment of reluctance, robbed them of every coin and trinket in their possession. All he wanted now was what was rightfully his. And not even that, so much, as a chance for his kinsmen to have a better life.

He also wanted to know the truth.

So why was his gut churning? And why did he feel so apprehensive about opening the door?

Bloody hell! He could stand on the doorstep for the rest of his life, but what would that accomplish?

Resolved, he shoved open the door, prepared to steal into his father's office. There were bound to be papers there that could shed some light on the truth. Besides, he wanted to know what was hidden in that damned drawer.

He half expected to encounter guards on his way to his destination, but getting into the office proved a far simpler task than Ian had anticipated.

As he stepped into the house, instead of a fat, burly constable with a looking glass shoved into his eye socket, a lovely servant girl with soft blond curls and cherry-stained lips accosted him. Her face was radiant as she revealed that, in his absence, a package had been delivered for him.

"It appears to be very, *very* important, Your Highness," she said, and batted long pale lashes at him.

"Really?" Ian asked, though naturally the unseen package wasn't intended for him.

The servant girl cast him a sultry smile and waved him forward, then hurried in that direction, obviously expecting him to follow. Ian did so, grateful for the distraction of another pretty face, so that he could eradicate a certain pair of defiant green eyes from his memory. Who Claire was and what she was after were not his concern.

Nor did it behoove him to dwell on the anguish she'd hidden behind her mask of anger, though never in his life had he witnessed such a look of despair.

As the servant made her way through the maze of halls, she cast flirtatious glances backward at Ian.

He smiled back, though he hadn't the least interest in dallying with her.

Neither did he care to recall the saucy sway of Claire's hips as she'd marched away from him, her ugly dress caressing that perfectly round bottom.

His immediate arousal had nothing to do with the servant girl's cute arse bouncing before him.

She ducked into his father's office and went to the desk, lifting up a small package and spinning about to face him.

Ian half expected to find his father seated behind the desk, but the room was empty.

"I hope you don't mind. It's from me," she said, her tone seemingly more intimate now that they were in private.

Ian looked at the neatly wrapped gift and felt ill at ease. Apparently, Merrick knew the girl on a personal level. She was cute, he was forced to confess, but he hadn't the least bit of interest in his brother's leftovers.

Her expression turned to one of concern. "Have I somehow displeased you? Do you not remember me?"

"I'm not upset in the least," Ian assured her and came

forward to accept her gift. "Of course…I—" *don't,* he interjected silently "—remember you."

Her smile returned. "I'm so glad you returned to London."

Ian stared at the gift. He was acutely aware that the girl had moved away and closed the door. She returned to his side, watching as he fumbled with the bindings.

"I knew you wouldn't like it if I visited you on your first night back, so I didn't. And then you left, and everyone was worried—especially me."

"I had business to tend to," Ian said, and continued to struggle with the wrappings. Evidently, she'd put quite some effort into the adornment of the package, because it was bound by more strings than a puppet. He tore away the last of the bindings and opened the box to reveal a modest wooden heart.

"I carved it myself!" she said. "Do you like it?"

Ian lifted the heart out of the box. "Yes," he said, examining it. It was handpainted—a little too lovingly for his comfort.

The servant moved around him and sat on the desk, casting him a naughty glance. Then, she lifted her skirt ever so slightly, revealing silky white calves. "Do you remember this?" she asked.

Most men would greedily accept her invitation.

Ian tried to determine how best to deny her.

When he didn't take advantage of her offer, her smile faded. "I know. You don't have to say it." She jumped down from the desk, her face darkening with color as she straightened her skirts. "I realize you've come to

London to choose a bride. I only thought…maybe…just once more wouldn't hurt anyone."

"It's quite all right," Ian said, realizing she must feel mortified. He put out his arms to offer her a hug and wondered what the devil was wrong with him that he was turning down a beautiful woman's invitation, when he'd never before felt inclined to. He loved women—all of them. And girls of her station knew, without explanation, that a dalliance was bound to be simply that—a dalliance. This sweet lass was quite the tasty morsel, besides, with bright blue eyes that watered as she withdrew from his embrace.

"Well, I should be going," she said. "I only wanted to give you a gift to remember me by."

"I shall never forget you," Ian swore, bending to kiss her temple.

He wished like bloody blazes that he at least knew her name.

She nodded, her lips quivering. "I'll leave you to work. I know you have much to do before tomorrow night."

Ian winced, wishing he could say something to soothe her feelings. He simply wasn't willing to make her body feel better; nor did he relish the reminder that tomorrow he would bind his brother to a perfect stranger. Despite his earlier resolve, he felt just a wee bit of guilt over it.

He moved around the desk, placing a barrier between himself and the girl, and then sat and watched as she shuffled toward the door. She hesitated in the doorway, and gave him a brief, sad smile.

He smiled wanly, aware that his arousal had vanished, and waved her away.

What the devil ailed him?

The girl was lovely—there was no question as to why Merrick had been drawn to her. And she evidently harbored no illusions; she wanted nothing more than a moment of affection.

Still, he'd let her go.

She closed the door behind her, leaving Ian to contemplate the irony of the situation. One woman glares at him, looking as though she'd like to pluck out his eyes, and he finds himself cocked and ready to fire. Another woman throws herself on a proverbial platter and serves herself up ripe, and he finds himself limp as a wet rag.

At least she had led him to the place he most wanted to be. And, better yet, he was alone.

He rifled through the drawers, looking for any financial or legal records that might be traced to Glen Abbey Manor.

It proved to be a wasted effort. He found nothing, save a vial of laudanum and a wrinkled portrait at the bottom of a stack of papers in the bottom drawer.

At least he thought he had found nothing, until he looked more closely at the stained, yellowed portrait. A scratch, as though from broken glass, marred the left eye, and ink bled through the forehead, but he recognized the face nonetheless. It was the image of his mother, though she was much younger.

Flipping over the portrait, he tried to make out the writing that bled through the thinning paper: It read "The sound of a kiss is not so loud as a cannon, but its echo lasts so much longer. I suffer a ringing in my ears that will not cease to torment me.

With all my love, Fiona."

Ian recalled the phrase from the letter Merrick had carried. He returned the portrait to its place in the bottom drawer, contemplating its meaning.

Why would two people who obviously longed for each other choose to live apart?

Unless they hadn't done so by choice?

Chapter Ten

The following evening, Claire dragged her two finest black evening dresses out from the wardrobe.

She was still in mourning, and it wouldn't serve to appear in public dressed in vivid plumage. But even with her choices narrowed to two, she couldn't decide which gown to wear. One was entirely black, made of silk crepe. She'd purchased the garment from Courtauld's before she'd realized the family's pockets were to let. The other was made of velvet—quite scandalous—with hints of black lace peeking beneath the hem and sleeves. It was slightly shocking, she knew, but her father would have been amused by the choice.

She laid both gowns on the bed and wished Alexandra would arrive to help her decide, but she knew Lexie would choose the silk crepe. It was the more proper of the two. If the truth were known, on some level, Claire wished she were more proper. She just couldn't bring herself to care overmuch what people thought about the fabric of her gown.

Anyway, why did it matter what she wore? She wasn't the least bit interested in gaining the prince's favor. And she wasn't really in the mood to be proper. It was enough that the dress was black, she decided, choosing the velvet and lace.

She dressed almost entirely without help before making her way below stairs to ask Mrs. Tandy to help her make the final adjustments.

With every passing moment, Ian envied Merrick less and less.

In fact, he was starting to pity the poor bastard.

In preparation for the evening's celebration, he'd been dragged about by the proverbial collar, scrubbed, trimmed and polished until even his nose shone. He'd been fitted with a pair of trousers and a jacket that had had to be adjusted to fit his width and breadth. Apparently, Merrick was of slightly smaller build, and the tailor had shaken his curly red head, wondering aloud if the prince had gorged himself during his absence from London.

Bloody hell, did they even dictate Merrick's diet?

It seemed they told Merrick what to wear, where to go, how to speak, whom to speak to and—he clenched his jaw—whom to marry. You'd think by the age of twenty-eight, Merrick could be trusted to make a few decisions for himself.

In contrast, even as a child, Ian had been allowed to run free. He woke when he wished, ate when he was hungry, and never, in his wildest dreams, could he imagine his mother dictating whom he should wed.

Ryo, for his part, had become his bloody shadow, always watching, his black eyes unreadable. Although Ian had managed to evade him during the brief outing to High Street yesterday, the servant had caught him in the hall outside his father's office and had remained by his side ever since.

A fish that nibbles at every bait will soon be caught, Ryo had warned.

More bloody riddles. Ian had had almost enough of his cryptic lessons.

With mere moments remaining before the evening's guests arrived, Ian ducked into the library, hoping for a moment's respite from Ryo's scrutiny.

As he entered the room, one portrait caught his attention. Something about it seemed oddly familiar. On closer inspection, he realized it was a depiction of Merrick standing in a field that looked like Glen Abbey's parklands—at least, he presumed it was Merrick. The image had been painted at a considerable distance and the figure was blurred. Perched on the young boy's arm was a white saker preparing to take flight. The bird was similar to one Ian had owned as a child. He tried to remember how he'd acquired the bird—a gift, perhaps—but he couldn't recall.

He continued studying the portrait. There was no house depicted. Were it Glen Abbey, the white house would have been directly behind the boy. But there was no house. And the portrait was painted at an odd angle, almost as though the painter were seated up high, looking down through a pane of smoky glass. Details were undistinguishable. Still, the woodlands in the background were familiar, and the field was covered with a purple haze that reminded Ian of a blanket of wild heather.

"That was a very, very good day," Ryo commented, appearing at his side. He joined Ian in perusal of the painting.

Ian frowned, peering down at the top of Ryo's balding head.

"You will be expected to join your father soon," Ryo announced.

"Of course."

"The duchess has arrived."

"Splendid," Ian said, his tone intentionally sardonic.

He returned his attention to the portrait, determined to make his way into the hall at his own pace. In fact, it was on the tip of his tongue to tell Ryo to go to the devil, but he wanted to learn more about the painting…and that *very good day.*

"There is an old saying in my language," Ryo said.

"I'm certain you'll share it."

Ryo seemed oblivious to his sarcasm. "'First I saw the mountains in the painting—then I saw the painting in the mountains.'"

What the devil was that supposed to mean?

And then, as though Ian hadn't the sense to decipher his annoying proverb, Ryo continued. "Not everything is as it seems."

That was rather obvious, wasn't it?

Ryo peered up at him. He opened his mouth to speak

and then closed it, as though reconsidering his words. He again focused on the painting, placing his hands behind his back. After a moment of silence, he said, "You were very pleased that day."

Ian cast Ryo an irritated glance. Of course Merrick would be pleased. He hadn't had to concern himself with his best friend dying of starvation or his mother sobbing herself to sleep every night.

Ryo's black eyes were sparkling. "Do you remember?"

As if the question conjured it, an image materialized in Ian's head. For an instant, he forgot it wasn't he who was depicted in the painting.

In fact, he remembered releasing his newly acquired bird from his arm, watching it soar high, laughing as he chased it across the field. He remembered his mother watching from a distance, her expression melancholy. And he remembered the joy he'd felt when the bird had returned to him of its own free will.

For a long moment, he was lost in reverie.

"It was painted just a few days after your thirteenth birthday, from the loft inside the carriage house," Ryo disclosed. "The year before it burned down."

Ian's lips curved at the memory. His mother had been convinced the carriage house was haunted. She claimed to have spied strange faces peering down at them through the upstairs window.

Ian blinked in momentary confusion.

It took him an instant too long to realize the images in his brain were real.

His focus snapped downward to find Ryo had slipped away.

If there had been a chair nearby, he would have sat down, so unsettling was the realization.

The carriage house had, in fact, burned down, the year after his thirteenth birthday. His mother had ordered the building destroyed to make room for her expanding garden.

Where did the lies end?

As much as he had uncovered, he still knew nothing at all.

What had his father done to anger his mother so that she would refuse him a presence in her life and in the life of their child? That she would burn down a building out of spite or out of fear?

Had she once been his mistress?

Had he discarded her?

Ian just couldn't imagine that his mother would allow herself to be entangled in such a sordid affair. She was entirely too proper, and far too proud, to be someone's kept woman.

But if the fault were entirely his father's, why would his mother allow him to raise even one of her children?

How could she have allowed Ian and Merrick to be separated?

Where did the truth begin and the lies end?

Chapter Eleven

Standing in the receiving line, Ian turned to look at his father's profile.

The Duchess of Kent—the influential Victoria—stood beside him, introducing guests as they arrived.

"Welcome," his father was saying. "Welcome."

He shook the hands of arriving gentlemen and patted the ladies' hands. To one he showed particular interest.

"Lady Stanford! So nice to see you again. And this—this cannot be your daughter!" he said, gesturing to the child hiding behind her. "My, how she's grown!"

He turned to Ian. "You do remember young Lady Margaret, Merrick? Isn't she absolutely delightful?"

"Indeed," Ian agreed.

And she was.

In fact, he would have been quite besotted by her, if only he were twelve.

Ian extended his hand to the woman, and then to her

child. "Very good to see you again," he said without feeling.

And so it progressed, one guest after another moving through the receiving line, until the room behind him was a crush of human life and the chatter of conversation drowned out the band.

He stood there, listening to the incessant drone, and wondered what the devil he was doing in this place, wearing his brother's clothes, his brother's shoes and his brother's name, when he could simply look his father in the face and ask the old man what he wished to know.

Because it isn't that simple, he reminded himself.

Someone led him away from the receiving line to the dais, so that he could better inspect the females being paraded before him. As he watched the procession—skinny women, fat women, young women and some who were long in the tooth—he was suddenly struck with a sense of regret so deep that he wanted to walk away not just from this wearisome party, but from London.

For all he knew, Merrick would have sent his father to the devil before subjecting himself to such a travesty. In fact, his brother's decision to leave London had very likely been, in part, due to these circumstances. And here Ian was about to choose a bride his brother would likely abhor.

His only comfort was in the fact that he wasn't about to walk anyone down any bloody aisle, and Merrick didn't have to go through with the farce if he didn't wish to.

"Do you see that young lady standing by the door?" the duchess was asking.

Ian turned his head in the direction she pointed but saw nothing but a sea of sashaying gowns. "Yes," he lied.

The duchess smiled. In her late thirties or early forties, she might have been handsome but for the plump figure and the ever-present censure upon her too-round face, and jowls that constantly jiggled in disapproval.

"That," she informed him, "is Von Munching's daughter. Her papa has a baronetcy in Germany and her mother is the daughter of the Earl of Berkshire. Very proper family, indeed."

Ian hadn't a bloody clue to which woman the duchess was referring. Everyone looked precisely the same. By the light of a dozen chandeliers, everyone was aglitter, like tiny fireworks winking insistently in his eyes.

And then he saw her.

She was a like a sultry shadow slipping through a rainbow. For the first time in more than a day, he felt the blood begin to pulse through his veins.

Gone was the peasantlike garb. She was dressed in black velvet—a black so rich it bordered on blue—with ebony lace spilling like Spanish moss from her sleeves. Her hair was twisted into a lovely but simple coif, with curls tumbling about her face. Her ears and neck were unadorned and her bodice was modest, though he did spy a hint of her creamy breasts from his perch high above the floor.

His reaction was immediate. His body heated with desire. His breath burned in his lungs, until he reminded himself to exhale.

God help him, if he'd thought her lovely before, she was unparalleled at this moment.

In fact, he couldn't recall seeing a more incredible woman in all his day.

It was all Ian could do to stand and pretend to listen to the duchess as she prattled on about barons and dukes and earls while his father listened.

"What about her?" Ian asked, interrupting the duchess in the midst of her monologue.

The duchess lifted her fan to her breast. "Who, dear boy?"

Boy? Ian thought, taking mild offense, though he smiled. If she thought him a boy, let her slip a hand inside his trousers and see if she still believed it. He was hard as a bloody stump.

"That one," he said, nodding in Claire's direction. She stood beside a woman dressed in mauve.

"Do you mean the lovely young lady standing next to the display?"

Ian realized, with a private smile, that Claire had chosen a spot in perfect view of the crown jewels.

"Yes," he said, watching her. She hadn't even bothered to look his way. And he didn't recall her coming through the line. She must have arrived late.

"That would be Lady Alexandra, Lord Huntington's only child," the duchess revealed. "She's quite lovely, I agree, and her lineage is impeccable, as well."

Ian frowned. "The girl in black?" he asked. "Her name is Alexandra?"

The duchess reared her head back. "The girl in black?" she repeated, looking befuddled by the question. Then she shook her head. "Oh, no, no, no, dear boy! That would be Lady Claire Wentworth." She turned to look more directly at Claire.

Claire was still studying the jewels, oblivious to their regard.

"Poor child," the duchess said. "Her mother passed when she was but a little thing, and her father turned his toes up some months ago." The duchess raised her fan to cover her mouth as she stretched up to whisper in Ian's ear, "I hear tell they are in quite deep."

So she was in debt.

That would explain much.

Ian turned to look at the duchess, and she nodded, fanning herself as she peered back at Claire. "She's lovely, I suppose, though her brother Ben inherited all the wit and charm—if nothing else, poor dear boy."

Ian couldn't disagree more. If Claire's wit were any sharper, he'd be six feet under by now.

"As I understand it, she's quite the bluestocking and keeps mostly to herself," the duchess added with unmasked disapproval.

"Really," Ian said. "No husband?"

The duchess gave him a shrewish glance and cackled. "What man would shackle himself to a penniless woman who cannot even abide by the rules of propriety? Why, look at that dress! I simply cannot believe she wore velvet tonight," she said, shaking her head. "It's quite disrespectful of her father, though I suppose it's to be expected with *that* one."

"I don't recall meeting her," his father commented.

"You wouldn't," the duchess assured him. "She

didn't attend the last soiree—though for the life of me I can't remember why."

It seemed to Ian that the duchess recalled quite enough. It was a wonder her nose hadn't stretched clear across Britain, as she seemed to have it in everyone's affairs.

The duchess added somewhat absently, "I haven't seen her brother around of late. I wonder where he's off to."

"At any rate, she doesn't appear to be the sort we are interested in," his father interjected. His dismissive tone grated on Ian's nerves.

Ian could bloody well speak for himself.

"Of course not," the duchess agreed. "You'd fare *much* better with Lord Huntington's daughter." And then she laughed and smacked Ian's arm with her fan. "But, you rascal, I'm certain you have no memory of your first encounter with the poor darling. You were—" she smirked, fanning herself a little faster "—less than interested, I should say. I heard it for months afterward from her mother—how you broke her daughter's heart."

Ian found himself nettled.

Devil hang him, he was sandwiched between two old shrews—one of the female variety and another who happened to have a bloody cock between his legs. No wonder they got along so famously.

In Ian's opinion, Claire was far more appealing than any ten women in this room together.

He watched as she spoke to the guard. Even from this distance, her gaze and stance looked flirtatious.

Something like jealousy pricked at him.

Obviously, she hadn't the least bit of interest in presenting herself to the prince; she had yet to even look his way.

Her true motive for coming was apparent.

She coveted those jewels.

She might be a lady, in truth, but she was also a beautiful, conniving little thief at heart.

He suddenly wanted nothing more than to drag her outside and slip his tongue between those sweet, red lips.

He wanted her, damn it.

And, in truth, this very instant, he wanted her more than he wanted the answers to all his bloody questions.

He was deaf and blind to the guests who approached him, the mothers introducing their daughters, the widows introducing their breasts.

He was focused only on Claire.

Then, suddenly, he stumbled on a perfect solution for everyone.

"Excuse me," Ian said, and walked away.

The jewels had been placed at center stage, inside a display case flanked by four guards. They were armed, though not in the conventional fashion—shiny scimitars were sheathed on ornate belts. All four guards were muscular, with billowing white shirts and loose black breeches that did little to hide their hulking forms.

Claire listened to the guard who was speaking, trying to ignore Lord Huntington, whose smiles and winks and brushes against her person had suddenly taken on new meaning.

"The queen, having lost her true love to the sea, was drawn to the shore where the lovers had spent so many hours together. Each day," the guard continued, "the queen wept, her tears spilling into the tide, and each evening when she retired, her handmaiden knelt where her mistress had stood, scooping up the evidence of her sorrow...her tears, which had crystallized upon striking the water."

"She must have wept for months!" Alexandra exclaimed.

Claire didn't believe it, of course, but she thought the fairy tale charming. She wondered how many times the guard had recounted it this evening already.

"There are so many jewels," she said, examining the sapphires, which were all precisely equal in size and shape. The tiara itself was covered with the brilliant blue gems and detailed with sparkling diamonds. The ring was a tear-shaped sapphire framed by three tiers of tiny diamonds.

Peering over her shoulder, Lord Huntington scooted nearer. He was so close now that Claire could almost feel the warmth of his breath on the back of her neck, and it repulsed her.

Alexandra scarce seemed to notice her father, or how he was carrying on.

"Alas, there was once a matching necklace," the guard disclosed. "But it was stolen some thirty years ago."

"Really?" Alexandra asked. She clucked her tongue and fluttered her eyelashes at the guard. "What, pray tell, is this world coming to, that people can justify stealing what belongs to others? It's simply a tragedy!"

Claire felt a tiny prick of guilt.

The guard returned Alexandra's smile. "Indeed, my

lady. It's terrible. In fact, for six hundred years, every Queen of Meridian has been portrayed wearing the entire set, except the last—Elena of Spain. The queen died very young, and His Majesty has never remarried. But, it is said that when the necklace is found, the king will find true love."

Alexandra sighed. "That is so romantic!" she declared. She elbowed Claire. "Isn't it, Claire?"

It was, indeed.

Claire sighed, realizing that no matter what wicked thoughts had brought her to this place, she could never steal from these people—from anyone. Like her grandmother's silver, and the sword hanging on the wall inside the pawnshop, these jewels were somebody's history, somebody's treasures.

She smiled wanly, reconsidering Lord Huntington's proposal.

When Ben's life was at stake, she had no room to bargain.

"I see you've acquainted yourself quite nicely with the crown jewels," a familiar voice taunted her.

Claire gasped at the sound. Her eyes snapped upward. "You, again!"

Those pale blue eyes seemed to penetrate her. "Do you find them to your liking?" he asked, his expression as mocking as ever.

Still, God save her, his slow smile was devastating.

Although her cheeks felt hot and her legs were liquid, Claire straightened her spine. "Sir, have you nothing better to do than to follow me and harass me?" she asked, hoping she sounded composed despite her private distress.

"My lady!" the guard intervened. "You mustn't—"

"It's quite all right," her tormentor said to the guard, lifting a hand to silence him, though his gaze never left Claire's face. And then he turned to the guard and demanded with palm outstretched, "Give me the ring."

To Claire's shock, the guard didn't argue. He opened the display case to retrieve it, and she had a sudden, sinking feeling.

"There you are, Your Royal Highness."

Your Royal Highness.

Claire groaned inwardly.

She wanted nothing more than to sink into oblivion. Alexandra was staring. In fact, Claire was acutely aware that *everyone* was staring.

She was too overwhelmed to speak. He seized her hand and slipped the ring onto her finger. To her dismay, she hadn't the wherewithal to resist.

"What are you doing?" she asked.

He winked at her. "A beautiful ring deserves a beautiful bride," he replied.

Claire blinked in horror at the sight of the enormous ring on her finger. Her face flamed. "But you mistake—"

He drew her toward the dance floor, out of Alexandra's earshot, and forced her to dance, despite the fact that they couldn't make out a single note of music over the sudden outburst of chatter.

"I mistake nothing," he said with great meaning as he drew her closer. "I am fully aware of the reason for your attendance this evening, Claire."

Claire didn't dare pull away from his steely embrace—not with so many pairs of eyes fastened on them—but she longed to. The warmth of his skin made her feel weak. And her heart was tripping so hard that she feared it would burst through her breast.

She said low, for his ears alone, mortified by her body's response to him, by the attention forced on her, "You really haven't a clue why I am here, *Your Royal Highness.* And it's Lady Claire Wentworth to you, thank you very much. Now, I demand you release me. This is entirely inappropriate."

He smiled, stealing her breath away. "Of course I know why you're here," he whispered. "And you are in no position to demand anything from me, madam."

Claire's face warmed.

It was true. She had, of course, come to *see* the ring. But she truly wouldn't have stolen it. She had only fantasized about doing so, hadn't really done anything but *look* at the jewels, and he hadn't a blessed thing to accuse her of. No matter what he thought of her, she wasn't a thief.

"I have a proposal for you, *Claire,*" he murmured. His raspy voice sent tiny tremors down her spine.

No man had ever affected her so.

Claire tried to remain calm, but panic bubbled up inside her. "And what, pray tell, might that be, *Your Royal Highness?*"

No matter that he took liberties with her Christian name, she wouldn't return the disfavor.

"I've no desire to marry you any more than you wish to marry me," he said, dropping all sense of pretense or tact. "In fact, I have no desire to wed anyone at all. And so, I'm willing to make you a proposal—one we will both profit from."

Claire tensed, afraid he would offer her the same proposal Lord Huntington had. "And what might that be?"

His eyes gleamed. "I will escort you to the dais to meet my father," he said, "and I will publicly announce that I have chosen my bride. You will flash those beautiful white teeth and the ring on your finger, stand by my side and try, very desperately, to appear pleased by my choice. At the end of this farce, you may keep the ring without question. You need only make up some reason as to why you cannot wed me. Perhaps you don't love me, after all."

"Of course I don't love you!" Claire protested. What a ludicrous notion! How could she love a man she didn't even know? "I've only met you twice!" she pointed out.

"Three times," he corrected her. "And that's enough to establish at least an attraction, don't you think?"

Claire gasped. "I am *not* the least bit attracted to you, I assure you!"

"Are you not?"

Claire's heart did a telltale flip. She was afraid he might feel it as well. "Not at all," she lied.

He grinned as though, somehow, he knew differently. "Pity," he said. "Because I'm quite attracted to you."

Claire felt as though she would swoon where she stood. In fact, she was quite afraid that the only thing keeping her from doing so was his firm embrace.

There was an awkward moment of silence between them.

"Any excuse not to marry me will do," he reassured her, as though he hadn't just made her skin prickle. "Perhaps you simply don't wish to leave England. And then, after you cruelly reject me, I shall depart London—a brokenhearted man—and return to Meridian to lick my wounds like a sad little puppy."

"I can hardly see that you would be heartbroken after such a brief engagement."

"Certainly, I would be disappointed," he countered, his tone disaffected. "After all, I managed to snare the loveliest woman in all of London."

Claire commanded herself not to blush over his false flattery, but her cheeks betrayed her.

His plan seemed far too simple. "Why would you do such a thing?"

"To buy time, of course."

Claire lifted a brow. "Time for what?"

"To find a more suitable bride, if I must. Evidently, I have exhausted everyone's patience and I am ordered to choose, tonight, the woman destined to bear me little princes and princesses. Have you looked about you this evening? We are surrounded by emptyheaded misses who, apparently, have managed to acquire more lace than wit in their lifetimes."

Claire choked back a bit of laughter. She had to confess that she rather agreed with his assessment of the ton.

"Do you realize that's the first smile I've ever witnessed on your beautiful lips? It's quite startling."

Claire ignored his compliment. He was proposing a business arrangement, not an *affaire de coeur,* and it behooved her to remember as much.

"Forgive me for pointing out the obvious, sirrah, but you haven't particularly given me any reasons to smile."

He winked at her. “We’ll have to remedy that, won’t we?”

Claire’s heart skipped another beat.

She didn’t *want* to be attracted to him and didn’t care what he thought of her. Nor did she believe he truly cared about her feelings. “And what if I should refuse your offer?”

He flashed her a disarming smile. “Then I shall be forced to regale everyone with tales of our first, very memorable encounter. It might prove to be somewhat awkward, don’t you think?”

Claire straightened her spine and tried to smile. “You would blackmail me?”

His grin only widened. “Of course. It’s hardly the worst thing I have ever done.”

Claire frowned at him. “You can tell anyone anything you like,” she declared, refusing to kowtow to him, though, in truth, she did care. Her face must be as bright as Alexandra’s dress, but it grew warmer still—in part from anger, because she couldn’t just turn down his offer. Too much was at stake to allow pride to prevail.

“Do it my way and we both walk away winners,” he urged.

Pride warred with good sense.

Claire peered up at him. “And you will not contest my reason for breaking our betrothal?”

“Absolutely not.” His eyes seemed to speak the truth. “Why should I wish to force any woman into wedlock?”

“And afterward, you will give me the ring without question?”

"Yes," he said. "Or a sum of money of equal value, whichever you prefer."

Claire sighed. "Very well."

"Famous! Now, smile, my darling, we have a very happy announcement to make."

Claire gave him a half smile.

"That's my girl," he said, and pulled her toward him for a brief cheek hug. Claire allowed him to lead her off the dance floor toward the dais, suddenly aware that the room was now so hushed one could hear oneself breathe.

It was all a ruse, she reminded herself.

There was no reason for jitters.

Still, her legs trembled as he turned to assist her up the steps. A single glance upward at his father and the duchess revealed their expressions of horror. If he hadn't placed his hand at her back to steady her, Claire might have swooned.

As he led her before his father and introduced her, Claire felt as though she were in a dream.

"Congratulations, my dear," the duchess said amiably, despite her earlier expression of disfavor. She kissed both Claire's cheeks. "You are quite the fortunate young lady. Your papa would be proud."

His Majesty said nothing at all, simply smiled and patted her hand, his eyes never lifting from the ring. He was clearly at a loss for words. Claire wanted to reassure him that it would all be over soon but his disapproval stung—though not enough to dampen her growing enthusiasm.

She peered down at the ring, wondering how much

it was worth. Never in her girlhood fantasies could she have imagined the prospect of becoming a jilted bride would make her so euphoric. Let everyone pity her in a month when it was over. She would walk away with a fortune. And, best of all, her brother would be free.

Now, she need only send a message to Ben's captors to plead for more time.

Chapter Twelve

By the following morning, everyone in London who was able to read, or who had ears to hear, knew the news.

Claire might have thought it all a dream but for the gargantuan ring on her finger—that, and the front page of *The Times* that greeted her when she opened her bedroom door. Jasper had the paper down in front of her door so that she was forced to face the morning's headlines.

A Crown For A Lady, the headline teased.

Bending to lift up the periodical, Claire shook her head, amazed that with all the crime and world events, a simple engagement should make the front page.

It wasn't even a true engagement.

The article declared:

HRH, the Crown Prince of Meridian and Lady Claire Wentworth are to be wed.

Last evening, at a ball sponsored by the Duchess of Kent, the engagement was made official, bringing Prince Merrick's celebrated three-year search for a bride to a stunning conclusion.

A spokesman for Meridian's royal house made the following statement: "It is with great pleasure that the royal house of Meridian announces the betrothal of its beloved son, HRH, the Crown Prince of Meridian, to Lady Claire Wentworth, daughter of the late Earl of Highbury and the late Countess of Highbury."

The seventh Earl of Highbury, the late Earl's only surviving heir, is expected to give away the bride. He could not be reached for comment.

In anticipation of the joyous event, the Archbishop of Canterbury has honored a request for a special license. The wedding, however, is to be held in Meridian, to allow the bride a respectful period of mourning.

Making her way downstairs, Claire turned to the society page. There she found another, longer article. This one detailed the entire evening, reprimanding her for her scandalous choice of dress—how dare she wear velvet while still in mourning—and implying that *now* she would be forced to learn proper decorum, as the Royal House of Meridian was likely to be far less forgiving than her too-permissive father. However, the article forgave her for her lapses in judgment, declaring that she "could scarce be blamed for her choices because of the absence of a proper female figure in her household."

Claire took offense. What was she, if not proper? Unlike many women, she'd never even kissed a man. She'd never worn revealing dresses or flirted with married men. In truth, she'd never flirted with anyone at all, and she doubted she would know how. She had never spoken ill of—or to—anyone, nor had she ever been disrespectful to her father. Perhaps she wasn't precisely political, but she was certainly proper!

Although the article rankled her, she continued to read, fascinated to know what the public thought about her and her unexpected betrothal.

Apparently, she was London's new darling, and mothers had offered to tutor her before her imminent departure from England. Claire frowned as she continued to read. She hardly needed *tutoring.* Her intellect was not lacking—she knew far more than most—and her manners were impeccable. Simply because she didn't enjoy soirees, gossip and shopping didn't make her a complete misfit.

The article dared to suggest that her brother should be grateful for the match, as it was rumored they were left deep in dun territory after their father's death.

There was also speculation about a longstanding affaire between Claire and the prince, but the Duchess of Kent had issued a statement of contradiction, attesting to the fact that before last evening, Prince Merrick hadn't even known Claire's name. However, the duchess admitted Prince Merrick had been enamored with Claire from the instant he'd set eyes on her.

Halfway down the stairwell, Claire sat on the steps to finish reading.

It wasn't true, of course, that Merrick was enamored of her. The duchess hadn't the first inkling how they'd met. She couldn't know that even his compliments were laced with mockery.

The article ended with fervent good wishes for the "happy couple" and declared that London had not witnessed such a fairy-tale coupling for ages. It concluded that all of London, from the very rich to the very poor, would follow the courting and transformation of Lady Claire Wentworth.

Part of Claire wanted to scream and toss down the paper. Part of her wanted to fold it neatly and stash it somewhere safe, because, if she didn't know better—know the real story behind it all—she might be drawn into believing the fantasy.

It did *seem* terribly romantic, if one looked only at the surface. Beneath the surface, however, the truth was far less glittery.

Still, she wondered why Merrick had chosen her when he could very well have offered the same proposal to anyone.

Unless he was just the tiniest bit attracted to her, as he claimed. And she was forced to confess, if only to herself, that that *was* a shockingly pleasant thought.

But it wouldn't serve to dwell on it, she told herself. In a short time, everything would be over; the prince would vanish from London, and she would be alone again—with Ben, of course—and no longer quite so destitute.

No matter what his reason for the proposal—perhaps he felt guilty for his mistreatment of her—Claire had awakened this morning feeling as though a tremendous burden had been lifted from her shoulders. And she would gladly play the part of a happy bride until the time arrived to end the affair. Then, she would claim she wasn't prepared to leave London to make her home in a strange land. She would end their betrothal and wish Prince Merrick well.

Then she would forget him.

"How's our reluctant guest?" Huntington asked.

"Full of complaints."

"Well, that's to be expected, isn't it?" Huntington asked. "I want you to raise the ransom."

He'd been thwarted by the most unexpected turn of events. Weeks before, when Ben had come to him seeking counsel and money, he'd referred the boy instead to the back room at White's, as he wasn't in the habit of giving away his bank notes. Ben's debts had presented him with the perfect opportunity to get what he really wanted.

Claire.

He'd coveted her from the moment she'd flowered into womanhood. Unlike the rest of the ton, his daughter included, Claire actually used her God-given wits for something more than calculating her social status. No, winning her would take far more than the promise of a pretty ring on her finger—or so he'd thought.

Last night's engagement had taken him aback. Had he thought it even remotely possible, he would never have sent Alexandra to convince Claire to join them for the evening.

The hireling lifted a brow. "But she can't pay what she owes as it is. An' she ain't got much left."

"How do you know what remains in her possession?"

"How d' ye think?" the man countered. "I took a gander with me own two eyes. The house is as bare as a baby's arse."

"I see," Huntington said. "Well, it doesn't matter. She'll either ask *prince charming* for what she requires, or she'll come running back to me." He lit a cheroot and sucked in a slow, deliberate drag, exhaling toward the shorter man's face. "In either case, we might as well get a little something extra for our efforts, eh?"

Huntington assessed his surroundings. Only the lowest of businessmen and the sleaziest clientele ventured this deep into the rookeries. And only the most ignorant or stupid were at ease here. He was vigilant but not afraid. To his way of thinking, it was not unlike being in the bush, where the hunter could, in the blink of an eye, become the hunted.

Unaffected by the smoke, the hireling shrugged, though his eyes betrayed a flicker of greed. "Naturally, I'll be expectin' me cut to go up."

"Of course." Though not if he didn't earn it, Huntington determined, and considered how best to utilize the man's services.

Stoic little chit that she was, Claire hadn't bothered to come to him until her "little gift" had been delivered. "The finger was a good touch," he remarked. "I trust it didn't actually belong to the lad?"

The hireling shook his head. "Nah. Belongs to some dead bloke who won't be missin' it where he's lyin'."

"Good. Just to make it more interesting, why don't

we give the lady another little fright tonight?" Huntington suggested.

The man smirked. "I can manage that."

"I have every faith in you," Huntington said and tipped his hat in a combined gesture of faux respect and farewell. "I believe that concludes our meeting, *sir.* And I shall look forward to hearing more about this evening's encounter. Just leave her intact," he advised. "Or you shan't be seeing a single penny."

The hireling waited until Huntington mounted his curricle and drove away, then spit on the ground. "Dirty bugger," he said.

Claire narrowed her eyes at the driver.

It wasn't enough that he had nearly run her down and then had blamed the accident on her. Now he stood at her front door, stubbornly insisting that she accompany him as though she hadn't any choice in the matter.

He announced, "Tonight's gathering is in your honor, madam. Prince Merrick is eager to present you to his guests."

For an instant, Claire wavered, but only for an instant. It was, after all, a false engagement, she reminded herself, and tonight's *gathering* was an unnecessary formality. "I cannot simply leap into your carriage and fly away with you, Mr.—"

"Ryosan."

"Mr. Ryosan..."

The driver shook his head. "Only Ryosan. In the country of my birth, *san* is the same as mister."

Claire frowned, wondering how in God's name the

conversation had suddenly become a lesson in foreign languages. "Yes, well, thank you very much for enlightening me, Ryosan, but I still will not accompany you. In *my* country, you see, when a woman's attendance is desired, an invitation—with ample time for preparation—is in order."

God's truth, Claire didn't consider herself the least bit vain, but the thought of facing Merrick in her present state left her stomach in knots.

No, she just wouldn't go.

She was certain Merrick wouldn't renege on their deal simply because she refused to accept a last-minute invitation to dinner.

"I understand," the driver said, smiling.

Claire thought he might be mocking her.

"But then we have a dilemma, as I have been instructed not to return without you."

"No, sir," Claire countered, her tone unwavering. "*We* have no dilemma at all. *You,* sir, have a dilemma." She smiled back at him, though not so coolly. "And I am quite certain you will find a satisfactory solution."

"Yes, madam," the driver replied, his tone respectful but unwavering. "And so, you must forgive me if I remain on your doorstep all night."

Fine!

Claire refused to be bullied.

"I shall deliver you a pillow," she countered.

The driver's dark eyes were unfathomable. "And a blanket, please," he added. "It will be cold tonight."

It would, indeed, but Claire wasn't about to admit to

feelings of guilt, despite the fact that she felt a momentary stab of it. She closed the door, her cheeks warming.

He really didn't have to remain on the doorstep *all* night, she assured herself. He had two legs, after all, and could leave if he so chose. Claire was certain Merrick wouldn't punish him for something not of his doing. After all, the driver couldn't very well drag her out of her house against her will, could he?

Then again, she hadn't a clue how they behaved in Meridian.

Perhaps they did drag their women about by their hair.

"Are you quite certain it is the right decision, madam?" Jasper asked her.

"Quite!" Claire declared. The last thing she cared to do this evening was to suffer *His Majesty*'s scrutiny—or Merrick's tongue, for that matter. "Give him a blanket and a pillow," she directed Jasper. "That is, if you can find one. And if anyone else should happen to inquire, I have retired for the evening."

Chapter Thirteen

Ian had requested the small, impromptu dinner under the premise that it would appear only natural for him to want his father and friends to acquaint themselves with his bride. But he was forced to acknowledge, as he sat at a table where the meal had already been served and cleared and every seat was occupied save one, that it had simply been a ploy to see her—a ploy that had, unfortunately, backfired.

The duchess pushed her tea away and said what no one else dared. "Well, dear boy, it doesn't appear she'll be attending, after all."

In keeping with her exalted opinion, the other guests offered apologetic grimaces and shrugs.

His father sat at the head of the table, his expression not the least unsettled. "Perhaps Lady Claire Wentworth isn't the right choice, after all," he said, clearly relishing the opportunity to alter present circumstances.

"So you have already said," Ian countered, an edge of annoyance to his voice.

The duchess defended his father. "Clearly, she hasn't the least respect for your wishes. Any normal woman would have been pleased to alter her schedule to attend a dinner in her honor, impromptu or not."

Ian clenched his jaw. "It was a last-minute invitation. I hardly expect her to leap to my demands."

Though, in truth, some part of him *had* expected her to come running. He'd been certain that, at heart, she was no different from the rest of her breed—willing to do anything in the pursuit of riches and fame.

Apparently, she wasn't willing to suffer his company for a single moment longer than she must. The realization stung enough that, instead of turning the conversation toward matters of true concern—Glen Abbey and his own affairs—he'd spent the entire dinner obsessing about a green-eyed vixen who'd soon enough disappear from his life.

It was hardly time well spent.

"I would not take it quite so personally," the duchess suggested. "As I've said, Lady Claire Wentworth has somewhat of a reputation for disaffection."

Not for the first time, Ian wondered why the duchess was so engrossed in their affairs. What stake had she in the outcome of Meridian's politics? Clearly, she was ambitious, but what else did she aspire to? Was she enamored of his father? Ian studied the two of them. His father didn't strike him as a man who was romantically inclined, nor did the duchess seem to be dangling over him. So, then, were they simply two greedy schemers looking for the "most propitious alignment"?

His brother must have nerves and patience of steel

to deal with these people. Or perhaps, like Ian, he just didn't give a damn, because he was bound to do whatever was necessary—within or without the law.

In fact, to blazes with propriety. Just now, while his father was otherwise occupied, would be the perfect opportunity to search the king's private quarters. Ian stood, tossed down his napkin and took a French leave, not bothering to supply an acceptable reason for retiring. He simply left the table and the dining room.

"Poor dear," he overheard the duchess say as he departed.

In this cavernous house there were no such things as whispers.

"I haven't a clue what devil has possessed my son," his father retorted, not bothering with hushed tones. "I'm afraid he's not himself these days. Please accept my apologies for Merrick's rudeness."

Ian shook his head, disgusted.

His father still hadn't a clue which son he was dealing with.

Old fool.

Unsure what awoke her, Claire opened her eyes to a still, moonlit room.

The curtains were drawn, though not entirely. A gap remained where, hours ago, she'd pulled them aside to peer outside. The driver had, indeed, made himself comfortable in his coach. Stubborn codger. The moonlight was bound to keep her awake, but she didn't really wish to get up and risk the night air reviving her and keeping her awake for the remainder of the night.

As it was, her brain was beginning to roil with unwanted thoughts.

Feeling guilty for refusing Merrick's invitation, she'd removed the ring from her finger and had tucked it underneath her pillow. Like a pebble in a mattress, its stony presence was making her sore.

How dare he expect her to come running at his command, like some silly puppy?

Sighing, she flipped away from the window and faced the wall, trying not to think about the way he'd looked at her whilst they'd danced.

He was using her, she reminded herself.

Though why would he invite her to a small, private affair, where hardly anyone would see them together?

Unless he simply wished to see her.

Poppycock, she chided herself.

He didn't know her, and he'd made it quite clear that the farce would be over soon.

She tried hard not to think about Ben either, because whenever she did, panic nearly overwhelmed her. She was so close to being able to free him, and that's what she must remain focused on.

As soon as the sham engagement was over, she could use the ring to pay the ransom. Reaching beneath the pillow, she fingered the precious stones, smiling despite herself at the way Prince Merrick had unceremoniously placed it on her finger. She'd been mortified at discovering his identity. And Alexandra had stared, openmouthed.

Her eyes drooped as she stared at the faded flowered wallpaper, a French design her mother had chosen to celebrate Claire's graduation from the nursery. Her father had suggested replacing it some years ago, but Claire had declined the offer. Although she wasn't a flowery sort of person, she liked her rose-scattered paper just the same.

Drifting toward more pleasant memories, she let go of the ring.

A shadow crossed the wall, and her eyes fluttered open. For an instant, she thought it was only the curtains slipping back into position, masking the moonlight, but the shape flitted past, revealing light once more. Instinctively, she turned to see what had moved.

A male hand covered her mouth. Claire was forced to turn and stare at a twisted silhouette on the wall, though not before she caught a glimpse of him. He was the same man who had followed her from the pawnshop.

"Don't say a bloo'y word," a raspy voice commanded her.

Claire's heart pounded.

"I'm not going t' hurt ye—not this time."

She tried to speak, to ask what he wanted, but her words, forced through the knot in her throat and muffled by the hand clasped about her mouth, came out indecipherable.

"Shh," he said. "Do ye wish t' see your brother alive, *princess?*"

Claire nodded.

"Well, then, *princess,* just gi' me the bloo'y ring."

Claire shook her head as he groped for her fingers. Finding nothing, he demanded, "Where is it?"

He loosened his grip on her mouth to let her speak.

"I—I don't have it," she lied, realizing that there would be no assurances that he would release Ben if he absconded with the ring now.

"I don' believe ye," he growled, and pressed her face into the pillow.

Claire's heart flipped as the ring dug into her cheek. He was pushing so hard that she could feel it cutting through the down. "It's true," she swore. "Prince Merrick is keeping it until after the wedding."

"Well, then, the sum is now two-hundred fifty thousand pounds," he told her, shoving his hand against her mouth once more and jamming her face way down into the pillow.

Claire cried out. She tried to turn to plead with him, but he shoved her forward and pinned her to the bed. She felt the prick of cold steel against the back of her neck. "Uh-uh," he said, his breath smelling of sour ale. "You just get me another fifty thousand pounds, or I'll be tying ye both up by the ankles and dropping ye into the Thames. And your spoiled prince won't be able to save you."

Claire wanted to assure him that she would have the money soon, but he buried his face into the back of her hair, and she swallowed every word she was about to utter.

"I'm going t' go now, but don't scream or turn about, or I'll be cuttin' my losses here and now. Do ye get my meaning, *princess?*"

Claire didn't dare tell him she'd already recognized him. She hesitated in responding and he licked the back of her neck, drawing a shudder of disgust from her.

"Understand?" he asked again.

Claire nodded.

"Good," he said, and released her at last.

She didn't hear him walk away, so thunderous was the beating of her heart, so silent were his footsteps.

She watched the retreat of his silhouette into shadow with bated breath. And then, even after he'd been gone what seemed an eternity, she did not stir. Only when she was certain she was alone did she turn. Finding the room empty, she seized the ring and bounded up from the bed, her heart racing as she made her way to the hall door.

Greeted by silence, she peered into the corridor. Finding it empty, she flew down the hall and down the stairs toward the front door. Only when she reached the foyer did she dare scream.

Chapter Fourteen

With Ryo gone to fetch Claire, and his father preoccupied with the guests, Ian headed to the master's quarters.

After searching the room thoroughly, he found a small box in the closet. It had been tucked away behind a stack of hatboxes. For some reason, its placement struck him as odd. He sat in the chair nearest the closet to sift through it. Its contents took him aback. The box was brimming with letters that had never been dispatched, all addressed to his mother.

He sat in the chair reading and hadn't the first inkling how long he sat, or how much time passed.

God's truth, he no longer gave a damn if he were discovered.

From the letters, he gathered that his mother had once been betrothed to his father, a fact that both relieved and dismayed him. In anticipation of the coming wedding, his grandfather had signed away Glen Abbey as a dowry gift. It was the only thing he'd had of value to offer. He'd been so thrilled to have his daughter marry so well that he hadn't considered the consequences were they to part, so he'd made no provisions for that possibility. From what Ian gathered, the wedding had nearly occurred but had been called off at the last moment. Though his mother hadn't quite been jilted at the altar, she'd been jilted nevertheless. Apparently, his father had been forced to keep a childhood engagement with a Spanish heiress of royal blood. Only by then his mother was pregnant, with twins. And his father had forced her to choose between her two infants, keeping one to claim as his heir.

It was unthinkable, and yet…

In reading the letters, it seemed his father felt some remorse and that he wished to absolve himself.

So why hadn't he?

More disconcerting than shocking, Ian found countless vials of laudanum in the box—empty ones, full ones. Was the king drugging himself into apathy? Or was he taking the drug to ease the symptoms of some illness?

Why the hell should Ian care?

And why, by God, was his father bound and determined to foist his same mistake on his son?

It was obvious he must have loved their mother. If the quantity of letters didn't betray it—so many it could be called an obsession—his words spoke volumes.

How could he justify forcing Merrick to marry for political gain when he'd clearly regretted his decision every day of his life? In fact, he had made his Spanish heiress suffer for it. According to the letters, she'd never borne him any children and had died a miserable young woman.

And Merrick—what sort of life had his brother led, when his own father did not seem to know him?

At least Ian had been gifted with his mother's love. His mother might have lied to him, and he wasn't pleased to know it, but she certainly wasn't as cold as the man who had fathered him.

Whatever truth Ian had set out to uncover, his discovery tonight was entirely unexpected.

He read from a letter dated November 23, 1816:

> I am sending Ryo with a gift of a saker for Ian's thirteenth birthday. You may tell the boy…

He couldn't refer to him by name?

> …it was a gift from whomever. I have also commissioned a portrait to be painted by a certain acquaintance, a man by the name of John Constable. Please allow him to record the moment of gift giving, as I would greatly relish the opportunity to further John's name and reputation. I think you will agree that his talent has been greatly overlooked and you should feel free to set aside funds to commission a piece for yourself while he is yet available.

The letter ended in an angry scribble of black ink that bled profusely into yellowed paper. A first draft, perhaps? Had he bothered to pen another? So his father wanted to further the man's reputation, did he? Was that his primary objective? Had he said as much to Ian's mother? Was that why she'd been angry enough to burn down the carriage house? Had she watched the man peer down at them, prying into their lives, and burned inside with rage?

Ian tossed the letter back into the box. Were it put to Ian like that, he might have strangled the poor messenger where he stood.

Ryo had been there the day Ian had been presented with the bird, he realized. Ryo knew everything and yet he'd never told Merrick.

The bedroom door opened. Ian didn't bother looking up. He twirled a vial of laudanum in his right hand, acutely aware of the fragility of its glass.

"Merrick?" his father said, obviously startled to find him in his private quarters.

Ian peered up at him, his eyes stinging.

"What are you doing?" his father asked.

Ian didn't blink. "Looking for answers."

It was time to face the truth, no more sorting through lies.

His father averted his gaze. "I see."

He saw nothing at all.

Ian stared hard, willing the man to look at him.

He refused. "Your *bride* has finally arrived," he said.

Ian blinked. "Claire?"

"Do you have another stashed somewhere?" his father asked, daring now to look his way.

"Do you?" Ian countered.

His father's eyes glittered. "She's quite distraught," he disclosed, changing the topic, maintaining his composure. "You should tend to her at once."

"She can wait," Ian snapped, annoyed that his father could dismiss the situation so easily.

"She's weeping," his father announced.

Dread ripped through Ian. He bounded up from the chair, dropping the vial of laudanum at his feet as he brushed past his father.

Chapter Fifteen

"She refuses to speak to anyone but you," the duchess announced as Ian approached the drawing room.

It was evident by the woman's florid complexion that she was agitated by her lack of command over the situation.

Ian could hardly blame Claire for holding her tongue. She was wise enough to realize nothing she said in the duchess's presence would remain in confidence.

Inside the drawing room, Claire was perched on the edge of the settee, her eyes red rimmed. She had, indeed, been weeping, but she was settled now, wrapped in a blanket that didn't quite conceal her bare ankles. Evidently, she'd left her home in quite a rush.

Ryo stood guard at her side, looking very protective of her, despite their previous dissention.

He wasn't alone in his solicitude.

If anyone had harmed Claire, Ian swore he'd strangle the fool with his bare hands.

Still attempting to manage the situation, the duchess followed Ian into the drawing room. "I took the liberty of sending the guests home," she explained, as though she were mistress of this house and not a guest herself. "And I sent for tea. It should help to calm her."

"I'd like to speak with Claire alone," Ian said at once, not bothering to wait until Claire requested it. It was obvious Claire had little to say in Victoria's presence.

The duchess halted, tapping her heel in a telltale gesture of disapproval. "Of course," she replied, but Ian knew he had offended her.

He didn't give a tinker's damn. If his father was concerned about Victoria's sensibilities, he could get his arse downstairs and pander to her all he wished.

Ian and Ryo shared a look of understanding, and Ryo moved forward to see the duchess out, closing the door behind her.

Claire waited until Ryo stepped out of the room, not that she minded his presence terribly. He'd been kind to her since the ordeal, coming at once to her rescue and whisking her away from the house. But she wanted to speak to Merrick alone. She needed to be certain he wouldn't refuse to let her keep the ring. It was her only hope for Ben. This morning, she had been so certain her troubles were nearing an end. She'd felt safe in her own home. Tonight, she felt violated and afraid—not merely for Ben, but for herself, as well.

These men were greedy and ruthless; that much was clear.

What if she were to give them everything they wanted, and *still* they wanted more?

She was grateful Merrick had sent the duchess out. It was horrid enough that the duchess had witnessed Claire dressed in a night rail, a blanket and little else. No doubt everyone would hear of it tomorrow. It couldn't be helped. Claire hadn't dared to go back into the house. She had insisted, even, that Jasper and Mrs. Tandy spend the remainder of the evening at their daughter's home.

Despite their earlier discord, she was glad to be with Merrick now. He was the first person she'd thought of as she'd run screaming out the door, the only person she could imagine sharing confidences with now. She didn't dare go to Alexandra or back to Lord Huntington.

"Thank you so much for seeing me," she said, knowing he must be piqued that she had refused his invitation. In fact, he seemed quite put out, towering above her now, his hands resting on his hips. She shivered, though she wasn't cold. "I—I realize it is late."

"Tell me what happened," he demanded, settling down beside her on the settee. He tucked the blankets about her, wrapping her tighter, and Claire wanted to fly into his arms. It wasn't rational. She scarce knew this man, but somehow, she felt safer in his presence.

"Claire?"

She was suddenly afraid to tell him, lest he think she had been abused. "Someone…attacked me," she said, though she dared not admit where. Never in her worst nightmare had she imagined someone would violate her in her most private space. She shivered again.

He gently placed a hand at her waist. It lent her strength and courage. "Where?"

"In my home." She looked away.

Ian felt as though someone had punched him in the gut.

He examined her naked, wiggling toes and her state of dishabille, and understood what she was reluctant to say. Fury ripped through him.

"Claire," he began, forcing himself to speak calmly. "Did he harm you?"

She shook her head and played with the ring on her finger. "No."

Ian released the breath he'd not realized he'd been holding. He reached out and gripped her chin, lifting her face, needing to look into her beautiful eyes. "Are you certain?"

She nodded, wearing the same vulnerable expression she'd had in the carriage the first day they'd met…and then again on High Street, when he'd rescued her purse from the raging dog. His suspicions had been validated; she was deep in the suds, and every fiber of his being wanted to come to her aid. His own troubles were entirely forgotten as he peered into her eyes. She was but a tiny kitten hiding behind a lioness's facade.

"Claire, I can't help you if you won't tell me what happened."

She blinked and he yearned to reach out and draw her into his arms, but he didn't dare. The feel of her would unman him.

He was deplorable, because here she was, completely distressed, and he wanted nothing more than to press his tongue between her lips. He'd spent too many hours imagining the taste of her.

He willed his thoughts away from her half-dressed body—even disheveled, she was a tempting armful—but his gaze betrayed him, sliding to her bare feet.

Devil hang him, because despite his best intentions, his governor had risen.

She seemed entirely unaware that she was sitting next to a hound.

"He stole into my house while I slept," she said finally.

Ian gritted his teeth. "Who?" A jealous lover?

She shrugged, her brows drawing together. "A man."

"Did you know him?"

Claire shook her head. "Please, will you release my chin?" she asked, without temper. "You're grasping it too tightly."

Ian dropped his hand at once, chagrined to have allowed his anger to manifest itself in such a rude manner. "I'm sorry, yet again."

"It's quite all right," she said, rubbing her chin with a dainty finger. She offered him a consolating smile.

Ian wanted to bend and kiss the small red spot where his fingers had pressed her. He resisted the urge, reminding himself that he had no right to such an intimate gesture.

"I did not know him, though I have seen him before," she disclosed.

"When?"

She tilted her head, her expression more self-assured, and her lips curved. She dared to bait him. "The day you ran me down."

Ian smiled back, amazed she could find her mettle even now. He amended his previous observation: She was a lioness hiding behind a kitten's facade. "You mean, rather, that day when you weren't watching where you were going?"

She laughed, the sound enchanting.

"Very well. I concede to *some* fault. Yes, that day when I was wasn't watching where I was going." And then she contorted her face. "At any rate, I was coming from the pawnshop…."

"Pawnshop?"

Her cheeks brightened as she proceeded to tell him about her father's debts, her brother's disappearance and his captor's demands.

"That's quite a load to bear alone," Ian remarked, astonished that she had done so for this long.

She shrugged. "I had no choice. They said no bobbies, and I'm quite certain they mean to carry out their threats." She told him about the finger. "And he demanded that I give him the ring," she said, lifting her hand to reveal the winking monstrosity. "But I didn't."

"Obviously," Ian remarked. "You are quite fortunate he didn't snip off your finger and simply take it."

"I wasn't wearing it," she confessed. "I told him I didn't have it. I was afraid he would kill Ben if he no longer had use for him."

Brave, levelheaded chit.

"You did the right thing for Ben's sake," Ian assured her. "Tomorrow we'll make another trek to High Street. Tonight you'll rest here. I'll have a room arranged for you at once. Agreed?"

She nodded, and he felt both relieved and tormented at the thought of having her under the same roof.

"Thank you," she said, and seemed to mean it. Her eyes glistened.

He reached out to take the ring from her finger. "I'll put it somewhere safe.

She snatched her hand away. "If you don't mind, I would rather hold on to it."

"Suit yourself," Ian said.

"But I do thank you for the shelter. I didn't know where else to go. I no longer feel safe…at home."

She hadn't a clue.

She wasn't *safe* here, either—no safer than that bloody ring was on her finger. But he didn't bother to point out the fact.

It was going to be a long damned night.

Chapter Sixteen

That night, Claire tossed and turned.

It was the first time in nearly seven years that she'd slept outside her home, and, after tonight's ordeal, every strange noise left her ill at ease.

She'd requested a room near Merrick's, and was comforted to know he was a mere shout away. Still, she couldn't seem to sleep.

Her mind raced with the night's possible outcomes. Had circumstances played out differently, she might be dead right now, or left violated. The man's breath had been repugnant. And the sound of his voice still echoed in her ears. He'd stolen into her room and he'd held her at knifepoint. He could have forced her to do unspeakable things. He might have taken the ring and then disposed of Ben entirely. She hoped her brother remained unharmed.

As for Merrick, God surely worked in mysterious ways to have put him not once, but no fewer than three times, in her path. She might have taken a cab to and from the pawnshop and never have met him. On High Street, she might have been afraid, or even somewhat more sensible, and decided not to go. On the night of the engagement—she despised galas of that sort—it would have been easy for her to decline Alexandra's invitation. But she hadn't. And now she was sleeping in his home—and betrothed to him, no less!

But not really, she reminded herself.

It was simply a ploy to buy Merrick the time he needed to find himself *another, more suitable bride.*

Even though she told herself his choice of words didn't bother her, they did.

Anyway, what was it that made her so *unsuitable?*

She frowned up at the ceiling. The thought of Merrick wedding someone else left her feeling sullen.

But that didn't make sense, because she couldn't have feelings for a man she hardly knew. And she shouldn't care one whit if he walked down the aisle with another woman.

The sound of footsteps outside her door made her bolt upright in bed. Her heart fluttered. She held her breath, listening.

What if they had come for the ring…here?

They wouldn't dare!

She bounded out of bed and hurried to the door to listen, ready to scream if the knob should turn.

Outside Claire's door, Ian stood, hand poised to knock. But he hesitated.

What more could he do tonight, except ask how she fared? Anyway, she was likely fast asleep by now. In fact, he'd waited hours in hopes that exhaustion would save him from making a fool of himself.

He just wanted to see her.

Frozen in indecision, he stood, considering the circumstances.

Earlier this evening, he had been prepared to disclose himself to his father, but the situation had changed. Now, he was no longer willing to jeopardize his position if he could somehow be of aid to Claire. And neither could he disclose himself to her.

Even if the situation were different, and if Claire didn't smack him for the thoughts he was entertaining, he risked ruining her reputation by visiting her so late without a chaperone.

Still, he was torn. His hand remained in midair.

He couldn't give her what she deserved. He couldn't even give her the money she needed to ransom her brother. Not yet.

Tomorrow would be soon enough to see her, he told himself. He forced himself away from the door, retreating, knowing it was the right thing to do.

Damn it all to bloody hell! Why did he suddenly have to grow a conscience?

The following morning's trek to High Street was a far different venture from Claire's first visit to the much-deteriorated quarter. Merrick ordered the driver to await them as he stepped into the bleary weather to assist her from the carriage.

"Perhaps you should not have ventured here again, *denka,*" Ryo commented as Claire alit from the vehicle.

Merrick gave the man a quelling glance.

"It is said the nail that sticks out is the one that gets hammered down," the man persisted.

"Whatever does he mean?" Claire asked beneath her breath.

"The man fancies himself a poet," Merrick snapped, ushering her away from the carriage. "Pay him no mind."

"Why does he call you *denka?*" Claire asked. "What does it mean?"

Merrick seemed to hesitate before answering, and then replied somewhat curtly, "It's simply a name, nothing more."

Claire frowned, wondering why the question should nettle him.

When they reached Cameron's office, Merrick held the door open and waited until she was inside before stepping in behind her.

His hand brushed her waist and Claire's skin prickled. She ignored the sensation, focusing her attention instead on the man seated behind the desk. She was simply nervous, she told herself.

Cameron stood and came around his desk, his eyes fixed curiously upon Claire, though his hand was extended toward Ian.

"So…what brings His Royal Highness to High Street on this fine day?" Cameron asked, finally looking at Ian.

He bowed to Claire and smiled.

Ian felt his jaw clench, and like a jealous lad, he wanted to step in front of *his woman* so that Cameron's greedy eyes could not violate her.

But she wasn't *his woman,* he reminded himself.

What the devil ailed him?

"Allow me to introduce Lady Claire Wentworth," Ian said. *"My fiancée,"* he added as Claire offered Cameron her hand bearing the tear-shaped sapphire.

Cameron looked up from the enormous jewel. He smiled. "Yes, I understand congratulations are in order."

Ian nodded. "News travels quickly."

"Indeed, it does. Though I'm certain this is not a social call," Cameron added, and turned again to address Claire. "You must excuse my boorish manners, my lady. It seems I have been mingling too long with the common folk. Please, make yourself comfortable."

He gestured toward an old wooden chair that could hardly be described as *comfortable* even under the most generous of circumstances, waited for Claire to seat herself, and then turned to Ian and asked, "How may I be of service to the *Prince of Meridian* and his lovely bride?"

The man was an arrogant bastard, Ian decided once and for all. With luck, his investigative skills were as sharp as his tongue.

Claire peered up at Ian, her green eyes stark and wide. It was the same desperate look that had moved him on that first day in the carriage.

Ian gestured for her to begin. It was her story to tell, after all.

She looked down at her lap. "Yes, well, whatever I say remains in the strictest of confidence, I assume—because it could ruin my family's good name."

Cameron seated himself upon his desk, crossing his arms. "I assure you, my lady, that I do not kiss and tell."

Ian cast the man an irritated glance, but held his tongue, allowing Claire to continue uninterrupted. She told her tale quickly, though she held her aplomb quite well, Ian thought.

"I wouldn't worry overmuch about the finger," Cameron suggested when she was finished. "I'm sure it belongs to someone else, not Ben."

Claire tilted her chin up, looking both strong and vulnerable. "Truly?"

Cameron nodded. "Ghastly as it may seem, there are men who have few qualms about disturbing the dead for monetary gain," he explained. "It happens quite frequently. And it's quite an elementary tactic, if you think about it."

Ian hadn't even considered that possibility. In Scotland, the dead were sacred.

Her green eyes glistened. "How can you be certain?"

"Because, if Ben were to bleed to death or to die of infection, he wouldn't be worth a single copper to them. I can assure you, they won't risk his good health, not as long as he is of use."

Claire breathed a sigh of relief. "Yes, yes, I see." She nodded. "That does make sense."

"How long has he been missing?" Cameron continued to interrogate her.

"Three weeks," Ian answered, though Claire had already opened her mouth to respond.

He was beginning to feel invisible and didn't like it one bit, particularly where Claire was concerned.

He was jealous, he realized.

Cameron eyed Ian with an annoying twinkle of

amusement, as though he sensed Ian's thoughts, and continued speaking to Claire. "Where did you last see him?"

Claire shrugged and her expression gave Ian reason to believe she'd been keeping something from him. She glanced at Ian. "Well, I was concerned that he was being secretive," she relented, after a long moment, "so I followed him one night."

"Where to?"

"White's," she answered, looking a little sheepish over the confession. "That's how I discovered he was gambling."

"That's certainly nothing out of the ordinary for a man of Ben's means," Cameron contended. "Who doesn't attend White's, madam—and not necessarily for the wagers?"

"But that's just it," Claire argued. "We were quite cleaned out. I don't really know how, but we were. Ben said not to worry, that he would take care of it. But then he would disappear at odd hours, and things would go missing along with him."

"I see," Cameron said. "So that was the last time you saw your brother?"

Claire shook her head. This time she kept her focus trained on Cameron. "Once more. I followed him the next evening to a house on George Street."

Raising his brows, Cameron looked at Ian. "That's hardly an area of the city a woman of your caliber should be venturing into," he said.

"So I've been told," she retorted, frowning.

Ian tried not to grin.

Fearless wench.

His grin faded on the heels of his next thought. That same fearlessness would be the death of her if she didn't take care.

"So that's the last time you saw Ben?"

"Yes," she said, "though I do know he returned that evening, because Mrs. Tandy—our housemaid—saw him depart the following morning. He told her that he was going to speak to someone and didn't have time to break his fast, and he never returned."

"It sounds as though someone may have led him to a private game," Cameron said. "And I can assure you, in that part of town, it was likely not a friendly one."

"Is there anything you can do?"

Cameron engaged Claire with a sympathetic smile. "How can I possibly refuse a lovely lady?"

Claire's cheeks stained a deep rose. Her gaze shifted to Ian, and she smiled—not for Cameron, but for him.

For an instant, he forgot where they were. He forgot what they were doing. He forgot to breathe. And he certainly forgot that their engagement was a complete ruse.

For the briefest instant, she was his beautiful, fearless bride.

And then Cameron's voice intruded.

"It just so happens that the first time His Royal Highness inquired about my services—" he cast Ian a meaningful glance "—I was unavailable. Naturally, to make amends, I accepted his father's assignment to locate Prince Merrick when he vanished. As you can imagine, however, my services were no longer necessary once he resurfaced."

Sudden clarity came to Ian. His suspicion was correct. Merrick and Cameron had met previously, he realized.

Cameron's attention returned to Claire, allowing Ian a moment to digest his affirmation.

"Helping his lovely bride is the least I can do after accepting such a handsome sum for doing absolutely nothing," Cameron was saying.

It all made good sense now.

Evidently, like his father, Merrick had attempted to retain Cameron's services, perhaps to investigate the letters their father had written to their mother. When Cameron had refused him, Merrick apparently took the task upon himself. In any case, Cameron would have realized after Ian's initial greeting that Ian hadn't recognized him. From there, it would have been easy enough to deduce that Ian wasn't Merrick.

Still, Cameron had remained silent. Why?

"Thank you," Ian said, pondering the man's possible reasons for holding his tongue. Extortion, perhaps?

Cameron was studying his reaction, he realized. "I'm certain you've been told the family resemblance between you and your father is uncanny," he remarked, smiling slightly.

"Never."

Cameron nodded. "I make it a policy not to intervene in familial affairs."

Ian understood the message.

Whatever Cameron's reservations, he didn't intend to interfere. It seemed Ryo and Cameron were both resolved to stay out of his way, and there was little danger of his father discovering the truth. The man was so mired in his own affairs that he hadn't an ounce of mind to spare.

Ian's only concern now was Merrick. His brother was certain to find his way home eventually. Ian should let Cameron help Claire, and settle his own affairs. But he couldn't walk away. Not yet.

Chapter Seventeen

Cameron wasn't simply an ace investigator, Claire discovered. Like his father before him, he was an accomplished artist as well.

The painting she'd spied in his back room had been done by his father, John Constable. Cameron had decided to put his inherent talents to "somewhat better use." Apparently, his father didn't quite agree. Neither did Cameron's peers, who considered the renderings "pointless and without scientific merit" according to the detective.

Cameron called his creations "composite artistry," and he explained how they helped him to visualize his suspects. It was rather astounding, really. With scarce more than Claire's description of her attacker, he had sketched out a portrait that was incredibly accurate, at least to her best recollection. The drawings made perfect sense. How could one apprehend one's suspect without knowledge of his appearance? Most criminals were hardly of a mind to pose for portraits. Cameron's technique was quite innovative, really, and for the first time in weeks, Claire felt hopeful.

After leaving High Street, she insisted on returning to Grosvenor Square, wanting to make certain that Highbury Hall remained secure and that Jasper and Mrs. Tandy hadn't returned. To her relief, they found the front door locked and the house still vacant, though Merrick insisted on searching inside. Claire was grateful for his service. And, though she scarcely knew him, she felt safer in his presence.

With Merrick leading the way, she peeked first into the salon and then into her father's office. Her heart sank as she ventured into the dining room and noticed the missing box of silverware. Her grandmother's silver was gone.

With a sigh, she moved forward to examine the table where she'd set the box, and ran her fingers over the fresh scratches etched into the table's finish. A butter knife lay on the floor at her feet and she bent to pick it up, peering up at Merrick.

"He stole my silver," she said, afraid she sounded like a sullen child.

"Did he have the box when he entered your room?"

Claire shook her head.

"Would he have had time to retrieve it after?"

Again, Claire shook her head.

It had seemed an eternity at the time, but, in truth, she'd left the house mere minutes after her attacker had fled her bedroom. No, the thief had either returned later, or he'd remained hidden in the house. The latter was most likely, since Jasper and Mrs. Tandy had surely locked the doors.

"Stay here," Merrick commanded.

He left Claire alone to contemplate the lone remaining piece of her family's cherished heirloom. In retrospect, she should have sold the set. As measly as the clerk's offer had been, now she didn't have the silver *or* the money. She set the knife on the table. She didn't have a clue how long she stood staring at the piece before Merrick returned.

"The back door was ajar," he announced.

Claire sighed, feeling far more violated than she could have imagined.

She was vaguely aware that Merrick approached her, arms extended. Without hesitation, she flew into his embrace, tears pricking at her eyes.

She felt so helpless. It was as though she had no control over anything. Even her home was no longer a sanctuary. God's truth, if Merrick hadn't remained by her side, she wouldn't have had the strength to bear any of it.

"Everything will turn out," he promised, hugging her. He kissed her pate and Claire shuddered at the tenderness of the gesture. She peered up, wide-eyed, confused by the sensations his kiss evoked within her body. She felt suddenly breathless.

For the longest instant, their gazes remained locked.

Ian couldn't turn away.

The look in her eyes made his belly ache.

In all his life, he'd never felt so fiercely protective of another human being. He'd taken to heart the needs of his people, but this woman he wanted to hold tight, reassure her that no one would ever harm her.

His body responded at once to her scent—roses and woman—and he was powerless to stop its reaction. He drew her slightly away, not wanting her to feel the little fellow stirring. The last thing he wished was to take advantage of the situation. But the one thing he did want, more than anything, was to taste her sweet mouth.

He was nearly unmanned as she clung to him instead of letting him push her away. He could nearly feel the heat of her lips.

She came to her senses suddenly and pulled away, gasping for breath, her breast rising and falling against his chest, teasing him beyond mercy. He tried to clear the cloud of lust from his brain.

"That was *much* too bold of you!" she declared, giving Ian a censuring look.

He refrained from pointing out that he hadn't been the only willing participant. "I see absolutely no shame in desiring a kiss from my bride," he said without remorse. He knew it was a feeble defense. There was no more hope of his wedding Claire than there was of him reclaiming past years or erasing his parents' lies.

Claire narrowed her eyes. "If only that were the case. But, alas, it is not."

His lips curved at the return of her feistiness.

"We both know it's all a sham."

It was. Ian couldn't deny it. What wasn't a sham was what was going on within his trousers. Not to mention his heart. "You don't expect an apology, do you?"

For the longest moment, she didn't respond. And then she asked, "Do you regret it?"

Her eyes glinted with challenge.

Ian smiled as he shook his head, feeling devilish.

She narrowed her eyes further. Something about her expression gave him the impression that she appreciated his lack of remorse. She sighed. "You're quite the cad," she accused. Her hand brushed his chest in what was likely supposed to be a punishing slap. It fell far short, managing only to tease his nipples through his shirt. Ian ignored the sensation it caused in his trousers.

He shrugged. "That's not the first time I've been told that."

"It wasn't a compliment."

Ian chuckled. He had half a mind to kiss her again. Lord save his rotten soul. He wanted nothing more than to back her up against her fine table, lay her down and taste another pair of even sweeter lips. He wanted to show her what wicked things his tongue could inspire. He wanted to bring her to a climax with his tongue buried deep between her velvety petals and her silken thighs pressing his cheeks. He wanted to drink in her sweet ambrosia and lap his lips like a satisfied hound after devouring a juicy bone.

"Ahem!" a male voice intruded.

Claire shrieked softly and turned toward the door.

Ian spun about, instinctively thrusting Claire behind him. In one fluid movement, he retrieved the knife he kept at his boot. He shoved it up his sleeve when he spied their gentleman trespasser.

"The front door was ajar," the man said, his tone curt. "Forgive the intrusion."

"Lord Huntington!" Claire exclaimed. "You startled us!"

Claire had not noticed the commoner's weapon that declared Ian an impostor—nor the practiced skill that was the legacy of a thief rather than a pampered prince—but the intruder certainly did. Yet he didn't seem to flinch at seeing the gleam of Ian's knife vanish up his sleeve.

Huntington's glance flicked upward, his eyes full of something like disdain as he met Ian's gaze.

"Forgive me," he said without feeling. "I came as soon as I heard. Thank God you were not harmed, Claire. I should have taken your concerns more to heart." He opened out his arms for a fatherly embrace.

But instead of going to him, Claire retreated a bit. "Thank you, my lord. I'm perfectly fine."

Ian watched the exchange with interest, wondering who this man was that he would assume such familiarity with Claire. The hairs at the back of his nape bristled.

"Lord Huntington," Claire said, her hand fluttering to her throat to hide the flush that was swiftly spreading to her face. "I would like to introduce you to His Royal Highness, the Crown Prince of Meridian."

Ian noticed that Huntington's eyes narrowed as he spied the ring on Claire's finger.

Claire turned to Ian. "Lord Huntington is a longstanding acquaintance of my family's. His daughter Alexandra has been my closest companion since I was but a child."

Despite his first impression of the man, Ian extended his hand in greeting.

Huntington hesitated only an instant before accepting it. "We met briefly at your celebration," he asserted.

Ian nodded once, still assessing the man. He didn't remember him.

But then, he remembered few faces from that evening, except for Claire's.

"I've come to offer you shelter, Claire," Huntington announced. And then, assuming her compliance, he added, "Alexandra is waiting in the carriage. She'll be pleased to see you."

"But, I ..." Claire looked up at Ian and seemed to be begging him with her eyes.

What did she have to fear from this man? What had Huntington done to put her so ill at ease?

Maybe she just didn't wish to leave Ian?

He pushed the notion out of his head, unwilling to entertain the possibility.

She was using him, as he was using her. It was a mutually agreed upon arrangement, and it was pointless to begin reading anything more into her motives.

"It would be far more appropriate for Claire to remain under my protection," Huntington said. "At least until such time as she takes her vows."

Ian didn't reply and Claire seemed to shrink away from Huntington. In his peripheral vision, Ian watched her retreat behind him.

Huntington didn't approve of the betrothal, he sensed. Though *why* he should disapprove was a mystery—that is, if Claire's best interests were truly his first concern. After all, Huntington couldn't possibly know that Ian was an impostor.

"I can assure you it is what her father would have desired."

Ian briefly considered giving Claire the choice to do as she wished, but his gut said no. Her pallid face and worried expression only validated his decision. She might know this man, but she didn't want to go with him.

"Claire is under *my* protection," he said, realizing it sounded possessive. He didn't give a bloody damn. It was, in fact, exactly how he was feeling at the moment. And he didn't care to analyze why.

Claire sighed at his side. In relief?

Huntington clicked his heels in what Ian surmised was disapproval. The older man turned to Claire. "Is this your preference, my dear?"

"My lord, I *do* appreciate your offer," Claire said.

"I assure you the accommodations are quite proper," Ian told Huntington. "If that is what concerns you."

"It's true!" Claire added. "We are very well chaperoned, my lord."

"So I've noticed," Huntington answered sardonically.

Claire's cheeks stained a deep rose under Huntington's scrutiny. She fidgeted, but held his gaze, even lifting her chin in defiance.

Ian thought she was adorable, as discomfited as she was, and he had to will his smile away.

"Well, then. I doubt your father would have approved, my dear, but I shall respect your wishes. Alexandra will be *quite* disappointed, I assure you."

Ian didn't like the man. There was something distasteful about him.

He was behaving more like a petulant child who hadn't gotten his way than like the concerned father figure he was obviously attempting to portray. "You have no choice but to respect her wishes," Ian told him, not caring that he sounded like an arrogant cock.

The man's face turned florid, but he held his tongue.

The two of them locked eyes. Ian didn't so much as blink. Nor would he have the least hesitation about planting his fist against the man's windpipe.

"Please excuse me," Claire said, brushing past Ian, then Huntington. "I'll go and explain to Alexandra."

When she was gone, Huntington turned to Ian. "I'm quite certain you haven't a clue what you are dealing with," he said.

"And you do?" Ian countered, lifting a brow in challenge.

"I *am* an accomplished marksman, I assure you, and I am quite proficient with just about any weapon you might care to hand me," he answered.

His boast, it seemed to Ian, was more of a warning than a defense.

"And you believe I cannot possibly match your skills? Is that what you're implying?"

Huntington ignored the question.

"I was not raised in London," Ian said truthfully. "You mistake me for a man of your standard."

"I don't care who you are. I am unimpressed with your title and your pitiful little country. I shall thank you to keep Claire safe, or you'll be answering to me."

He clicked his heels, turned and marched away before Ian could respond, leaving Ian to wonder about his interest in Claire. It was evident the man's feelings ran far deeper than that of a familial friend.

Jealousy reared up like a two-headed beast.

It wasn't like him to feel so green.

He was getting far too close to Claire, he realized. And it would behoove him to keep his distance, lest he find himself far more embroiled than he already was.

Chapter Eighteen

The week passed without news and without incident. Claire was both disheartened and relieved. Cameron had yet to uncover news about Ben. And Merrick was nowhere to be found.

In fact, she was beginning to wonder if Merrick had lost interest in her cause entirely, as he fled each morning without breaking his fast and returned far too late for a proper discussion.

She was beginning to feel like an unwanted guest in his home.

Bored, worried and growing more anxious with each passing moment, she paced the gallery, perusing portraits of strangers whose faces all reminded her of Merrick.

She couldn't seem to stop thinking about the afternoon at Highbury Hall—of the way Merrick had kissed her, of the warmth of his lips so near her own.

Nor could she seem to forget the way she had clung to him. Good Lord, it was no wonder that he didn't wish to face her now. He probably thought her a complete wanton.

She stared at the portrait of a woman she assumed was Merrick's mother. The woman appeared young, though her face showed a trace of age—solemn wrinkles about the eyes and mouth. If the Mona Lisa wore a slight smile, this woman wore a slight frown, along with Meridian's crown jewels. Claire recognized the tiara. It was a perfect match for the ring shackled around her own finger.

"My late wife," the king said, coming up behind her.

"Oh! Your Majesty!" Claire started at his abrupt appearance. "Forgive me, I didn't hear you approach."

He stood looking at the portrait without responding.

"She's quite beautiful," Claire remarked uncomfortably.

His Majesty nodded agreement, but said nothing. There was another awkward moment of silence and Claire turned again to regard the painting. "I do believe Merrick has your look," she suggested, thinking it must be a compliment.

Once again, he didn't respond.

"How young was the queen when she passed?" Claire persisted. The king was quite uncongenial, she decided.

"Young," he answered without elaborating, and turned to observe her.

Claire fidgeted under his intense scrutiny. He had his son's uncanny talent for staring at her as though he could read her thoughts. "You must have been terribly sad," she offered, searching for something more meaningful to say. Nothing came to her.

He must think her an absolute ninny.

It wasn't rational, she realized, but his father's rudeness gave her a prick of annoyance toward Merrick.

It was obvious the king didn't approve of her. Though he was polite at mealtimes, he rarely conversed with her. That he was doing so now was a surprise.

Then, again, he wasn't *really* conversing. He was simply staring at her back. He seemed to enjoy making her ill at ease.

Once again, he didn't respond, and she had to look to be certain he hadn't left her standing alone in the hall.

He was just watching her.

Claire tried not to frown as she glanced back at the portrait.

"I am so very sorry for intruding," she felt obliged to say.

She was beginning to regret having accepted Merrick's hospitality. At least with Lexie she could have been herself, and she might have been able to avoid Lord Huntington completely. It wasn't too late to go.

Another uncomfortable moment of silence passed.

"Where is my son?" he asked her.

Claire shook her head. "I don't know." It was the truth. Merrick didn't seem the least inclined to share his itinerary with her.

"Well, we have something in common, it seems, because it appears my son has ceased to confide in me altogether," His Majesty complained.

"Really?" she said, and she tried not to sigh. It wasn't her place to hear this, nor did she wish to intrude. This wasn't her family, nor would it ever be.

"He hasn't spoken to you, has he?"

Claire forced herself to face Merrick's father. "No, Your Majesty," she answered. "In fact, I've barely spoken to him in days."

He nodded, seeming to believe her. "I see." Then, more silence. "Ryosan tells me Cameron is searching for your missing brother? Is this true?"

"Yes, sir," Claire replied.

She was beginning to feel as though it were an inquisition, not simply a chance afternoon conversation.

Merrick and his father were both arrogant, she decided, but at least Merrick was far less starchy. In fact, he was even rather common at times—nothing at all like his father.

Her thoughts returned to their afternoon kiss and her hand flew to her lips as her cheeks warmed.

"In fact, Cameron's father painted that particular portrait," the king revealed. "I've commissioned quite a few from him."

"He's quite gifted," Claire remarked.

"Quite," His Majesty agreed. "Cameron is, as well, though his father seems to feel he has bastardized his gifts. Then, again, Cameron's a bastard himself, so it's rather to be expected." Again, he stared at her, as though prying into her thoughts. "Sons are bound to disappoint, it seems."

Was he baiting her? Why would he tell her these things?

Claire held her tongue.

"So what, exactly, is the ransom?" His Majesty asked, and his tone held the slightest accusation.

Or perhaps her own sense of guilt simply supplied one?

Claire swallowed hard, feeling horribly discomfited.

Did he suspect their ruse? Did he know she had accepted Merrick's proposal for money?

Her voice wavered a bit. "Two hundred and fifty thousand pounds."

"I see," he said, and seemed to consider the sum a moment. His attention fell to the ring. "Don't grow too attached to that," he warned with a single nod. "Marriage is a business arrangement. My son has no interest in petty infatuations, and you would do well to remember that business arrangements can be easily dissolved."

He walked away, leaving Claire to wonder whether he was warning her not to get too attached to the ring, or to Merrick. In either case, it was rude and perhaps even a bit cruel.

She watched him go.

Stupefied by their exchange, she turned to stare blankly at the portrait, wondering if her growing feelings for Merrick were becoming so obvious that his father should feel the need to counsel her.

In any case, His Majesty was a bitter old fool. It was no wonder Merrick was an acerbic bounder.

Ian hadn't felt this much at ease since leaving Glen Abbey. They'd been following a trail that had led them deep into the rookeries, down a filthy alley that reeked of wastes. Surrounded by seedy types, Ian felt more in command of his senses than he'd felt in weeks. The blade he kept at his boot pressed into his leg, comforting him with its presence. It was within easy reach and he knew he could wield it more quickly than most could cock a pistol.

The building's windows were shaded black and the men who disappeared within were not the sort most would wish to face in the broad light of day, much less in the deep of night. But Ian felt the thrill of the chase. He'd like to say he was doing this solely for Claire's sake, but now that he was here, he wasn't so certain. If he didn't think of her—if he pushed her out of his thoughts, as he must—and he must—he still felt alive in the moment.

Cameron, the hound, had stumbled on the perfect vocation. Once Ian settled his affairs at Glen Abbey, he planned to propose a partnership with him. If Ian could put his skills to use along this vein, instead of in his usual thievery, he would find himself both challenged and accomplished at once.

That he wouldn't have Claire was a given. She wasn't the sort to love a man of his stature.

It didn't matter.

Even if she loathed him for his lies, he could live with that fact as long as she was safe and as long as he had helped her save her brother.

And they were close. So close.

The man whose portrait Cameron had drawn under Claire's direction had disappeared into the building they were now keeping under surveillance. They'd followed him from a nearby pub, where Ian and Cameron had overheard the bugger boasting about a payment to come. Now, they needed only to determine what business was done within and how best to get inside.

"Do you think he realizes he was followed?" Cameron asked.

Ian shook his head. "I doubt it. The bastard's too cocksure right now."

"Well, we can't very well just pop into the building and tip our hats at them," Cameron said. "One of us should stay the night and keep watch."

"I'll do it," Ian volunteered.

Cameron tipped him a curious glance. "Won't you be missed?"

By whom, Ian nearly asked. The man still hadn't a clue about Ian's circumstances. He hadn't revealed anything because the time hadn't been right. Miraculously, Merrick had yet to return to London, and Ian couldn't afford to risk exposing himself until this task was finished.

"Don't you have some gala to attend?"

Ian had forgotten. The Duchess of Kent had, indeed, planned another soiree—this one in Claire's honor. Though she still might not approve of Claire, Victoria seemed fond of the attention *The Times* was showering upon her. After Claire's "incident" had reached the papers, the duchess had somehow been assigned as her patroness by default. And suddenly, even the duchess's worst critics had given her a nod for taking such a compassionate stand in defending London's newest darling. The politics of these people was almost unpalatable.

"I'd forgotten," Ian confessed.

"I'll stay," Cameron suggested. "It's what you're paying me for."

Ian nodded, though he wasn't paying a single penny.

"If I didn't know better, I'd think you were avoiding

the girl," Cameron suggested, as he removed a cheroot and flint from his waistcoat pocket.

Ian didn't respond. He stared at the building's facade, wondering how Claire fared in his father's domain. More than anything, he'd like to see her snap at his father like the little fox she was. It would serve his father right. He was no match for Claire's quick wit if Ian still bore wounds.

Saucy, beautiful chit.

"If you're tired of her already," Cameron remarked, lighting his smoke, "I'd be delighted to take her off your hands."

Ian cast the man an irate glance.

"You'll be doing nae such thing!" he snapped, a bit of his brogue coming through in his anger.

Cameron grinned.

Chapter Nineteen

Glen Abbey, Scotland

The manor was in ruins.

Everything had been destroyed in the fire—from the portraits in the gallery to the ledgers that had been abandoned in Fiona's room.

Merrick, the son she had not set eyes on since he had been but an infant, had risked his life to save her, dragging her out through the flames.

The feelings she had experienced in that moment of discovery had completely overwhelmed her.

After the fire, Merrick, Chloe and Fiona had retreated to the hunting cottage, where Merrick had assured her that he'd had no knowledge of those ledgers. It should have been Fiona's first clue that the ledgers remained on the estate; not a single one had been forwarded for Julian's inspection. Edward, their crooked steward, had merely used the books as a tool to control the estate's finances, she had realized only belatedly, and she berated herself for not discovering it sooner.

Sorrow and regret nearly overcame her.

She'd spent most of her sons' lives grieving over the loss of her own father and her estranged son, and feeling sorry for herself over being jilted by Julian. Because of her, both her sons had suffered and Glen Abbey—their ancestral home—was no more. For four hundred and fifty years, her kinsmen had called Glen Abbey Manor their home. The history of her people, childhood memories, the nursery where she'd nursed Ian and where she'd hoped to see her grandsons tucked into the very crib she'd once used as a bairn were all reduced to ashes and rubble.

How could she have been so selfish?

How could Merrick ever forgive her?

And Ian—her sweet boy might never speak to her again, once he learned the truth.

Their father was a heartless bastard to never, even once, have come to face her after the day he'd forced her to choose between their two infant sons. In his stead, he'd sent perfect strangers to depict the precious moments he hadn't had the guts or compassion—or even love enough—to experience for himself. But Fiona knew she was just as much to blame, and now it was time to do what she should have done years ago. It was time to face the truth. Time to face Julian.

He was in London, Merrick had revealed to her. He'd come so that Merrick could choose his bride from among England's finer families and make a marriage of convenience.

Och, but hadn't Julian learned his lessons yet?

Fiona was so pleased that Merrick had fallen in love with a poor sawbones' daughter. He and Chloe were to be wed soon, and Fiona intended to hurry the ceremony lest Julian find a way to spoil it for them. And once Merrick and Chloe had exchanged their vows, she planned to march into London to face Julian and beg Ian's forgiveness.

She wondered how Ian fared.

While Fiona contemplated what she would say to her son and her once-cherished lover, Merrick and Chloe practically waltzed into the room, holding hands, laughing together, oblivious to Fiona's presence in the chair by the hearth.

Fiona smiled, remembering a time when she, too, had been that in love. Oh, to be young again. Someday, she hoped the same for Ian—that he would find himself a sweet girl to care for him and love him. Ian was always risking himself for others. It was high time someone took care of him.

"Mother," Merrick said in surprise. "I didn't see you sitting there." And then, noticing her smile, he commented, "You're looking rather radiant today."

"It pleases me to see you two happy," she said honestly. "Where have you been?"

"For a lovely, lovely walk," Chloe replied. "You should have come," she added in a chiding voice, though without the least bit of ire. "It would do you far more good to get the blood flowing through those legs than to sit there musing over what-ifs or what-could-have-beens!"

Fiona's legs were, in fact, still weak, but it was her

own fault. She'd spent far too much time in that blessed invalid chair without good cause. Her deception had cost her the strength of her limbs. With Chloe's help, however, she was growing stronger and stronger each day. By the time she headed to London, she was determined to stand and face Julian without a single wobble in her step.

"I was *not* 'musing'!" Fiona said, denying the charge, though she had been, in fact. "I was visiting with Constable Tolley—he only just left."

"Really? That's the fourth visit this week," Merrick commented, and Fiona ignored the heat that climbed into her cheeks.

"I do believe he has set his cap for you," Chloe teased.

"Poppycock! Don't even say it. I am entirely too old for an *affaire de coeur!*"

"I don't believe that," Chloe argued.

"So what did the constable want?" Merrick asked.

"Nothing much. He wanted to know how we fared. And he wished to inform me that Edward had not yet been found, though he assured me he has, in fact, fled Glen Abbey."

Chloe perched herself on the settee facing Fiona, crossing her hands and leaning forward to listen. "How can he be so certain?"

"Well, it has been weeks now, Chloe. As you know, this is a small town. No one would shelter that man, considering what he has done, and no one has seen him. No, Constable Tolley feels certain Edward has fled and we have seen the last of him."

"Perhaps he has," Chloe agreed, sounding hopeful.

Fiona peered up at Merrick, who had yet to come into the room and make himself comfortable. He stood watching the two of them from the doorway. "Merrick, dear? What are you thinking?"

"I was wondering if Edward had reason to go to London."

Fiona blinked. "Why ever would he?"

"To seek out Father."

Fiona shook her head. "I can't imagine why he would do such a thing. There was no connection between the two of them, except that Julian assigned Edward the position of steward for Glen Abbey Manor."

Merrick remained silent.

Fiona's brows drew together. "Is there something you know that I ought to?"

Merrick shook his head. "I just can't quite figure out Edward's motives."

Fiona sighed. "Isn't it enough that he's gone?"

Merrick scratched his forehead and shook his head. "I don't know, Mother. Something plagues me, and I just can't place it. It's probably nothing."

"Well, I can assure you Edward would have no reason to face your father," Fiona told him with conviction. "Julian is not one to be trifled with and Edward knows it. To be certain, Julian has nothing to fear of anyone but me—that is, once I am strong enough to face him. No, Edward is long gone—and good riddance to him!"

The Princes's Gallery at Vauxhall Gardens was the destination of the evening. All of London had been invited for the celebration, though the admission fee had been raised to an exorbitant six shillings to keep out the dregs of society.

Fifty thousand lanterns had been lit for the occasion and were now festooned in the foliage. To the lament of young lovers and the relief of some mothers, the dark walks were not quite so dark this evening.

The duchess had spared no expense. And yet, Victoria couldn't seem to spare two minutes to give Claire direction or even to enlighten her about whether Merrick planned to attend. The evening's festivities were as much a farce as the engagement itself—all for show without one ounce of meaning.

Claire forced herself to smile at passersby who tipped their hats and waved. And yet, she was forced to confess that, on some tiny level, she rather liked the fact that London seemed suddenly to adore her—if only because it validated her sense of self-worth in the face of Merrick's father's avid disapproval and Merrick's neglect.

Dressed in a proper, black satin dress that reflected her mood, Claire stood conversing with Alexandra for the first time in more than a week. Her attention, however, was centered on the crowd.

Where was he?

Even though their engagement was a sham, he was an absolute villain to treat her with such complete disregard. In fact, she had already heard apologies for Merrick's absence from no fewer than half-a-dozen guests.

Humph! So much for believing he was "attracted" to her.

She sighed, trying to make sense of Alexandra's prattling.

"Don't you think so, Claire?"

Claire nodded absently, gazing up into the night sky. At least the evening was temperate and the sky was clear. That should please Victoria, as the duchess had planned a midnight fireworks display. Too bad Merrick would miss it.

Well, if he didn't care to suffer her company, he could at least have taken pity and given her news of her brother. For all Claire knew, Ben was already dead and she was standing for naught in the midst of a faux celebration, pretending to be joyous when she felt more like weeping.

Papa, she asked silently, *how could you have left us so destitute?*

She eyed Lord Huntington who seemed distracted for the moment, regaling his present company with tales of his misadventures in India.

"Good Lord, Claire," Alexandra exclaimed. "Don't look so glum. It really doesn't suit you!"

Claire cast Lexie an irritated glance and continued to search the crowd, sipping anxiously at her beverage.

"You shouldn't drink that arrack punch so quickly," Lexie advised her, returning a frown. "You aren't accustomed to it and it's quite strong."

"I don't feel a thing," Claire swore.

Nothing except acute disappointment.

"Cheer up, Claire! Soon you'll carry his name—and his credit," Alexandra said. "Then you can do whatsoever you wish. Just think of all the dresses and shoes you will have!"

Claire took another sip and tried not to roll her eyes. Traditionally made with arrack, dark rum, fresh lime juice and syrup, the punch was, indeed, quite heady. This evening, it happened to be her saving grace.

"At any rate, you can't have expected him to behave differently," Alexandra was saying.

Oh, yes, she certainly had—and not because she had any ill-conceived notion that Merrick might care for her, but because they had an arrangement. Claire bristled.

"You *do* recall the way he treated *me,*" Alexandra seemed obliged to recount. "He was arrogant and quite rude."

Claire couldn't help but remember their own first meeting, when he'd not so subtly impugned her honor and then had insulted her integrity.

He was arrogant and rude.

Still, she would have liked to believe things were different now.

Somehow.

Something like sadness curled up in her belly and settled, heavy as stone.

She was nothing but a fool.

Why should she care? she asked herself. All she truly desired was her brother's safe return. What did she care about Merrick or silly weddings or shoes?

"Lady Claire," someone called out to her.

Starting at the interruption, Claire nearly spilled her punch as she turned to face a young man who appeared no older than sixteen. He was huffing and puffing as though he'd run some distance.

"How rude!" Alexandra declared, no doubt taking offense at the lad's bedraggled appearance more than at his interruption. "Did you not see that we were conversing?" she asked him.

The young man ignored Alexandra. "Here, madam," he said, handing Claire a small, folded parchment that appeared to be some sort of crude invitation. "I was told to give this to you."

"Well, I thought they'd banned his sort tonight," Alexandra remarked, as though the lad were completely deaf.

Really, they hadn't banned anyone at all, simply made admission to the gardens unaffordable for most. Claire cast her longtime friend a withering glance, wondering how she could have borne Lexie's self-important demeanor all these years. If Alexandra hadn't wished to take the chance that some poor devil might speak to her, then she should have declined the invitation to this party. They were in a public venue, after all.

In any case, Ben's ordeal had taught Claire more than she'd ever cared to learn about life. And she scarce had any patience remaining for those who didn't appreciate their blessings. In truth, there wasn't much difference between Lexie and Claire and the young man standing before them, except that the lad probably had far more common sense and a greater appreciation for every breath he took.

In fact, all that was standing between them was a matter of fortune, good or bad.

She thanked the young man, opened her purse, and found and offered him sixpence.

He grinned and tipped his hat. "Thank you, madam!" he exclaimed, then bolted before she could change her mind.

"He looks just like a rag-mannered footpad," Alexandra complained, scrunching her nose.

"He simply looks hungry to me," Claire countered, unfolding the missive.

It read "If you seek news of your brother, meet me at the west end of the quadrangle at 11:30 p.m. Come alone."

"Wait!" she called after the boy. "Who gave this to you?" But he had already vanished into the crowd.

"What does it say?" Alexandra asked, skirting closer to peer over Claire's shoulder.

Claire folded the makeshift invitation. She considered sharing the missive but quickly reconsidered. She might be a fool, but she was desperate to hear something—anything—about Ben. The instructions said to come alone, and it was nearly midnight now. What if they were watching?

The crowd was beginning to gravitate toward the east end of the quadrangle in hopes of gaining a better view of the fireworks display.

"Where are you going?" Alexandra asked.

Claire couldn't gather her thoughts enough to respond. She held her breath, praying that she was doing the right thing as she started toward the west end of the quadrangle.

"Claire!" Alexandra shouted after her.

Chapter Twenty

Trying to calm her stuttering heart, Claire waited anxiously near the northwest colonnade in the quadrangle.

She'd discarded her glass of punch along the way and stood empty-handed, waiting to discover who had summoned her. A few couples wandered past her into the Dark Walk area, but she didn't dare venture further from the crowd.

Ten minutes passed and still no one approached her, though she had the distinct impression she was being watched from afar. With every turn of her head, it seemed a shadow flitted back into the gardens. She told herself it was only the punch. But she was suddenly afraid she'd made a terrible mistake. It was far from secluded here, but with the fireworks about to begin, a scream would be lost in the night.

"Expecting someone?" a familiar voice asked.

Claire spun about to face Merrick.

He raised a familiar brow. "A lover, perhaps?"

She straightened her spine, both relieved by his presence and affronted by his question.

"Hardly!" she retorted. "It's about time you arrived. You may not care one whit about me, sirrah, but it's quite rude to leave me alone to manage *your* affairs. I agreed to *accompany* you when necessary, to buy you time to find someone more suitable, but not to shield you from your duties or be your agent!"

He grinned at her. "You missed me, I see."

Claire bristled. "How can you think such a thing!"

He leaned close and whispered, "Because you're behaving like a wife."

Claire's cheeks heated. "I most certainly am not!"

"You are," he countered, and seized her hand. "Come, let us explore the Dark Walk, my lovely bride."

Despite her pique, Claire's body quivered at his words. She told herself it was only the chilly night air, but even headier than the punch, his compliment had gone directly to her head, dizzying her.

She tried to ignore the shocking sensation of his strong, warm fingers laced through her own. Only her father had ever held her hand. Her brother had simply used her braids to get her where he wanted her to go.

"Where have you been?" she asked, trying to sound calm though bedlam had just erupted in her breast.

"Looking for your brother, of course."

Lamplights and chatter faded behind them, and the night darkened the path that continued before them, greeting them with silence.

"We shouldn't go this way," Claire protested, nipping

at her bottom lip. She had never walked apart with any man, not even in daylight.

"It's perfectly safe."

For whom? she wanted to ask.

She shivered, realizing that while she inexplicably trusted *him,* she didn't quite trust *herself* in his presence. Somehow, Merrick managed to turn her brain into something like mush and her knees to liquid.

Where was her anger when she needed it? All it seemed to take to diminish that shield was a single kind word or compliment. It was pure insanity. She wasn't thinking clearly, and the punch wasn't helping.

She tried to draw him back to no avail. He was stronger than she was. He kept walking, tugging her along.

"We'll miss the fireworks," she said, sounding far too desperate for her own liking.

He turned a very disarming smile her way, challenging her with a wicked glance that made her swallow. "What's the matter, princess?" he asked, winking. "Afraid to be alone with me?"

Claire relented at once, relaxing her grip on his hand. "Of course not!" she lied.

Good Lord, her father had always thought her too proud; now she knew it was true, because she continued walking despite her better judgment.

"Of course not," he mocked her, his smile vanishing. He released her hand. "A little less fearlessness would serve you far better," he reprimanded her.

Claire's brows drew together. "Perhaps," she agreed, turning up her chin. "But a woman must do what a woman must do!"

Without a single glance backward, she quickened her pace to catch up. "Anyway, it's not as though I have anyone else to turn to."

Ian's heart twisted at her honest defense. She'd said it as a matter of fact, without bitterness. He tugged at her hand. "You have me," he said, and meant it.

"For now," she said.

The resignation in her tone gave Ian a pang.

It was true. She didn't have anyone at all, he realized—except her brother, if the bugger wasn't already dead. And what good was the wastrel if he couldn't even keep his own arse out of difficulty? How could he possibly protect Claire? What would she do once Ian was gone? That time was bound to come sooner rather than later.

He decided that once he had settled his own affairs, if she didn't loathe him for his lies, he would take her home to Glen Abbey.

He would marry her in truth.

It was the only way he knew to keep her safe.

And if she didn't wish to wed him, well, he could walk away with a clear conscience, knowing that he had done all that he could.

Anyway, if she said no, it wasn't as though his heart would break. He was only doing it for her, because it was the right thing to do.

This section of the garden was nearly abandoned. Everyone had gathered close to the fireworks tower to await the night's promised display. He pulled Claire aside and turned to face her, trying to determine how best to say what he wished to say.

His tongue grew thick in his mouth.

For a long moment, they stood staring at one other in silence.

"What is it, Merrick?" Her expression suddenly grew fearful. "Is it Ben? Have you found him? Have they harmed him?"

Ian shook his head. "We haven't found Ben yet, though we think we've found your attacker."

Claire sucked in a breath.

Merrick seized her by the arms, holding her gently, wanting her full attention. "Claire, if he realizes how close we are, he may be a danger to you. Promise me you will not wander off alone without—" *me,* he wanted to say "—without someone to protect you."

Her delicate brows slanted. "I promise."

He would beg Ryo to guard her. He didn't need the man's continued presence. Ian was a grown man and was accustomed to fending for himself. By now, Ryo must realize that Ian would never harm his own flesh and blood.

Claire was staring up at him, her beautiful face lit by the moon, her cheeks pale.

How would he ever tell her the truth?

"We should be getting back now," she suggested, her voice trembling.

His breath growing shallow, Ian inched closer. "Are you cold?" he asked her.

She shook her head, her chest rising temptingly between them.

Ian tried desperately to ignore it.

She was giving him that look again, the one that had

so moved him the day they first met. She stood straight and proud, in the stance of a warrior princess; only those green eyes revealed weakness.

A few curls escaped her otherwise perfect coif, flying irreverently in the soft evening breeze, beckoning his fingers to tame them. Ian resisted the urge. Devil rot his soul. Despite the polished appearance, she looked much as she had when she'd lifted herself up from Drury Lane, brushed herself off and reprimanded him for his lack of manners—defiant and noble. She was so beautiful, so unaffected, so unlike other women of his acquaintance. He could just as easily see her romping in the heather with his children as he could see her as mistress of his home.

The thought made his cock stir.

Her black satin dress revealed nothing of the curves he knew existed beneath the crisp fabric. Her décolletage was modest, hiding the pebbling of those buds. His mouth longed to taste her skin, roll those sweet nipples between his teeth.

His body reacted swiftly, sending fire seething through his veins and heat into his loins.

Heaven have mercy, he silently begged.

But he couldn't help himself. He drew her closer, needing to feel the curves of her body.

"Merrick," she murmured. To his dismay, she didn't resist, only whimpered as he drew her against him.

Claire grew dizzy as he pulled her against the hardness of his body, pressing his broad chest into her breasts.

That face was like a guardian angel peering down at her. His blue eyes glittered like crystals.

His lips were so close now that she could scarcely breathe. And then he whispered her name. "Claire," he said, and it sounded like a cry for help.

God forgive her, she knew he was going to kiss her. She knew she should stop him, but she couldn't. She *wanted* him to hold her and chase away the chills and the darkness.

And she wanted something else she couldn't name.

"Claire," he whispered between her parting lips.

Claire swallowed, vaguely aware that her fingers clenched the crisp, white shirt beneath his jacket. How they found their way there she hadn't a clue.

Maybe she wasn't so proper after all, she lamented, as his lips touched hers gently, because her body convulsed in places she dared not even think about.

His tongue slid into her mouth, shocking her with its velvety warmth. She responded instinctively, mimicking his foray between her lips, sparring with him with her own tongue.

He swore and drew her against him, clutching her body close as he ravaged her mouth with a fierceness that both surprised and thrilled her.

Somewhere in the distance, fireworks exploded and people cheered. Or maybe it was just inside her head, because something sensational exploded throughout her body, sending shards of color bursting behind her lids.

A shadow flitted before her eyes, slipping back again into other shadows, but Claire was certain she imagined it in the dreaminess of the moment.

Chapter Twenty-One

"There you are! Confound it, Claire. You had everyone worried!"

Dazed and breathless, Claire turned to face Lord Huntington, her hand going to her lips, though not out of shame. God save her, she didn't even have the presence of mind to feel embarrassed, though her mouth felt bruised and swollen from Merrick's kiss.

"I—I am sorry," she offered.

"Alexandra said you received a strange message and left in a rush. Considering the circumstances, what were we supposed to think?" Lord Huntington continued to rebuke her.

"As you can see, she's perfectly fine," Merrick interjected. "On the other hand, you seem to have a rather annoying habit of turning up at just the wrong moment. Tell me, Huntington—have you nothing better to do with your time than to follow my fiancée about?"

Lord Huntington scowled at the question. "It does

seem someone must chaperone her, since her *prince charming* is hardly a gentleman!"

"You see something amiss with a man wanting a kiss from his bride?" Merrick asked, stepping forward, his stance confrontational, his hand clenched at his side.

"She's not your bride yet," Lord Huntington countered.

Claire might have panicked about the possibility of their coming to blows, but she bristled at Merrick's question, and her anger took precedence.

She'd had just about enough of both men.

Botheration! She might have remained calm if only Merrick hadn't said *that.*

While Lord Huntington might actually have cause to defend her honor, he certainly couldn't know it. And Merrick—well, he had no cause at all to expect a kiss from her. She wasn't his bride! She lifted her skirts so as not to trip in her flight from the garden. She was anxious to escape their presence, but not before giving each a small piece of her mind.

"I am a grown woman," she reminded Lord Huntington with as much aplomb as she could muster. "And *you,* sirrah, are *not* my father."

She turned to Merrick, raising her voice slightly. "And you!" She cast a glance at Lord Huntington and the words caught on the tip of her tongue. She turned back to glare at Merrick. "You!" she repeated in frustration, and spun away, marching toward the quadrangle.

The truth was that she wasn't certain who she was angrier with—Lord Huntington for hounding her, or Merrick for speaking so flippantly about something so precious as a kiss *and* for affecting such a casual attitude toward their situation. More than anything, she was angry at herself for thinking any kiss from Merrick could be precious.

Completely sobered by the exchange, she vowed to keep her distance from Merrick and to guard her heart. This was a business arrangement, after all, not a love affair, even if the man had a disarming smile and a voice that made her heart trip.

He was using her, she reminded herself, and she was using him. It was mutually beneficial, and that was that.

Sucking in a breath and pasting on a false smile, she refused to look back. She couldn't care less if either man followed her. Lord Huntington could twiddle his thumbs and Merrick could go straight to Jericho!

"Not an ounce of steel in that one," Ian commented.

Huntington cast him a baleful glare, but didn't reply. Without another word, the man turned and followed Claire's dust back to the festivities like a lovesick hound.

Bloody bastard.

Something like jealousy curdled in his belly as Ian watched them go. Still, he was in little hurry to join them. Claire would be safe enough with her watchdog nipping at her heels and he wanted to savor the moment. His heart was still hammering and his flesh was still throbbing over the intimacy of their kiss.

She was a termagant for certain.

Who the devil would have thought he'd lose his heart to some hot-blooded city chit who could kiss like a temptress one instant and nip at his arse like a rabid dog the next—and that he would like it, no less.

He wanted her even more than he wanted restitution from his father, he realized. In the end, if he could have Claire, and a little surety for his kinsmen, all would be well.

The hedge rustled almost imperceptibly behind him. Ian spied the movement in his peripheral vision.

"You can come out now," he said to Ryo.

Ryo hesitated only an instant. When he emerged, the little man was smiling with something that could be mistaken for pride, if Ian didn't know better.

"Very good, *denka,*" Ryo said, using that damnable appellation Ian couldn't quite gauge the meaning of. To begin with, he'd called him *denka-sama,* eventually dropping the *sama.* It was a title of sorts, he was nearly certain, though what it meant, he couldn't begin to imagine.

"How did you know I was there?"

"I saw the moon shine off your pate," Ian lied. In fact, he'd only guessed. Who else would be keeping such a close watch over him?

Ryo chuckled.

It was the first time the bugger had shown the least bit of mirth or even cracked a bloody smile. In his own surroundings, Ian hardly knew how to converse without looking for the humor of a situation. And no matter how desperate his men grew, they were always jesting and laughing together.

Ryo gazed upward at the pyrotechnics finale. "The lady's temper is as…expressive as those fireworks, *hai?*"

Now it was Ian's turn to chuckle.

They shared a moment of camaraderie while the last

of the rockets flickered and disappeared into the night sky. It was the first bit of ease he'd had since leaving Glen Abbey. They might have been friends, Ian thought, as he considered the man standing beside him.

Ryo stood staring at the sky, his hands clasped behind his back in a military fashion.

There was so much Ian needed to know, so much he could never ask his father or his mother. Still, he hesitated, reluctant to speak openly about what they both already knew.

Curiosity won over better judgment. "When did you realize you had the wrong passenger?" Ian asked, dropping all pretenses.

"The first night," Ryo replied. "When we stopped at the inn."

"How?

"A simple deduction, *denka.* Your ring finger did not bear the royal crest. *Denka-sama* would never willingly remove it."

"Denka-sama?"

"He is the crown prince. It is his title."

"And *denka?*"

Ryo met his gaze and said, as a matter of fact, "You are your father's son, but not his heir." His attention returned to the night sky.

Ian nodded and asked point-blank, "If it's such a simple deduction, isn't it curious my father hasn't noticed the missing ring?"

"Your father is preoccupied, *denka.*"

Ian couldn't keep the sarcasm from his tone. "That's painfully obvious."

Ryo peered up at him, tugging thoughtfully at his beard. "In my country," he began, responding to the comment with yet another riddle, "it is said that four things come not back—the spoken word, the spent arrow, the past life and the neglected opportunity. Your father is haunted by three of these ghosts."

The canny Asian remained silent while Ian digested the information. Clearly, the letters revealed regret. It was obvious that harsh words lay between his parents. And yet their entire lives had passed without either attempting to make amends. How many opportunities had each let slip by?

"You must take care that you do not follow his path," Ryo added.

In the distance, a pair of lovers strolled their way, spotted them, giggled and veered onto another lane.

Ian thought of Claire and felt a stab of impatience.

He had never been one to waste opportunities. He'd be damned if he'd let anything slide by: not Claire, not the chance to confront his father, not this moment to uncover more truth. With the fireworks over, it wouldn't be long before guests ventured back into the Dark Walk. "Why did you not go back after Merrick when you realized your mistake?" he pressed.

"What makes you think I did not?"

Ian arched a brow. "And still you left him?"

Ryo nodded.

"Why?"

"Life is the wisest teacher, *denka*. My greatest concern was for his welfare and your friends took him well in hand, so I left him to follow his chosen path."

Ian had had little doubt his men would lead Merrick to safety once they recognized his face. "They're good men," he acknowledged. "But that doesn't explain why you didn't reveal me. For all you knew, I may have intended harm. I didn't exactly welcome Merrick with open arms."

Ryo's eyes narrowed. "It is said that when the character of a man is unclear, one need only to look to his friends. I knew."

The question slipped from Ian's tongue. "Who are Merrick's friends?"

Ryo lowered his gaze. "*True* friendship is rare, *denka.* In this way, you are a far richer man than your brother."

Ian felt a keen pang of loss for Merrick—for the friend and brother he might have had. "Tell me, Ryosan. What role do you play in my brother's life that you know him better than does his own father?"

"I am *his* sensei…his teacher."

"And his only friend?"

Ryo's black eyes twinkled. "I believe it's time you made an appearance at your celebration, *denka,* or your *bride* will soon greet you with her own manner of fireworks."

"In other words, the lesson is over, old man?"

Ryo shook his head. "I can only advise you," he countered. "If you do not soon listen to your heart, I'm afraid your lessons will only have begun."

Chapter Twenty-Two

It was nearly three in the morning before the party left Vauxhall Gardens. His father, accompanied by the duchess, led the convoy of carriages returning to Berkeley Square. In the following carriage, Merrick and Claire rode in silence, in much the same mood in which they had ridden together the day of their first meeting, with one notable difference: Claire was coming home with him. That fact kept Ian grinning despite the baleful glances she continued to cast in his direction.

She had yet to forgive him for some imagined slight and they'd spent the remainder of the evening standing side by side, making idle chatter with well-wishers while she tossed verbal daggers at him beneath her breath.

In spite of that fact, Ian was enjoying the sight of her sitting so primly before him. He admired the spitfire in her. Somehow, she filled his moments; when she was near, everything seemed vivid and full. When she was not, he felt a strange void he'd never known had existed before now. He could easily grow accustomed to her presence, he thought. And it would be incredible to see her face every evening before going to sleep and each morning when he awoke.

Och, he was smitten, and he hadn't the first qualm about admitting that simple fact.

She was tired, he could tell by her drooping lids, and he longed to tell her to lay her head upon his lap, so that he could remove her pins and run his fingers through her silky hair.

"What was it like to have a brother?" he asked, trying to make conversation, wanting to know more about her and curious as to what he had missed as a child.

She tilted her head, peering up at him quizzically, brows drawn together. "Why do you ask?"

"I simply wondered."

She crossed her arms, rubbed them, and turned to stare out the window, even though there was nothing to see but darkened houses. "Ben and I are only two years apart," she yielded. "He took care of me. He vexed me. But he was always there for me." She sighed. "I only hope he's well."

"As do I."

She met his gaze, her irritation softening just a bit, her green eyes filled with anguish.

"You don't blame yourself for Ben's circumstances, do you?"

She shrugged. "When my father died and Ben discovered the debt we were in, he was concerned mainly for me. He worried something would happen to him and that we'd not have the means to support me through my old age." She turned again to stare out into the night. "He and Papa used to jest that no man would know how to handle me—even were I not such a solitudinarian and I chanced ever to meet someone."

"A what?"

She shot him an embarrassed look. "I don't really like to be around strangers," she explained.

"You don't strike me as being particularly timid."

"I'm not. I simply despise idle chatter. And I don't like frilly dresses, shoes or politics." She lifted an accusing brow. "Or, for that matter, rude people."

Ian smiled, amused by her mettle. Even as fatigued as she seemed, she had the heart to reprove him. "And what is it you *do* you like, lass?"

"Philosophy," she said, narrowing her eyes. "Science, solitude, and *truth.* And butterflies. Tell me, why do you have such a strange accent? At times, it sounds slightly...Scottish."

Ian considered his answer in light of her revelation and chose not to lie. Instead, he changed the subject. Soon enough, he would reveal the truth. "Why butterflies?" he asked her.

She shrugged again. "Because they are born absolutely hideous and reveal their beauty only after time and to those who linger to see it."

He considered her explanation. The woman was, by far, one of the most beautiful human beings he'd ever encountered, but she seemed to take great pains not to call attention to that fact. Her dress was understated, she wore no face paint and her coif was simple.

"Are you a butterfly, Claire?"

Her head snapped up, her eyes were slightly glazed. "What I am is fagged," she replied tartly, dismissing the question. "If you don't mind, Your Highness, I would rather not share my private thoughts with you. I continue to be grateful for your help but would very much appreciate keeping our arrangement on a professional level." Then she turned again to stare out the bloody window.

Ian was taken aback.

"Certainly," he relented, and sat back to mull over the evening, trying to determine what he had done to anger her. Kisses didn't lie—she must have *some* feeling for him. He must have said something stupid to hurt her, but for the life of him he couldn't think what it could have been.

Ian was already gone the following morning when Claire descended below stairs to break her fast. The scent of sausage and bacon drifted out into the foyer, making her ravenous, despite the fact that she had a small, lingering headache after last night's imbibing. Alexandra had warned her she might experience a little twinge.

In the dining room, His Majesty sat perusing the morning paper. Claire hesitated in the doorway, reluctant to disturb him.

"Good day," the king said, peering up from *The Times.* "Please join me, Claire."

"Thank you," she said, and entered the dining room, whispering good-morning to the attending servant as she chose a seat at the opposite end of the table. She was hungry, certainly, but there were boundaries she didn't wish to cross, and disturbing Merrick's father at his breakfast was one of them.

"Why don't you sit closer," he suggested before the attending servant could pull out her chair. The servant immediately pushed the seat back under the table. Giving her an apologetic look, he barred its use by placing his hand firmly upon the back as though she would tussle him for it. She gave him a puzzled glance and chose a seat closer to His Majesty.

Apparently, His Majesty's every request was law, she thought with some amusement and felt instantly sorry for the child Merrick had been. No wonder he didn't know how to *ask* for anything. He'd had a rotten example. Her own father would never have forced his will upon either of his two children.

"You are, apparently, quite the darling this morning," he said, pushing a section of *The Times* toward her. Something about his expression provoked her.

The headline read: Rags To Riches?

She drew it closer to read.

The article cited rumors about her brother and hinted at possible scandals of financial debt and gambling problems. But, overall, it was a somewhat more positive recounting of Claire's fairy-tale engagement, though she took exception to the reporter's comment that she was not to be blamed for her brother's suspected extracurricular activities. In the same breath he hailed Claire as "London's darling" and called her an English success story. In great detail, the article expounded upon her very proper choice of dress and highlighted the evening's festivities, which were offered through the "boundless generosity" of the Duchess of Kent, with the remainder of the account being a rather boring list of "attendees of consequence."

"I wonder if people believe everything they read," she commented, trying to keep the contempt from her voice. She pushed the paper back gently, so as not to offend him.

"Of course, they do," His Majesty assured her, eyeing her. "Have a biscuit. Those are my favorite."

Before Claire could reach out to take one from the platter before her, the attending servant retrieved one and placed it on her plate.

Claire eyed the biscuit a little warily.

Good Lord, what if they had poisoned it?

It was a ridiculous notion that somehow didn't seem quite so ludicrous as she squirmed under His Majesty's scrutiny.

His Majesty's plate, on the other hand, was filled to brimming with sausage, eggs, bacon and just about everything else that was available.

"I must tell you…I engaged in a bit of rebellion once upon a time," His Majesty began.

"Really?" Claire asked, her attention still centered on the lone biscuit sitting on her plate.

"You understand rebellion," he proposed. "As I hear tell, you have a history of noncomformist behavior."

Claire's brows drew together at his implication. She looked at him, confused by their dialogue and slightly annoyed by his casual assassination of her character. Just because she needed the money and had agreed to this farce didn't mean that she should be forced to suffer such rudeness.

It will be over soon enough, she consoled herself.

Still, she couldn't quite hold her tongue. "With all due respect, sir, I don't think I would describe *reading* as any sort of rebellion. And my dear father, God rest his soul, never had the first objection to my exploring the sciences. In fact, he had very few objections to any of my interests. His only lament was that I wasn't more sociable, like my brother."

He lifted a biscuit from his plate, waving away her objections. "Yes, well, that brings me to another matter entirely, but I digress."

Claire braced herself. She had the sudden sense that she had walked right into the middle of an ambush.

"Let us not mince words," His Majesty proposed. "You must realize that my son only chose you, Claire, because you were the *least* suitable candidate. In fact, we were discussing your lack of merits," he explained, "when Merrick simply decided without a proper discussion. Well, I could hardly object publicly. Though, in the end, my son will do the proper thing, I assure you—as did I. And, naturally, you will only have gained a reputation for gold digging after your brother's antics are made public. I really don't think that's your intent, is it?"

Claire sat, stunned by his frankness.

At least he wasn't being coy like the duchess would have been, smiling to her face and stabbing her in the back the instant she turned about. Her skin was tingly and moist and her stomach felt as though it would sink somewhere beneath her chair.

"What I am proposing, you see, is that *I* give you the funds you require, now, so you can ransom your brother at once. For that payment, what I would require is that you pen my son a letter giving him your deepest regrets. And then you simply go. Leave the ring, of course."

He allowed her a few moments to digest the offer.

Her head began to spin and her heart beat frantically.

Claire swallowed. It was what she most wanted, after all—her brother's safe return. If he gave her the funds now, there would be no more waiting. She could free Ben and put an end to this farce once and for all.

"Naturally, I would also require your complete discretion, as my son should never know."

Claire thought she might be ill. She stared down at her hand on the table, at the enormous ring on her finger.

He was offering her a way out, so why was she hesitating?

And why did she suddenly feel as though she would retch?

"The ransom is two hundred and fifty thousand pounds," she reminded him, thinking that he would surely object.

He straightened in his chair. "I'm willing to provide five hundred thousand—enough to ransom your brother and a little extra to help repay your family's debt."

There was nothing more she could say.

"Yes, of course," she agreed for Ben's sake, feeling instantly ill-used and sickened by the arrangement. Though, God's truth, why she should feel so horrible about accepting Merrick's father's proposal and not Merrick's was beyond her. Both were cut from the same cloth.

"Excellent!" His Majesty exclaimed, sounding more chipper than he ever had before in her presence. "I shall have the funds drawn at once!" He popped the remainder of a biscuit into his mouth, brushing the crumbs off his hands into his plate. "Well, that should conclude our business," he said after he had swallowed.

Just like that, he dismissed her.

"Thank you," Claire said, and tried to rise from her seat without embarrassing herself. Her legs felt weak. Dazed, she turned to go.

"Oh, and Claire…as a courtesy to my son, let me reemphasize that we should handle this affair as discreetly as possible."

"Of course," Claire agreed. He needn't continue to emphasize discretion. What did he suppose she would do? Shout it from the rooftops? She held onto the table for support, unable to look at him.

"And I shall be certain to squelch whatever rumors may arise concerning your brother's activities and your subsequent engagement to my son," he added.

"Thank you," she said again, and walked away before she could disgrace herself by weeping.

Ignoring the prick of tears behind her lids, she hurried away, refusing even to look at the attending servant as she passed him by.

"He's not going to lead us to Ben," Ian said, trying one of the doors and finding it locked. They'd had Claire's attacker cornered, both he and Cameron blocking entrances and exits to the alley, but the man seemed to have realized he was being pursued and had, somehow, eluded them, slipping into one of the alley's back doors. "He knows he's being followed."

"Then we'll just have to beat it out of him," Cameron countered, trying yet another door.

Ian chortled, though Cameron likely wasn't jesting. Actually, Ian would do it, too, if only he were certain it was the same man who had attacked Claire. He would do it simply to make him pay for mistreating the woman Ian loved.

Damn her, by the way.

Why had she turned so sullen last night? Whatever he had said or done to upset her, there must be something he could do to make it up to her.

"You seem distracted," Cameron said.

When wasn't he of late? "Just tired. Last night was enough to curdle one's liver."

"You're just not accustomed to it," Cameron told him, trying another door and finding it unlocked.

Ian's brows shot up as the door clicked open. "Probably," he admitted, and cast Cameron a questioning glance.

From inside, the sound of clinking glasses and drunken voices drifted out to the alley. High-pitched female laughter made both of them wince.

"Sounds like a pub."

"Shall we enter?"

"I could use a shot of cheap whiskey," Ian replied.

"On one condition," Cameron bargained. "I never drink with blokes until I know their names."

Ian chuckled. "Ian," he supplied, "though I'd rather you call me bloody bastard than use my given name just now."

Cameron shook his head. "*I'm* the bloody bastard," he contended. "But will 'whoreson' do?"

Ian grinned.

"Whoreson it is, then," Cameron announced. "Now let's go have that shot of rotgut. Maybe we'll happen upon our little friend while we're at it."

Chapter Twenty-Three

Ian stumbled into the house in Berkeley Square somewhere near midnight, completely soused.

It felt damned good to speak his mind to someone with some bloody common sense. Cameron excluded, these city bastards were nothing like his kith and kin.

He tried not to wake anyone as he made his way upstairs, but he slipped on the bottom step, landing on his face. At once, he checked his pocket to be sure he hadn't damaged his gift for Claire. Finding it intact, he smiled and gently patted his coat. Pulling himself up, he stumbled up the stairwell, cursing himself for drinking so damned much.

The last time he'd come home this foxed he was but a green boy with too many oats to sow. Well, he still had oats to sow, damn it all, but the problem was that he only wanted to sow them in one place.

Och, what was wrong with him? He was a fine braw lad, wasn't he? Why wouldn't Claire want to marry him?

He found her door, intended to knock, but somehow forgot and pushed it open. "Hey hinnie," he said. "Did ye miss me?"

Claire sat upright, crying out, startled by the intrusion. "Merrick?"

"Iss jus me," he reassured her, tripping across a small rug.

"Merrick!" she exclaimed as he stumbled forward onto her bed. "What are you doing? Get up! You can't stay here. This isn't seemly!"

He rolled over onto his back, lying across her bed, grinning. "I came tae gi' ye a wee bitty gift."

"You're jug bitten!" she accused him.

"Nah," he proclaimed, slapping his chest. "I jus hadda wee dram is all." And he pinched his fingers together, holding one eye closed as he tried to show her the amount.

He was more than a trifle disguised, Claire realized.

Botheration! She'd spent most of the day sobbing since speaking to his father. She had been praying, hoping, Merrick would return with good news, so she might tell them *both* to keep their blessed money…so that she might do what her heart urged her to do.

Obviously, Merrick had spent the entire day and night deep in his cups.

She glowered at him. "*Where* have you been?"

"Chasing a verra verra bad man," he explained, and closed his eyes, slapping both hands on his chest.

Her ire faded a bit at his explanation.

Suddenly, he lifted up one hand, and said, "Gad! I hope I didn't kill your present!"

"You brought me a present?" Claire couldn't keep the surprise from her tone.

"Aye, lass."

She didn't really want to care that he'd thought about her, but she did. It pleased her immensely. Curiosity got the best of her. "What did you bring me?"

He grinned a lopsided grin and gingerly opened up his coat pocket to search inside. Spotting what he was looking for, he slid his fingers within to retrieve it. "Look…it's a butterfly!" he exclaimed, holding it up for her inspection.

He seemed proud of his captured prize.

Claire squinted to better see it, and tried hard not to laugh, but she couldn't suppress a smile. She wasn't entirely certain she should tell him the truth, but she couldn't resist. "It's a moth."

He frowned. "Nah, my love, it's a wee butterfly!"

He'd called her *my love.*

It was nothing more than drunken babble, but it tripped her heart nevertheless. She reached out to take the poor insect from his fingers. The moth was still, it's wings turning to powder. She didn't have the heart to tell Merrick it was already deceased. "Thank you," she said and meant it. "It's lovely."

"You are lovely," he whispered.

Despite the chilly night air, warmth spread through her body, creeping up into her cheeks.

He was staring at her, smiling crookedly, looking at her as though his heart were right there in his eyes, and Claire suddenly felt acutely aware of her lack of dress.

She set the dead moth upon the nightstand.

She knew she should ask him to leave, but she really didn't want him to go. Not yet.

"There is so much I want to tell you…but I jus can't …"

"You don't have to say anything at all," Claire assured him.

It wouldn't matter anyway, she lamented. Soon enough, it would all be over. Then he could choose a bride his father would approve of and she and Ben would return to their ordinary lives. The thought devastated her.

Who would have thought she'd grow to love the arrogant knave lying beside her?

They stared at each other.

Moonlight sifted in through the window. Diffused through billowing drapery, it fell across Merrick's face. Lying as he was, his lashes cast long shadows over his magnificent cheeks and his hair shone like spun silver. He was beautiful. She would sorely miss that crooked smile and sharp wit. And she would crave his kisses long after the taste of his mouth and the warmth of his touch had faded from her memory.

"I suffer a ringing in my head that'll not cease to torment me," he blurted.

Claire cocked her head at him. "Are you ill?"

"Aye," he said. "I am, lass. I'm addicted to your mouth…your lips."

Claire's cheeks burned. "What has that to do with the ringing in your head?" she asked, ignoring the tiny thrill his admission gave her. But she couldn't contain her smile.

"Something about cannons and kisses," he muttered.

"I read it in a…book…once. Only now I understand what it means."

She was relieved he understood what it meant, because she didn't comprehend a single word coming out of his mouth. Still, she was glad he'd come to her. They wouldn't have many more opportunities to be alone together. Tonight might be the last time.

"What time is it?" she inquired.

"Do you want me to leave?"

"No," she confessed.

"Very well, then. I'll stay, if you insist." He grinned. "But only if you'll kiss me." He closed his eyes and puckered his lips.

Claire laughed, reaching out to caress his cheek with the back of her hand. "Silly, silly man."

He seemed to be waiting for his kiss, and then his face relaxed. He blew a hearty sigh that ruffled the hair on his brow and she knew at once that he was asleep. She bent forward, touching her mouth to his lips. He didn't stir.

"I love you," she whispered.

He didn't respond.

Tears pricked at her lids. And, for a long moment, she simply stared at his face, trying to imagine how things might have been.

He began to snore.

Claire considered waking him and asking him to leave, realizing that her reputation would be at stake if she were to allow him to remain. But at this moment, she really didn't care. When all was said and done, she didn't think she would ever love anyone again. This feeling had accosted her just when she'd thought her heart was immune.

Adjusting her pillow beside him, she laid her head down and set her hand upon his chest, closing her eyes, feeling safer lying next to him than she'd felt in all her life. When she was old and gray, she would recall this moment and there would be no regrets. She thought of the moth lying at her bedside and smiled a bittersweet smile. She fell asleep with Merrick's heart beating soundly beneath her palm.

Chapter Twenty-Four

Ian awoke to the sound of smooth, even breathing not his own. Claire was lying beside him…as it should be…as he wanted it to be for the rest of his days. He knew her scent without opening his eyes. Roses and woman.

His head ached, but his groin ached more.

Lord, he wanted her.

The blood rushed into his loins as he thought of taking her. His heart began to pound as he thought of burying himself between her sweet thighs.

He opened his eyes.

It was dark.

She was like a chimera curled up beside him on the bed, her beautiful face buried against the pillow, the moonlight lucent against her white gown, revealing everything and nothing at all. As she took each slumbering breath, her breasts teased his arm. His palms ached to cradle the plump little delicacies.

Heaven help him, she should have asked him to leave. Now, he was afraid it was too late.

He was a bloody rotten hound for coming to her so late, as though she were no more than a bit of muslin. But he hadn't been able to help himself. Like a siren's song, her presence under the same roof was a temptation he couldn't resist.

He didn't want to resist her.

He gently pushed the pillow off his shoulder, trying not to disturb her sleep. He considered leaving, but he was powerless to stop himself from bending to touch his lips against her mouth. The taste of her was like manna to his starving soul.

He hardened fully and his trousers grew tight as he watched her sleep. Her face was like that of an angel, her lashes long against pale cheeks. Her hair was free. He'd never seen it undone. Like dark silk, it spread across her breasts and spilled over the white sheets. Enthralled, he reached out and twirled a strand between his fingers, wondering if her mons would be so silky soft.

He wanted to taste her.

All he wanted was to give her pleasure.

As though it had a will of its own, his hand reached out to cup one breast and she moaned at the touch, rising toward it instinctively.

It was more than Ian could bear.

He wasn't strong enough to walk away tonight. And why should he? If she didn't want him to love her, she could ask him to leave and he would go.

Her nipple pebbled beneath his hand and he groaned inwardly, trying not to wake her. Not yet.

He loved her. Her skin, her body, her mouth, her hair...everything about her, including her incredible wit.

"Claire," he whispered, knowing he shouldn't touch her without permission, but afraid she would ask him to leave.

She stirred, murmuring. The sound made him throb.

"Claire …"

Claire awoke to the shocking weight of a hand on her breast. He squeezed softly, sending lightning currents throughout her body, stirring something wicked deep inside her. His touch made her body convulse in places she'd never known existed. Her breath quickened and she swallowed, afraid to protest lest he go, afraid not to protest lest he think her a wanton.

"Claire," he whispered again.

Her heart tripped, but she ignored him, not wanting him to realize she was awake.

His hand paused over her pounding heart, as though to measure its beat. And then again his hand squeezed her. Claire arched into his touch, desperate for something she couldn't name.

Without warning, his hand fluttered down her belly, toward her private place, and lower, to the hem of her night rail. He lifted her gown slowly and Claire's heart slammed against her ribs.

Stop him, her conscience railed.

Heaven forgive her, she didn't want to.

She squeezed her eyes shut as he lifted her gown, sliding it up her thigh until she was revealed to him. And then he descended upon her, his warm mouth embracing her in a kiss that sent her pulse skittering. She cried out in shock as his tongue slid into her body, dancing within. Her body clenched around his tongue as it swirled deeper. Instinctively, she leaned toward his caresses, her leg shifting to give him better access.

It was wicked…so very wicked…but so very wonderful…

Ian groaned with pleasure as she spread her legs for him, letting him feast on her body.

She was warm, sweet, silky…

He hardened fully and he pressed himself against the bed, trying to imagine what it would feel like to penetrate deep into her body. She was tight around his tongue and he nearly unmanned himself as he thought of sinking into the velvety depths of her.

Her sweet, feminine perfume filled his nostrils and the taste of her dizzied him.

"You are luscious," he told her, devouring her, his heart hammering. "So luscious!" he declared. And then he couldn't speak any longer. He dove into the depths of her, lapping, sucking, tasting. He didn't know how to say it, but he begged her to hear what his heart and his body were trying to tell her…that he cherished her.

Reaching up, he kneaded her breasts while he buried his tongue deeper inside her. She was wet and ready for him. When she didn't resist and, instead, whimpered and arched into him, he pulled himself upward, needing to look into those green eyes.

They were wide and drunk with pleasure.

Claire swallowed.

She was thrilled by the desire on his handsome face, the glint in his blue eyes. His lips shone, wet from his kisses. The sight of it made her shiver painfully.

"If you tell me to go," he swore. "I'll go."

She shook her head and he growled low in his throat, pulling her gown up over her head and stripping it off. "I want to see you, Claire."

Claire couldn't deny him.

She didn't want to deny herself.

Something had begun to ache deep within, something she knew only he could cure.

"Do you understand what this means?"

Claire nodded. She understood that she was giving him something precious and that after tonight, it would be gone and that there would be consequences.

He reached down and touched her where his mouth had caressed her and bent to whisper into her ear. "This is mine. Only mine. Do you understand?"

Again, she nodded, her breath constricted within her breast. She couldn't imagine giving herself to anyone else.

"Say it," he commanded her.

"It's yours," she swore.

He rewarded her by slipping a finger inside her body, swirling it gently, and she whimpered with pleasure, throwing her head back. "Yes," she cried softly. "Oh, Merrick..."

Ian was beside himself with lust. Even the sound of his brother's name on her lips didn't temper his desire.

Damn his head and damn his conscience.

Tomorrow, he would make everything right.

He unbuttoned his shirt and kicked off his boots.

Tonight, he wanted only to bury himself deep inside her, feel her body tighten around his shaft.

He undid his trousers, freeing himself, then pinned her hands above her head, kissing her breasts, her neck, nibbling at her flesh, undulating against her belly, letting her feel his arousal against her bare skin. He wanted her to fully comprehend what it was he was about to give her. If she wanted him to stop, now was the time to say so.

When she didn't protest, he shed his trousers and positioned himself lower, seeking entrance to her body. His shaft glistened with the evidence of his own desire. She lifted her hips, inviting him in and he groaned, shifting upward and thrusting into her.

She cried out and he stilled, shuddering, his brain fogged with pleasure. Ignoring his own body's demand to stroke himself between her sweet petals, he kissed her lips, her chin, her eyes, her throat, until he was certain her pain had eased.

Claire's fingers pulled at the soft curls on his chest, reveling in his bare male flesh.

He had begun to fill her but had stilled, teasing her with the promise of more.

She clung to him, tears slipping from her eyes. And then, just as quickly as the pain had appeared, it vanished, and she needed him deeper still. She curved upward to tempt him, crying out when he answered her plea, plunging inside her.

"Claire," he rasped, and then slid his hands beneath her bottom, holding her, thrusting harder and harder.

It was like nothing Claire had ever experienced before.

It was like nothing she had ever imagined.

He drove inside her again and again, harder and harder, until his body reached its culmination and she could feel it pulse deep inside her.

Crying out, she spread her legs wider, arching into him, needing her own release. Pleasure shattered within her. Her body convulsed. She clung to him, unable to speak, unable to stir. Tears streamed from her eyes. Without a word, he withdrew and rolled onto his back, groaning with satisfaction as he pulled her atop him.

"Tomorrow, we'll make this right," he swore.

Claire's heart squeezed, because tomorrow promised only pain. Still, tonight, she didn't have to think about that. Tonight, she was still lying atop him and she wanted only to make believe the morning would never come.

She laid her head on his chest, while he caressed her back, his hand combing through her hair.

She lay atop him so long that she felt him stir once more, growing hard between her thighs and her heart beat a little faster.

"Can we do that again?" she asked a little timidly.

He chuckled. "Again?" he asked.

Claire lifted herself up and peered down into his eyes, nodding.

"I believe I can accommodate you," he said, grinning. He reached out and lifted her, settling her back down upon his hardened shaft.

"Oh, my!" she cried out.

She hadn't thought she could feel him any deeper.

"Ride me, Claire," he commanded her as he undulated beneath her. Claire answered his rhythm with her own, matching his deliberately slow stroke.

"Oh, my," she sighed, and sat upright, bending backward to accept him more fully, the need for communion making her bold.

"That's my girl," he encouraged, reaching up to stroke her breasts.

"I want to do this again!" she whispered. "And again!"

He laughed and patted her on the bottom, grinning boyishly. "Patience, lass, we haven't even finished this one yet. There will be many, many more opportunities."

He didn't understand. *There would be no more opportunities,* she wanted to tell him. But she closed her eyes and refused to be saddened. She had this moment, and memories of this bittersweet union would carry her through a lifetime.

Chapter Twenty-Five

"You can't keep me here!" Ben shouted, rattling the cell bars in desperation.

He hadn't had a bloody bath in nearly two months and his own stench was beginning to rival the stink of the prison. The pungent scent of urine filled his nostrils and the squeak of rats screeched in his ears until he thought he would go mad.

He'd never realized people could live, and die, in such squalor. Just yesterday, a man was discovered lying dead in his own feces.

"How many times ha' ye been told?" a cellmate called out. "This is Fleet, boy. They can do whatever the hell they want. Now, get some sleep, will ye? Ye're keeping the lot of us awake."

Ben reared back and rammed the cell door with his entire body, screaming out in frustration.

Damn it.

The bloody worst of it was that he didn't even know

how he'd ended here. He'd been in engaged in a card game—and had won, damn it all! After a long losing streak, where he'd nearly lost everything, he'd won. He banged the cell door again. The sound of it reverberated throughout the prison.

"Shaddap, ya bleedin' infant!" another cellmate demanded from somewhere down the dark, rank corridor.

"Take your lumps like a bloo'y man," shouted another. "No one is comin' for ya, can't ye see, ya blockhead?"

Disheartened, weary and hungry despite the slop they'd provided him for the day, Ben collapsed on the floor near the wall. A rat shrieked out of his way, scurrying toward the shelter of his bed. He didn't care if he flattened the little vermin. Every day, it lay in wait, ready to snatch his food when he wasn't looking.

Sweat ran down his brow, mingling with silent tears he refused to acknowledge.

He'd been drugged. There was no other explanation for it.

He tried to recall. Who had attended the game?

The usual cast and crew, Lord Huntington included. Huntington had introduced him to the bunch, warning him that he would be no match for their practiced skills. Huntington himself had lost his money early on and had departed the game to save what was left of his pride and his pocket. Ben had remained because he was winning. He pulled his hair, trying to remember, as though the effort would extract some clue from his fogged brain.

How long had he been confined here now?

Days? Weeks? Months?

He had won, blast it all! He'd won!

Who put him here?

Who?

He smacked his head in frustration, trying to remember.

Claire must be beside herself with worry by now. She likely thought him dead. He'd wanted only to set them both free of their debts. Instead, look what he'd done. He'd made a bloody mess of everything.

The last thing he remembered about that night was taking a victory shot of rotgut whiskey. The next thing he remembered was waking in debtor's prison. No chance to pay back funds, no holding cell, nothing. Just darkness and stink and slop for dinner.

But he had won. Why should he be here at all?

He heard footsteps approaching down the hall, but didn't bother to crawl into his flea-infested bed. Instead, he curled into a ball and buried his head in his arms. Let them harangue him for keeping the other prisoners awake. Let them bring him before someone—anyone who could give him bloody answers.

The footsteps halted at his cell. "Highbury?"

Ben didn't answer. Let them come in after him so he could plant his fist against some bugger's windpipe.

"You have a visitor," the guard announced, and walked away.

Ben raised his head, squinting to see through the filthy darkness. His lids were heavy with exhaustion.

"Tsk-tsk. What a bloody mess you seem to be in," a familiar voice remarked.

Recognizing the voice, Ben bounded to his feet and ran to the cell door. "Thank God, man!" he exclaimed.

"Huntington! I thought I'd rot here with no one the wiser!"

"That's entirely possible."

Ben's brows drew together in confusion. "I don't understand. Why am I here?"

"You lost your arse in a card game."

Ben shook his head. "But I didn't—I won. I won!"

Huntington's expression was smug. "That rather depends on how you look at it, doesn't it?"

Ben swallowed the knot that tightened in his throat. "I don't understand."

Huntington tapped the cell bars. "Well, you're in gaol," he said, pointing out the obvious.

"But you don't understand. There was no formal accusal. I wasn't given the opportunity to pay anything back. I don't owe anything! I simply awoke on a bed of filth, surrounded by men who'd rather foul their trousers than stir the feathers."

Huntington peered into the cell. "You have feathers in there?"

"What the hell do you think?"

"What a relief! One would wonder about the justice system if they provided such plush accommodations to common thieves and debtors. At any rate, I'm certain that, in time, you'll come to feel the same as the rest of these chaps. It's always best not to rouse the dust, lest one find himself eating it."

Ben stepped away from the cell door, appalled. "So, you didn't come to free me?"

Huntington shrugged. "That depends on you," he answered in a voice a little too self-satisfied for Ben's liking.

Understanding came to Ben in a flash. "You put me here."

Huntington was silent, neither denying nor confessing to the charge.

Ben seized the bars, enraged. "Why? Why would you do such a thing?"

"Come now, let us not jump to hasty conclusions. I came to offer you a bargain, Ben."

Ben clenched his teeth. "What sort of bargain?" he asked, enunciating every word.

"I believe I know someone who might be persuaded to release you, if you'll agree to a simple exchange."

"Exchange?"

"Did you know that Claire is to be wed soon?" Huntington asked.

"What the devil you are talking about?"

"She had to raise the funds for your ransom somehow, Ben. Unfortunately, my little plan backfired. She didn't appreciate my offer and went elsewhere. But it doesn't matter. What I want is for you to put an end to the wedding and to convince your stubborn sister to be with me instead."

"You can't marry Claire," Ben argued, confused. "Have you forgotten you're already married, Huntington? I think your wife might take exception to you installing another woman in her bed."

"Lady Huntington is of no consequence. We keep separate residences and, I assure you, my wife could care less who I *install* in my bed. Anyway, you mistake my meaning," Huntington clarified. "I don't intend to *marry* Claire. I just want her available whenever I wish."

"You've got maggots in your head!" Ben suggested, disbelieving his ears. He and Claire had viewed Huntington in much the same light as they had their father. The man had stood by their side and comforted the both of them while they buried the late earl.

"Claire would never agree to such an arrangement," he assured Huntington. "My sister has far more sense than that. She's not a Haymarket ware!"

"Humph! You could have fooled me. You should see the way she clings to that cocksure fiancé of hers. He rams his tongue down her throat every opportunity he gets and Claire simply allows it. She's nothing more than a trollop."

"You're a bloody bastard!" Ben told him with conviction. "You can go straight to hell. I won't help you."

"Then you'll rot here, after all. Guard!" Huntington called without hesitation. "I'm ready to go now."

The door at the end of the corridor opened, letting in the only light Ben had seen in days. Huntington strode toward it.

Ben shouted, cursing him, trying to convince the guard while he had the man's ear that he didn't belong in this place, but the guard simply cackled and slammed the door behind Huntington, casting him once again into filthy darkness.

Claire hadn't thought His Majesty would gather the funds quite so swiftly, but it was obvious he wanted her out of his home.

She had no choice but to comply.

No matter what she and Merrick had shared last

night, circumstances remained the same. His father didn't approve of her, and Merrick had merely been using her to gain more time.

At least he'd never lied to her.

And now, the sham was over—not on Merrick's terms, but on his father's.

Well, it didn't matter. She had the means to free her brother, and she was going to do just that. That she'd lost a piece of herself in the process was simply a consequence of their circumstances.

She stared down at the ring on her finger, admiring it. It was beautiful, but it wasn't intended for her. Someday, another woman would wear it. That woman would bear Merrick's children and share his bed. And Claire would hear about their visits to London and read about their royal affairs in the paper. And she would become a faded memory. People would point to her and whisper about her tattered fairy tale. And she would remember sweet, wicked kisses and a shimmering night when everything had seemed a perfect dream.

Well, she was wide awake now, and there was no point in avoiding the inevitable.

Ryosan had already gathered her belongings and taken them to the carriage. She inspected the room one last time, spying the small, lifeless moth on the nightstand.

Poor creature.

Tears pricked at her lids as she lifted up the delicate gift. Opening her reticule, she placed it inside, determining that it would not die in vain. She would cherish it always, along with the memories it would engender.

Resolved, she went to Merrick's room to leave him

the ring. She placed it in a small velvet pouch and set it down on the perfectly made bed. Beside it, she placed the note she'd written. It read simply, "It's over. I'll tend to my own affairs from here on out. Thank you for everything, but please do not seek me out."

And then she lifted her chin, straightened her spine, turned her back and walked away.

Chapter Twenty-Six

"I believe I've pinned our man down," Cameron said when Ian sauntered into his office. "He's a nighttime guard at Fleet. His buddies tell me he's been known to take a bribe now and again."

Ian contemplated the new information. "Is it possible he could have smuggled Ben inside?"

"Anything is possible," Cameron replied. "And it would explain why no one has seen Ben, and why every trail leads to a bloody dead end. Inside those prison walls, I doubt anyone looks at anyone's face. And you can't bribe or browbeat a man to talk about what he doesn't see."

"At this point, what are the possibilities?"

Cameron lifted both brows. "That he's already dead, of course."

Ian winced. Claire would be devastated.

"But that's not what my gut says," Cameron added at once. "I really don't think they would continue to ransom a dead man."

"They might," Ian argued. "If they were greedy enough."

Cameron shook his head. "Let's think about this. If he's alive, Fleet Prison would make perfect sense, considering Ben's activities of late. I hear tell of gooneys being posted at the more serious games to discourage nonpayment. What if that's what's happened here? What if Ben lost a fortune to someone with connections and they used the opportunity to extract that debt from his family? Fleet would be the perfect place to imprison him. When and if the poor bugger is released, he can't very well point his finger at anyone, now can he? He was in debtor's prison, after all, not locked away in someone's attic. Chances are he'll want to keep it mum."

"So, if he's there, how do we find out?"

Cameron winked at him. "Getting in is never the trouble," he said. "It's getting out that usually poses a problem. I know someone and it should be simple enough to find out. And if he's in there, we'll have him out by nightfall."

"And if he's not?"

Cameron shrugged. "Then we haven't any more leads aside from that bastard prison guard, and we'll be shoving a barking iron up his arse when he leaves his post at daybreak. Either way, we'll be getting the answers we're looking for soon."

Claire wasn't bacon-brained enough to carry the money on her person. Once she was certain she was dealing with the right person—and only then—she would hand over the banknotes. To that end, her only lead was the house on George Street where she'd last spied Ben before he'd disappeared. She was halfway there before she realized she was being followed.

This man, however, wasn't the same one who had attacked her in her home. This man was at least a head taller and much leaner, and appeared to be older. He also wasn't nearly as adept at concealing himself as her attacker had been. She'd first noticed him outside Merrick's home. He'd stood across the street, watching while Ryo packed the carriage.

When the man quickened his pace, she ducked into a dress shop whose doors were about to close.

"Just a moment, please!" she begged the plump female face behind the closing door.

"Oh, my!" the shopkeeper exclaimed, obviously startled. "I was just about to close."

"Please," Claire persisted.

The woman smiled suddenly. "I know you! Come in! Do come in!" she insisted and dragged Claire into her shop by the hand. "At least I feel as though I know you."

"You do?" Confused, and a little unnerved, Claire peered back at the door left ajar.

"I used to sew for Lady Huntington," the woman explained. "What a wonderful surprise to see you, my dear. Tell me, have you come to purchase your wedding gown?"

The question took Claire by surprise. She shook her head.

The good-natured woman tilted her head in obvious disappointment, but said, "Oh, I do understand! It's a grand occasion and I'm certain you'll be going to someplace more elegant, like Courtauld's. Still, you *must* allow me to measure you for a day dress."

"That's really not necessary," Claire assured the woman. "I only wanted to come in and rest a moment."

"But I insist!" the woman said, clapping her hands in glee. "It would be my wedding gift to you. Everyone has been following your story in the paper. I must say, it couldn't have happened to a sweeter girl. And don't you listen to a thing those nincompoops say!"

Despite the queerness of the situation, Claire couldn't suppress a smile. She didn't have the heart to tell the woman the truth. Anyway, just for the moment, while she waited for her pursuer to leave, it felt good to pretend that there might be a wedding after all. "Very well," she relented. "But I must insist on paying."

"Poppycock!" the woman declared. "I can certainly afford a few yards of cloth for a woman of inspiration!"

Claire laughed. She refrained from pointing out that getting married was hardly a grand accomplishment.

"It's about time you stopped wearing mourning," the seamstress said. "It's time to celebrate! Pink or violet?"

"Neither," Claire replied, peering back at the door, grateful for the safe haven. "Have you something nice in green perhaps?"

"Of course!" the woman said, heading toward her back room. "Come and choose your favorite!"

Claire hurried to the door, closing it. And just for good measure, she locked it, then hurried after the seamstress, peering back over her shoulder at the window.

* * *

Clearly, the daytime guard was uneasy about their arrival, but he didn't protest as his superior commanded him to unlock the cell-block door.

The corridor revealed to them was long and dark. The guard entered first, leading the way, lantern in hand. Cameron and Ian followed.

He stopped at the first cell, where a man sat on the dirt floor chewing his toenails. He was an older chap with matted gray hair. "Not him," Ian said with certainty and they moved on to the next cell and the next.

Halfway down the block, they came to a man who lay sleeping on a dirty pallet. His dark hair was matted and his face was black with grime, but his profile bore an uncanny resemblance to Claire.

"This the man?" the guard asked.

"Ben?" Ian called out.

The man on the cot opened his eyes and turned his head to view them. "Tell Huntington I said to go hump a camel. My answer is still no," he said with malice.

"Huntington is behind this?" Cameron asked, raising his brows.

The prisoner sat up. "Don't you know who the hell butters your bread?"

"Open the door," Cameron commanded the guard. "This is the man we're looking for."

The guard complied, casting wary glances over his shoulder at Cameron. In his cell, Ben stood and came forward from the shadows.

"Let me introduce myself," Ian offered, stepping into the cell once the door opened.

Ben had the same stark green eyes as his sister. Ian and Cameron exchanged glances of relief.

"I'm Ian MacEwen," he said, "Your sister's...fiancé."

Ben's expression twisted. "I'll be damned!" he exclaimed, scratching his filthy chin and then flashing perfect teeth. "Then it's true?"

"Well, man, are you just going to stand there gossiping?" Cameron asked him. "Or do you want to get the hell out of here?"

"Get the hell out, of course!" Ben replied without hesitation and brushed past them toward the door, scratching his matted head. "I'm one hungry, dirty bastard," he declared, chortling.

Ian stood back and let the man pass. "Pew!" he said, getting an unexpected whiff. He waved a hand under his nose as he met Cameron's gaze and laughed. "I'll vouch for that, lad. You need a bloody soak."

Chapter Twenty-Seven

After leaving the dress shop, Claire hailed a hansom and returned to Grosvenor Square.

Though her pursuer seemed to have fled, she'd completely lost her nerve and hoped Lord Huntington might agree to accompany her to the house on George Street.

A woman must do what a woman must do—humph! Claire couldn't believe she had once said that. She felt like a complete ninny.

She would have gone to Cameron, instead, but didn't dare face Merrick. She suspected the two had become fast friends, and she just couldn't bear to see him again.

The only thing keeping her strong was the knowledge that Ben needed her. Otherwise, she was afraid she would melt into one giant puddle of tears. Her heart was thoroughly broken. And *how* she'd managed to get it that way was beyond her, because she'd thought she was keeping herself well guarded.

Obviously, she hadn't guarded herself well enough.

But she refused to feel one ounce of guilt over last night. It had been the most incredible night of her life. Let the consequences fall where they may. And if the bittersweet memory haunted her the rest of her days, then it was a price she was willing to pay.

Still, once she freed Ben, she planned to escape to the country until Merrick and his party left London. And she vowed never to read the paper again. She didn't want to hear news of him, didn't want to know when he visited London or when he chose his new bride. The mere thought of him wedding someone else made her stomach turn.

The cab dropped her in front of Alexandra's house. Their longtime servant answered the door. "Shall I summon Lady Alexandra?" he inquired.

"No," Claire said, nibbling her lower lip. "Is Lord Huntington receiving, perchance?"

The servant smiled. "He will be pleased to see you, my lady. Please come in."

Ian couldn't wait to see her.

Ben had insisted upon returning to Highbury Hall to repair himself, and Ian couldn't blame the man. The plan was for Ian to retrieve Claire and to take her home to her brother. Ian was so charged with the news he could barely contain himself. He couldn't wait to witness their reunion, and he considered how best to break the news. Briefly, he considered not telling her and letting her just see Ben for herself. But he decided it would be far too cruel to make her wait. She was so worried about her brother. Every second he kept the knowledge from her was a second too long.

He spied Ryo in the foyer. "Where is Claire?"

Ryo shook his head.

Ian had a sudden, sinking feeling in his gut. "Where is she?" he asked again.

Ryo simply stared at him. He glowered at the man and bolted up the stairs to Claire's room, shoving the door open. It was devoid of her belongings, every trace of her removed.

Where would she go?

Why would she go?

She must have at least left him a note, he reasoned, panic welling in his chest.

He hurried to his own room, finding a note on his bed, along with a small brown velvet pouch. He opened the pouch and turned it upside down, dumping the contents. His heart twisted at what spilled onto the bed.

It was the ring he'd promised her—completely intact, with not a stone missing.

Confusion furrowed his brow. Why would she leave it? They'd had a bloody bargain. Bloody hell! He'd not slept day or night trying to keep it. He lifted the note to read it and his jaw clenched.

He stood staring at the note in disbelief, trying to make sense of the words.

She wouldn't leave, he told himself, not after what they'd shared last night, not with Ben in trouble. Not unless she had been given other means…or an ultimatum.

His mind rattled off questions.

The answer to all of them seemed to be the same.

His father—selfish, rotten bastard! The old man had

wanted Claire gone from the instant she'd arrived in his home. And he had the means to achieve it.

Ian crushed the note and tossed it to the floor, clenching the ring in his fist until the stone cut him.

What if Claire had gone after Ben herself?

What if she had gone to Huntington for help?

His heart hammered against his ribs and his gut wrenched at the possibility.

Furious, he flew downstairs and made his way to his father's office, intending to confront the man once and for all. This was not the way he'd intended to do it. Somehow, after meeting Claire, he had mellowed. He had no longer been angry, simply prepared for the truth. But at this moment, he was more infuriated than he'd ever been in his life.

The old man was seated behind his desk. When Ian walked in, slamming his closed fist upon the door as he passed, the king looked up.

The ring sliced into Ian's palm, but he didn't give a damn. He tossed the obnoxious piece of jewelry on the desk.

"Where is Claire?"

"I believe Ryo said she returned home," his father said pleasantly, with no trace of guilt.

Ian clenched and unclenched his fist at his side. "Why?"

His father shrugged. "How should I know, Merrick? She simply left." He peered down at his papers once more, as though to dismiss Ian.

"Liar!" Ian shouted, smacking his hand down on the papers on the desk. "Why?"

Obviously alarmed by Ian's temper, his father raked

his chair away from the desk. "I don't know," he insisted, clinging to ignorance.

"I don't believe you," Ian said with conviction. "You're a rotten, selfish bugger who doesn't know how to breathe a word of truth!" He lifted his hand, revealing a spot of blood where his palm had been.

"Merrick!" his father said, eyeing the bright red stain. He stood up and took another step backward in self-defense.

Ian glared at him. Every ounce of ire he had pent up came to the forefront.

"Blind auld fool!" Ian said, shaking his head in disgust. "Even now, you haven't the first bloody clue, do you? Do you have any notion how sickened by you I am?"

"How can you speak to me in such an insulting manner?" his father asked, looking wounded by Ian's actions and words. "I raised you better than that!"

Ian leaned over the desk, seething with contempt. It radiated from his skin like fire. If he were a bloody dragon, he'd incinerate the self-serving codger where he stood. "Look into my eyes," he demanded. "Look deep and tell me what you see, auld man!"

His father began to quake. "I see an insolent, ungrateful son who has little respect for his elders."

"Wrong!" Ian said. "You conceived me, aye, but *I* have *no* father!"

"You can't mean that!" the old man argued. "She can't be worth this much to you, Merrick. Can she? She's just a silly woman!"

"My name is *not* Merrick," Ian returned scornfully. "It's Ian, auld fool!"

The look on the old man's face at the revelation was one of absolute horror.

"And, yes," Ian assured him. "Claire is worth a hundred thousand of you. So you'd better pray she went straight home, because if she's come to any harm at all—any at all—I will hold *you* personally responsible!"

His father stepped forward, cocking his head. "You are Ian?"

Ian turned and walked away, afraid that if he remained even one more second in his father's presence, he would strangle the bastard with his bare hands.

"Thank you," Claire said, and meant it. She would be eternally grateful for Lord Huntington's service. Despite the fact that she had treated him coolly, he had, at once, come to her rescue. And he'd been a perfect gentleman, besides.

"It will be my utmost pleasure," he told her. "I'm so glad you've come to your senses, my dear. I'll warrant Meridian is a far cry from England."

"I'm certain," Claire agreed, sighing, trying hard not to think about Merrick at all.

She was anxious to arrive at the house on George Street, eager for answers. She fidgeted in her seat, averting her gaze, uncomfortable with Lord Huntington's regard. "Where is Alexandra this afternoon?" she inquired.

She'd not spoken to Lexie since the evening at Vauxhall, and then, she hadn't been entirely civil. Even though Claire didn't agree with Alexandra's views, they'd known each other far too long to let that stand in the way of their friendship.

Besides, she hadn't many friends to lose.

She wondered if Merrick would miss her even a little, and chided herself for dwelling on something so pointless. It was over, she told herself. She had understood the consequences when she'd agreed to the ruse to begin with. And she had realized the import of her actions last night. She was no longer a virgin, but what did it matter? She had never intended to marry anyway. She didn't want to marry any man. None would ever be as tolerant as her father.

"Gone to the country to visit her mother," Lord Huntington revealed. "I would have thought she'd have told you."

Claire thought it curious their servant hadn't remembered that when she'd come to their door. The man had asked Claire if she was there to see Alexandra and he'd been ready to fetch her.

Claire shrugged. "Well, I'm certain I must have upset her," she admitted. "I shall have to apologize when she returns."

"I'm certain it will be entirely forgotten by then," he reassured. The carriage came to a halt. "We're here!" he announced.

Claire peered out the window, surprised to spy the docks. "I'm afraid the driver has the wrong address," she said, and turned to face Lord Huntington.

"Not at all," Lord Huntington said with a smile that unnerved her. As he reached out to cover her nose and mouth with a putrid cloth,

Claire tried to scream, but the effort only managed to fill her lungs with stinging ether.

Ian knocked on Claire's front door.

When there was no immediate answer, he let himself in, far too on edge to wait for someone to admit him.

Ben was descending the stairwell, clean shaven and smiling, his face startlingly similar to Claire's.

"Where is she?" Ian asked without preamble.

The look on Ben's face was hardly reassuring. "I thought she was with you."

Ian swallowed. His gut turned. "She's not here?"

Ben shook his head. "No."

"Are you certain?"

"I've gone through the entire house."

"Bloody hell!" Ian exclaimed, and covered his face with an arm. Something like pain stung the back of his eyelids. Fear clutched at his chest.

"Ian?" Ben asked. "Where is my sister?"

Ryo entered behind him, answering the question because Ian suddenly couldn't speak. "We suspect she went to pay your ransom."

Ian's voice shook as he faced Ben. "Is there anyplace else she might have gone? Any place at all?"

He and Ben shared a look of utter fear and Ian knew before Ben said it what his answer would be.

"Only Huntington," Ben replied.

Chapter Twenty-Eight

"Why have you brought me here?" Claire asked. "I don't understand!"

Her hands were bound and she was in the windowless brig of what she assumed was a trade vessel, with nothing more in her possession than the dress upon her back.

"You're taking a little vacation abroad," Lord Huntington disclosed.

"You can't do this!" Claire told him, trying to get her hands out of the bindings, but even as she said it, she realized it wasn't true. He could do whatsoever he wished.

Who would stop him?

Who would look for her?

Her stomach roiled at the answer to that question. She'd asked Merrick to leave her be and not to seek her out. Never in her life had she hoped more than she did this instant that someone would completely and disrespectfully disregard her request. He was her only hope.

Huntington seated himself beside her, reaching out to caress her hair. Claire cringed, moving her face away from his touch, unable to bear it.

"You might enjoy it more if you simply tried, Claire," he said gently. And then he shifted to lie beside her.

Claire panicked. Remembering Jasper's instructions, she kicked, aiming low.

He reeled backward, howling, cursing profusely.

Claire watched, stunned by his reaction. Red faced, he finally straightened, and said, "You will come to regret that, Claire!"

He moved to the door.

"What about Ben?" she demanded to know, realizing now that he must have had a hand in Ben's disappearance. "What have you done with my brother?"

"Ben is perfectly fine," he assured her, confirming her suspicions. "A little indisposed, but fine, nevertheless."

"Where is he?"

"Right where he belongs—Fleet Prison."

At his disclosure, Claire felt a mixture of relief and terror. Ben was alive. But she'd heard horror stories about the residents of Fleet. Once behind those walls, all prisoners were treated with equal disdain. It was the dread of all men, commoners and gentlemen alike.

"Why would you put my brother in such a place?"

"I'll untie you when I return," he said, ignoring her question. "I'm afraid this impromptu journey has left me somewhat in a pinch. There is so much to do before we set sail."

"Alexandra will wonder where I've gone!"

"I'll be sure to give her your regards," he said, and

opened the door. "If you're a good girl…and you learn to appreciate my efforts, I'll see to it that Ben is released *unharmed.*"

Claire's eyes shot him with venom. "And if I don't?"

"Then, it's quite the pity, but good men die in prison every day." He left her to mull over that fact, slamming the cabin door and bolting it from outside.

Claire lay back upon the hard bunk, taking measure of her surroundings. It was a very, very small cell, with just a bunk, a blanket and nothing more.

Why would any man want to possess a woman who didn't want him? she wondered.

"Merrick," she whispered. "Where are you?"

Huntington made his way homeward, preparing his story. Alexandra had yet to leave, but he would, indeed, send her packing to the country to visit her ungrateful mother.

Gad—all women were thankless bitches!

Still, he was a little angry with himself. Things had gone a bit awry. He hadn't intended to snatch Claire. He just hadn't been able to resist the opportunity once it had presented itself. Having Ben arrested and put away was one thing. This was another entirely. She wasn't some common bat he could dispose of after dawdling with her. She was someone of consequence, and despite the fact that she had made herself unavailable to most people, she *would* be missed.

And what if Ben were to be freed somehow?

What if his bloody highness came searching for her?

No, he couldn't set her free now, even if wished to.

And he truly didn't. For too long, he'd wanted her. He'd loved the chase, and now that he had her right where he wanted her, he wanted the spoils of victory.

He wouldn't leave for a few days, that's what he would do. He'd keep her on the ship until suspicion was cast conveniently elsewhere. And then, once it was safe to depart, he would take her somewhere far away.

His body hardened at the thought of taking her. He wondered if she would enjoy it a little rough…a choke around the neck.

The first time he'd done *it,* it had been entirely an accident. It was simply a game he'd played with an experienced paramour. He'd squeezed too tightly and forgot to let go. Poor wench. After that, he'd grown quite addicted to the thrill of it.

He peered out the window, spying Merrick and Cameron walking toward his door—along with Ben.

"Drat!" he said, and called to the driver. "Keep going! Don't stop!"

Edward had been following the girl since she'd left Berkeley Square. He'd been in London long enough to know who she was. How ironic that Julian hadn't realized the brothers switched places. He wondered how Merrick and Ian had discovered the truth.

Whatever the story was, he was sure he could use the situation to his advantage. He just didn't know how yet.

Anyway, he couldn't go back to Scotland. Since he had burned down Glen Abbey Manor, the authorities would be searching for him there. It seemed pleading mercy to Julian was his only option, though he knew his half brother well enough to know he must have something of value to offer the king in return, or Julian would never allow him to return to Meridian.

He watched the *gentleman* depart the ship alone, and realized his suspicions had come to fruition.

He knew a desperate man when he spied one; it took one to recognize another.

He waited and once he was certain the girl would not be moved, he returned to Berkeley Square, certain that her whereabouts must be worth something.

Chapter Twenty-Nine

Cameron placed Huntington's house under surveillance, while Ben brought his servants home to be sure someone was about in case Claire returned. Together, he and Ian sought out the prison guard, who swore—after a sound beating—that he hadn't the first clue where Huntington had fled.

If anything should happen to Claire, Ian would never forgive himself.

He had yet to speak to his father after confronting him, and doubted he would ever forgive the stupid bastard. If he hadn't sent Claire away, she wouldn't be in this predicament now.

Lord, he loved her.

And when he saw her again, it was the first thing he intended to tell her...along with the remainder of the truth.

There would be no more lies—*ever.*

His life as Merrick was *done.*

His parents' deceptions were *over.*

* * *

Julian Merrick Welbourne II sat at his desk, letters strewn before him, contemplating past decisions. He stared at a vial of laudanum, not touching it. The drug had assisted him through years of regret, numbing the pain. Now, it offered little relief.

Somehow, he'd made a terrible mess of things…his own life…Fiona's…his sons, not to mention that of the wife he'd never loved.

If Ian was here in London, then Merrick must also know. Surely, he'd lost both of his sons.

Where had things gone so wrong?

"What a tangled web we weave when first we practice to deceive!" he'd once heard a man say.

His entire life, he'd only wanted to do the honorable thing. He'd ceded to his father, marrying Elena, because he'd believed it was true that his duty was first and foremost to Meridian. Not all men were born to follow their hearts; some were born to a higher burden.

Still, he had offered Fiona a life of luxury under his loving care, and she had rebuffed him. And still he had given her the opportunity to raise at least one of their sons, while he'd made the other his heir instead of Elena's progeny. In the end, it hadn't mattered, because Elena had despised him, avoiding his bed as if it harbored the plague, and she hadn't borne him any children at all.

Meanwhile, he had even sent his half brother Edward to keep Fiona safe, knowing Edward would care for his blood as though it were his own. He and Edward might not have been very close, but Edward had spent his entire life shadowing Julian, trying to overcome his baseborn beginnings. Julian had wanted to give him the opportunity to prove himself, to feel worthy. He had entrusted two of his most precious possessions to him. And somehow, in the process he had lost Edward, Fiona, Elena and, now, both his sons.

And further, Ryo had informed him that Claire had gone missing.

Ian would never forgive him. The hatred in his son's eyes was something Julian had never witnessed before. It cut him to the core.

How would he ever make things right?

"While we consider when to begin," Ryo advised him upon entering the office, "it quickly becomes too late."

Ryo knew him too well. Julian considered the loyal servant's counsel. He knew Ryo was right, but the problem was that he didn't know *where* to begin. "I fear it is years too late," he countered.

Ryo shook his head. "It is never too late, *heika,* as long as you have breath in your lungs."

"Why didn't you tell me, Ryo?"

"And if I had told you," the servant asked, answering the question with a question, "what would you have done?"

Julian shrugged.

"A good teacher merely opens the door," Ryo said. "A pupil must enter of his own free will. You did not ask me to detail your journey, *heika,* only to guide it."

"I have failed," Julian lamented.

There was no pity or condemnation evident in Ryo's tone. "Everybody fails, *heika.* The greater question is not whether you have failed, but whether you are content with your failure and what you will do about it."

"You know that I would give anything to make things right," Julian swore.

"Then you may wish to receive a guest."

Julian raised his head, surprised by the announcement at such a late hour.

"Who is it?"

"Merely a stepping stone," Ryo answered in his usual cryptic style.

"Show him in."

Ryo left and returned shortly, standing in the doorway, motioning the guest to emerge from the shadows of the hall.

"Edward?" Julian said with surprise when he saw the man's face—older, but still very similar to his own.

Edward entered the room, his face devoid of expression. "I know where the missing girl is," he said, getting directly to the point of his visit.

Julian shook his head. "How?"

"It doesn't matter. If you want her, I can show you where to find her…for a price."

Julian didn't hesitate. "You can have whatever you want," he agreed, rising from his chair. The last thing he'd intended was to cause the girl harm. If he could save his relationship with at least one of his sons, it was worth any cost. "Take me to her at once," he demanded.

He turned to Ryo and added, "Ryosan, please go tell my son."

Lord Huntington returned soon after leaving her. As promised, he untied Claire's hands and then abandoned her once again, leaving her to wonder about his intent.

A woman must do what a woman must do, she'd once told Merrick. So, what must she do now?

Humph! She wasn't nearly as brave as she would have liked to believe. In fact, she was terrified. And utterly confused. Everything she had ever known to be true had been turned upside down: her quiet life, her family and friends.

Someone unlatched the door.

Huntington entered, urging her to get up, waving a pistol in her face. "Change of plans, my darling," he announced. "We're going someplace safer."

Claire arched a brow, eyeing the pistol. "Safer for whom?"

"Don't argue with me, woman! Get up!"

Claire stood at once, taken aback by his language. He was obviously still quite angry with her for kicking him earlier. No one had ever spoken to her so harshly—not even Merrick's father, who despised her.

"Let's go!" he said, seizing her by the arm and dragging her toward the door. "Behave yourself. You would do well to remember I have your brother at my disposal."

Claire tried to shrug out of his too-firm grip. "I am perfectly capable of following your lead. I need not be steered like cattle!"

He released her. "Don't cause a scene," he warned her, poking her hard with the pistol. "Or you'll surely regret it."

Claire clenched her jaw, trying not to sob. She was

hardly a simpering miss, but it was almost too much to bear.

Huntington led her off the ship and onto the docks where dockhands were busy at their given tasks, despite the fact that night had fallen. They cast curious glances in her direction but didn't stop their laboring. And why should they? A man with a gun was likely a common sight in these parts and they knew better than to meddle in the affairs of others.

Whatever needed to be done to save her, she would have to do herself, she realized.

She checked about, casually slipping out of one shoe, leaving it behind a crate. She scarce broke her stride and Huntington didn't notice. It was growing darker. She considered tossing off the other shoe and fleeing down the alley, but the thought of Ben rotting away in some prison cell made her waver.

"Where are we going?" she asked when they reached his carriage.

"I've already told you," he said. "Someplace safe." He urged her into the vehicle, jabbing the barrel of his gun against her spine. She hoisted herself up, but not before slipping out of the other shoe, leaving it in the gutter.

Again, Huntington didn't notice. He climbed in behind her, pushing her into the seat and slamming the carriage door. He rapped the rooftop, signaling the driver to go.

Chapter Thirty

Ian found one black slipper lying behind a stack of crates. "I think it's Claire's," he said, inspecting it. It was quality leather, just a little worn. The inside of the shoe was still slightly warm. It hadn't been long since she'd shed it.

Ryo had come to inform them that Edward, of all people, had arrived with news of Claire's whereabouts. Whatever the hell his steward was doing in London and how he should know anything about Claire, Ian couldn't figure, but it didn't matter right now. Finding Claire was his only obsession.

Ben seized the shoe. "It's Claire's," he confirmed. "My sister hasn't bought a new pair of slippers in five years. I'd know those scuffs anywhere."

Ian was already searching for its match.

"Here's another shoe!" Cameron shouted.

Both Ben and Ian rushed to where he stood.

The black leather slipper was lying in the gutter.

"They must have traveled by carriage," Cameron deduced. "The shoe is turned toes facing the street, which tells me she must have been heading in this direction and her walk ended right here."

All three men considered the evidence. In one direction, the street ended in a dead end. In the other, it veered toward…

"I think I may know where he's taken her," Ben said, grimacing.

"George Street?" Ian asked.

Ben seemed surprised by his quick answer. "How did you know?"

"Your sister is far too fearless for her own good," Cameron said.

"If he took my baby sister there, he's a dirty, rotten bugger," Ben said. "And I'll kill the man with my bare hands."

"Not if I get to him first," Ian assured him.

Claire recognized the little house on George Street at once. The sight of it gave her a tiny prick of hope.

Both Cameron and Merrick were already aware of its location. She'd given them the address when they'd first hired Cameron to search for Ben. Lord Huntington couldn't know she'd been here before, and she certainly wasn't about to reveal as much now. She jumped down from the carriage, hoping he wouldn't notice her bare feet, and prayed she'd not step on anything too sharp. More than that, she hoped Merrick would discover the clues she had left for him.

"What is this place?" she asked.

He seized her by the arm and pushed her toward the house. "You might consider it a playground, of sorts."

He shoved her through the front door and stepped in behind her. The front room was dark and musty, reminding her somewhat of the scent of the pawnshop—things old and well used.

"It hardly seems a playground of any sort," she muttered beneath her breath.

He pulled her toward the stairs, lit a lamp at the bottom of the stairwell and then ushered her up.

A glance over her shoulder revealed a messy front room with dark shades drawn over the windows.

Upstairs, it was slightly tidier. They passed one room furnished with gaming tables and another with a bed. And yet another bedroom. And another. He pushed her into the last room at the end of the hall and entered behind her, setting the lamp down on a small table.

Claire scrunched her nose as she looked about the horrific room. A huge bed occupied the center. Filled with gadgets and swings and things she couldn't even begin to consider, it reeked of something unhealthy and sour.

Claire shuddered, rubbing her arms in revulsion. The floor was sticky beneath her feet. "Where are we?"

"You might say it's a place where a man might feel free to explore his vices," Lord Huntington explained.

Claire didn't truly comprehend his meaning, until she spotted a small book lying open upon a table. Sitting next to the book was a wooden statuette. Curious, she perused the book and lifted the novelty to inspect it. Her face turned hot. The book was filled with images of men and women in contorted positions. She looked more closely at the statuette in her hand and dropped it, shrieking. After last night, she understood exactly what it was.

She turned to look at Lord Huntington, shocked and repulsed. He was smiling and Claire's heart began to pound. Whatever danger she had thought she was in, she suddenly understood the full extent of it.

"You are debauched!"

"Everyone is a little debauched, Claire. Only I am willing to confess to it." He approached her, bending to lift the wooden figure from the floor. "Don't tell me you haven't been dreaming of Prince Charming inside you?"

Horrified even by the prospect, Claire backed away from him, looking desperately at the door behind him for an escape. Her heart leaped when she saw the face peering into the room from the shadow of the corridor.

It was Merrick—but it wasn't Merrick.

His father came into the room. "Let her go!" he demanded of Huntington.

Claire had never been so thrilled to see another human being in all her life—no matter who it was. If she could have leaped over the bed, she would have flown into his arms in gratitude.

Lord Huntington turned the pistol on Merrick's father. "Well, look who it is."

"Put the gun down," His Majesty commanded.

Claire shook her head, warning him to be wary. "He's depraved," she said, and gasped, spying a stranger in the hall. The stranger drew a pistol out of his jacket.

"Stay where you are," Huntington demanded, panic in his tone, dropping the wooden figure.

Claire hadn't the first clue to whom he was speaking—the stranger or Merrick's father.

Apparently, His Majesty was unaccustomed to commands. He took another step forward and Huntington aimed…

It happened so fast, Claire hadn't even time to scream.

In a hideous moment of deafening silence, she saw the man in the hall dive forward to push Merrick's father onto the bed. The pistol exploded and bright red stained the stranger's shirt as he collapsed atop Merrick's father.

Huntington muttered something unintelligible and stumbled out the door.

Her heart thundering in her ears, Claire stared at the bodies piled atop the bed before her.

"Oh, God!" she cried, and reached out to push the stranger from atop Merrick's father.

His Majesty stirred, peering up at the man lying beside him. Clutching at his shirt, he gave a low, keening cry that tore at Claire's heart.

"Edward!" he sobbed.

But it was too late. Edward opened his mouth and blew out a rattling sigh, then closed his eyes.

For the longest moment, Claire stared down at the pair while His Majesty sobbed over the stranger's lifeless body.

"Who was he?" she asked, trembling.

"My half brother," His Majesty confessed. Silent tears streamed down his face.

Spying a sudden flutter of activity, Claire looked up at the doorway, afraid that Lord Huntington had returned.

The first face she spied was Merrick's. Then came Ben. It was too much to bear. She took a step forward, her heart beating furiously, and cried out as her feet crumpled beneath her.

Then the room went black.

Claire awoke in her own room, surrounded by familiar flowered wallpaper.

For just an instant, she was certain it had all been nothing more than a terrible nightmare—until she spied Merrick seated at her bedside. "Claire," he said softly, smiling. "Welcome back."

Claire was relieved to see him. "Where is Ben?" she asked.

"Your brother is fine. Though you took a rather nasty fall—quite literally," he added, seeming to struggle to keep his smile from widening into an outright grin.

She furrowed her brow. "I don't understand why that should seem so funny."

"Let's just say that you were so excited to see Ben that you slipped over a statuette…one of somewhat unnatural proportions and suggestive design."

Claire realized what he meant. She'd been so happy to see them both that she had run to greet them. Apparently, she'd forgotten about the foul monstrosity lying on the floor. Her cheeks burned hot.

"You're absolutely lovely when you blush," he told her.

Claire blinked, embarrassed. "And Lord Huntington?" she asked, changing the subject.

"Cameron nabbed him before he could get away. He's right where he belongs…in gaol."

Claire sighed in relief, though she was concerned for Alexandra. "I'm sorry about your uncle," she offered.

"Me too," he confessed, and sadness flashed through his blue eyes. "Though, in truth, I had no idea he was my uncle." He shook his head. "So many wasted years."

"Where is my brother?"

Ben rose from his seat and came to sit on the bed beside her. He reached out to take her by the hand, his expression sober now. "I'm sorry for everything I must have put you through, my dearest, Claire."

It was evident Merrick was saddened by what he'd learned of his uncle. Giving him a moment to reflect upon his loss, she turned to address her brother. "All that matters is that you are safe now," she reassured him.

Ben's expression grew impassioned. "I would have rotted in that gaol were it not for you...and Merrick," he continued. "When I think of how foolish I have been..." He shook his head.

Claire squeezed his hand to counter her rebuke. "You certainly will the next time you worry me so."

"Merrick told me everything," Ben said, meeting her gaze directly, his eyes glazed. "I am so thankful you were not harmed. I simply cannot express my gratitude."

Claire's sense of sarcasm returned. "You might not be quite so pleased when you discover everything I've sold."

Ben grimaced. "I had my suspicions the moment I walked in the house, but it doesn't matter, Claire." His voice softened, filled with self-condemnation. "For putting you through such trials, it's the very least I deserve," he lamented. "Upon my honor, there will never be a next time. And I thank you from the bottom of my heart for never forsaking me."

Claire's eyes misted. "You are my only brother," she told him. "You need not thank me at all. You would have done the same for me."

And then, she said, more passionately, "You're *all* I have left."

Ben cracked a smile. "Not quite," he countered, and cast a glance at Merrick, who sat quietly, listening to their discourse. He stood abruptly. "On that note," he offered with a private smile for Merrick. "I believe I shall take my leave and give the two of you a moment of privacy."

Before Claire could protest his sudden departure, her brother was at the door. "Remember that I do have pistols at the ready should you attempt anything untoward," he assured Merrick. "Either that, or I shall hold you to that wedding," he said flippantly, closing the door.

There was a moment of awkward silence once they were alone in the room.

Merrick smiled. "It seems Ben has long admired Huntington's daughter."

Claire held his gaze. "Yes…I know. I believe Alexandra feels the same."

"He should tell her," Merrick advised. "Before he loses her…"

Claire held her breath. She had never expected to see Merrick again. And now that Ben was safe…she was certain he would go. She tried to find the words to say what was in her heart before it was too late. She wanted to tell him how much his help had meant to her, how much *he* meant to her. "Thank you…for everything," she offered lamely. "For saving me."

"You can thank Edward and my father for that. Ben and I came later."

Claire nodded. She had never been one to mince words. "Now that it's over, you're still here. Why?"

They locked gazes.

"Because I love you, Claire."

"Oh, Merrick," she whispered, tears welling in her eyes. Nothing he could have said would have pleased her more.

He screwed up his face and cleared his throat. "About that name," he said. "It's not mine." He thrust out his hand as though to greet her, looking more than a little sheepish. "Let us begin anew. My name is Ian MacEwen. Pleased to meet you, miss."

"Ian?" Claire sat up, confused. "I don't understand."

He sighed, and put his hand down, looking her straight in the eyes. "Merrick is my twin," he said, much more soberly.

After a moment of trying to digest his confession, her brow furrowed. "So you're not a prince?"

He shook his head.

"And you won't be going back to Meridian?"

He shook his head again. "In fact, I've never stepped foot out of Britain in my life…or, rather, not to my best recollection."

"You lied?"

He nodded. "With good cause, but aye."

Claire had never been more relieved to learn she'd been lied to. She wasn't meant to be a princess, and certainly not a queen!

"What do you say, lass? Now that all is said and

done, do you think you could be happy with a poor, ill-tempered Scotsman? Because the *truth* is that I *want* to marry you."

Claire wasn't certain she was hearing him correctly. "Why?"

He smiled. "Well, you see, Claire, I was just a hideous little caterpillar when I met you. And now—well, I'm still just a hideous little caterpillar," he admitted. "But I think I can grow to be that butterfly you so admire…with you in my life."

It was the most beautiful proposal Claire had ever heard—not that she'd heard many, but it was certainly better than her first.

She choked on a giggle.

"I'll never lie to you again!" he swore vehemently, moving to the edge of the bed. "And I'll buy you a thousand books—you can read them any time you like. And I promise you'll never have to wear shoes again if you don't want to." He lifted his brows. "Or even dresses, for that matter."

Claire gasped, covering her mouth, laughing as fat tears slipped down her cheeks.

"What do you say, lass? Will you be my wife?"

Claire nodded and flew into his arms. "Yes!" she exclaimed, throwing her arms around him. "Oh, yes!"

But then she suddenly pushed him away. "What will your father say?"

"I wouldn't worry overmuch about him," Ian reassured her, reaching up to wipe away the tears from her cheeks. "He's on his way to making his own amends. And if I know my mother, she'll keep him far too preoccupied with restitution to worry about either of his wayward sons."

Claire choked on another giggle, joy overwhelming her.

He pushed her gently back down upon the bed. "You, on the other hand, *must* worry about this particular son quite a lot!" And he bent to kiss her on the mouth.

"I love you," he said again.

"I love you," Claire confessed, laughing against his puckering lips. "And, yes, I will marry you...on one condition."

"And what might that be?"

She clutched his shirt, pulling him down atop her. "You must never, never stop kissing me," she demanded.

He chuckled low, the sound heartwarming. "I'd like tae see you try and keep me from it," he warned her, pressing his mouth against her lips once more.

She whispered in his ear. "Not like that..."

He lifted his head and tilted her a curious look, spying the wicked expression on her face, the glimmer in her eyes. "I see," he said, raising his eyebrows and laughing as he dove beneath the sheets.

Epilogue

The sky was uncharacteristically blue, belying the soberness of the day. More appropriately, there should have been another gray London sunrise.

Julian Merrick Welbourne II stood staring at the grave where his half brother lay. The freshly packed soil was rich and black, speckled with upturned clippings of brilliant green—a stark symbol of life and death, and the swiftness and violence with which life could be upturned.

He'd buried Edward without ever having acknowledged their relation.

It seemed pointless to confess it now, when the man was dead and there was no hope for atonement.

He'd like to have shed a tear, at least. But his eyes remained dry for the brother who, despite the fact that he'd been denied kinship, and in spite of his obvious unresolved anger, and despite the fact that time and distance had placed wedges between them, had taken the bullet meant for Julian.

Blood was, indeed, thicker than water.

Somehow, that fact left him feeling hollow as he stood alone in a final, anonymous tribute to a man he'd never really bothered to know. He had sent Edward, his father's "mistake," away. He had also banished Fiona—his "lapse in judgment," as his father had called her—and he'd kept one of their twin sons to raise in a house full of lies. Merrick had never suspected. In the end, the guilt had driven Julian nearly to madness.

He stared at the ground, clearheaded for the first time in months, maybe years.

Edward had been the last of his blood kin except for his sons. And both of them surely loathed him now, after discovering the truth.

After their encounter with Lord Huntington, Ian had left London without ever giving Julian the opportunity to explain himself. Apparently, he felt he knew all he needed to know. And, evidently, there had been little love lost between him and Edward, as well, because Ian hadn't even considered remaining to see the man put into the ground.

And Merrick…if he didn't already despise Julian after facing his true mother for the first time in his life, Ian would surely turn his heart once he returned to Glen Abbey.

Julian removed his hat and tossed it down upon the grave, then walked away, disgusted—more with himself than with anything else.

Someday, his own funeral would not be so different, he feared. Perhaps, perforce, strangers and acquaintances would pay him respects, but his own *family*—the word was somehow alien to him—would be painfully absent.

Would he look down from some higher place and see blank, unfamiliar faces?

Shuddering, he walked out of the cemetery to find Ryo waiting by the carriage. The loyal servant spared Julian the benefit of his wisdom, for the moment, and simply gave a sober nod as he opened the carriage door.

Julian gave the cemetery one last backward glance. Though they spent a great deal of time in London, their family had no official parish here. Members of the Meridian Royal House were traditionally laid to rest on familial soil. But because Edward was, to everyone's best knowledge, nothing more than a servant, Julian had had him interred in Kensal Green's All Souls public cemetery. At least he had a gravestone that bore his name. At this point, that was all Julian could do. He mounted the carriage and closed the door.

The return trip to Berkeley Square was dreary, despite the sunny day. Once home, Julian went to his office, pulled the drapes and withdrew the image of Fiona from his drawer. He set it down upon the desk to contemplate. It was only then that he noticed the package that had been delivered and placed on one corner of his desk. It was a small, wrapped handkerchief with a dirty note attached to it.

He untied the handkerchief and unwrapped it, revealing its contents: Merrick's ring bearing the royal crest of Meridian.

A multitude of emotions assaulted him at once. At the forefront came self-disgust. He'd never, even once, noticed the ring missing from Ian's finger. He'd been so self-involved, and so concerned with Merrick fulfilling his duty to Meridian, that he hadn't paid a single moment of attention to what his son was saying, or, more importantly, what he wasn't saying.

With trembling hands, he lifted up the note. It read "My dearest brother, wear it in good health." And it was signed J. Merrick Welbourne III.

Merrick had disowned himself.

All these years, the fear of loss had led Julian to commit acts that now tormented him. And his son had so easily discarded his position, along with everything that went with it.

Stunned, he stared at the ring, trying to determine what could be so bloody important that a man could walk away from *everything*.

It was almost more than he could bear.

"Ryosan!" he shouted.

As though he'd been waiting just outside the door, Ryo popped his head in at once.

Julian could feel his face heating. "What is this?" he demanded to know, pointing at the filthy handkerchief cradling the royal insignia ring.

Very calmly, Ryo approached the desk. "It appears to be *denka-sama*'s ring," he said, announcing the obvious.

Julian stood. "I *know* what it is!" he returned, smacking his hand upon the desk. "What I want to know is *how* it arrived here!"

Unaffected by his anger, Ryo's deep black eyes twinkled. "It was delivered earlier this morning, before the funeral, by a man who called himself Rusty Broun. The package was addressed to Ian, but since *denka* has gone, I thought it best be given to you."

As the import of the missive fully penetrated, Julian sank back down into his chair.

Both of his sons had abandoned him.

He was completely alone.

Everything that mattered in this world was in Glen Abbey.

"Where did I go so wrong?" he asked aloud.

"Saru mo ki kara ochiru," Ryo said in his native tongue.

The words penetrated, but Julian hadn't a blessed clue what the man was trying to say. Everything with Ryo was a bloody riddle. "Even monkeys fall from trees?" he translated, confused.

"Even experts make mistakes," Ryo enlightened him. "It is what you do with the mistake once you become aware of it that is the true measure of a man's character."

Julian blinked, trying to make sense of the events of the past months…of the emotions assailing him now.

He'd met Ryo during a diplomatic visit to Siam when Merrick was merely five. The Asian had come to serve him after his own master had threatened to have him beheaded for thievery. In fact, it had been a very, very inquisitive little Merrick who'd taken the master's carved ivory dragon's egg. Having hidden the fascinating bauble with the express purpose of spiriting it away to Meridian, Merrick had watched, wide-eyed, as Ryo's master had accused him, then sentenced him in the same breath. Ryo had known the thief's true identity, but he hadn't revealed it. And Merrick had scurried away then, returned at once with the egg in hand, confessed his *crime* before Ryo's master, and begged that Ryo be spared. Though they wouldn't have harmed him, Merrick couldn't have known that, and he'd earned himself a lifetime servant and friend for confessing to a crime that would have resulted in most men's heads being served upon a platter—literally. Saved from his fate, Ryo had pledged to become Merrick's sensei, teaching him the ways of the world. The two had been inseparable ever since.

Julian stared at the ring.

Perhaps he should take a lesson from his son.

Maybe it wasn't too late to confess himself.

It might even earn him his sons' forgiveness.

At worst, well, it could be no worse than the fate laid out before him now: to live the rest of his years alone, without anyone who mattered.

At best, well, he couldn't count on that…but it was worth a try.

"Prepare the carriage," he commanded Ryo.

Ryo's eyes glinted. "Where shall we go, *heika?*"

"To Glen Abbey," Julian announced.

The last time Fiona saw her sons together they were infants in Meridian, twin little golden-haired cherubs sharing the same crib and the same sweet little smile. Now, they were grown men, uncannily similar in appearance—only side-by-side was it possible to see that Ian was slightly larger of build, that Merrick's skin was slightly lighter, Ian's hair a little more sunkissed. But instead of seeming distant and cold toward one another, or even merely cordial, they were like true brothers, she mused, debating philosophies, sharing secrets, teasing one another and laughing heartily. It was as though by wearing the other's shoes, each brother had come to know the other in a way that even years together could not have accomplished.

And now, both had women who adored them, whom they adored in return. It was all a mother could hope for—someone to love her sons as much as she did.

What was more, both Chloe and Claire seemed to be fast friends, and Claire had begun to accompany Chloe on sick visits to the villagers' homes. At the moment, the two were busy planning Chloe's and Merrick's wedding, which was to be held in the little chapel that had once safeguarded the Stone of Scone. She'd left her sons to discuss their renewal plans for Glen Abbey, as they were overseeing the manor's reconstruction together. Once the manor was restored, they intended to begin construction on a new hospital. Chloe was beside herself with joy over the prospect.

Fiona dismissed the distant sound of hammers and saws as she immersed herself in the peace of her rose garden. A butterfly flitted past, then landed gently upon a fat green leaf. For Fiona's part, she was relieved just to have salvaged her roses from the fire. The garden was her tribute to a distant time, when love was hers to cherish and hopes were still as high and strong as Meridian's peaks.

But enough about losses. She was eternally grateful for the second chance to see her sons live out their lives and to know her grandchildren. Chloe was expecting a

Christmas baby. And she was both saddened and relieved to learn that Edward had passed away—she refused to dwell upon that, however. There were no dark clouds on the horizon on this fine, brisk day.

Noticing a hint of bright red amid the green foliage, she hurried toward the promise of a bud. In all her years of trying to coax her tiny, exotic roses to flower, she had merely a handful of successes. This bright morning, with the sun warming her shoulders, the mere possibility of finding a healthy blossom elated her.

She bent to inspect the tiny bud, breathing in the scent of greenery and just a wee hint of perfume. This time, instead of plucking the blossom, she would leave it to grow. Maybe in whisking past buds indoors to coax blooms from the protection of her vases, she had prevented their flourishing. No, this time, she planned to watch the bud stretch wide so that butterflies and bees could dance upon its petals. She would leave it to soak in the dew and to dry in the sun…and maybe next year she would be rewarded with many more blossoms.

No more secrets.

No more fear.

No more sorrow.

It was a new day.

"Fiona?" a distantly familiar voice intruded.

Fiona's stomach twisted. She stood and turned to face the man she had both loved and feared for so many years.

For the longest moment, she could only stand there, staring, her heart hammering.

She had not looked into those pale blue eyes in nearly

twenty-eight years, but she knew them. They still held her enthralled.

Though he was handsome still, his face was just a bit too gaunt. Otherwise, he was largely unchanged, except for a few lines etched about the eyes and mouth.

But she was not the same.

She was a mature woman and she'd lived a lifetime without him. She certainly didn't need him now. She turned away, her tone steady, despite her shaking limbs. "What are you doing here, Julian?"

"Forgive me," he begged her.

An aching moment of silence passed as Fiona refused to look at him.

"I suffer a ringing in my ears that will not cease to torment me," he said, his voice breaking.

It was hardly the first thing she had expected him to say to her.

A sob caught in her throat. Her legs felt weak. Tears pricked at her eyes.

She had once sent him a portrait signed in that fashion, wanting him to know how much she missed him, how terrible the distance was between them.

Despite her resolve to keep her barriers intact, his statement penetrated her defenses. Tears welled in her eyes.

"I've been a fool," he said, his eyes glistening. "A stupid fool. Can you ever forgive me, Fiona?"

For just an instant, she was again that young girl who would have given anything to hear those words from his lips. She had to remind herself that too many years had passed, that she could never so easily dismiss the pain he had brought upon them all.

"Do Merrick and Ian know you are here?" she asked.

"Not yet," he told her. "But you have my word I'll not interfere. I've resolved to accept whatever decisions our sons have made, and I am desperate to prove myself to you, if only you'll allow it."

Fiona shook her head. "I don't know," she answered honestly.

What had he expected her to say? Too many years had passed to simply fly into his arms.

"I have something to give you," he said, producing a package from behind his back.

It looked like an ordinary hatbox—an old one, at that. Did he think he could ply her with presents?

Fiona lifted her chin. "I don't need any gifts from you," she assured him. "I have everything I could possibly desire."

Almost everything, a little voice countered.

"But this was yours to begin with," he persisted. "I am merely returning it."

The only thing Fiona wanted returned was the deed to her ancestral home—at least, what was left of it. She tilted her head.

He took a step forward. "Will you accept it?"

She hesitated a moment, then accepted the package from his outstretched hand, still afraid to hope. Eyeing him suspiciously, she held the box in one hand and opened the lid with the other, revealing a familiar piece of parchment lying atop what seemed to be a collection of letters. Her heart tripped at the sight of it, and she peered up at him, surprised. "The deed to Glen Abbey?" she asked.

He nodded.

"Why now?"

"I want you to be completely free to follow your heart after you read the accompanying letters."

She placed the deed inside the box and lifted one of the letters. It was addressed to her. They were all addressed to her, she realized—so many of them!

"I should have sent them long ago," he lamented. "I never stopped loving you, Fiona."

Confusion stole away her thoughts. "I…I don't know what to say."

"Say nothing. Simply read them," he requested of her. "Afterward, if you feel you wish to see me, I'll be waiting at the inn. If you choose not to, send word and I will go." He turned to leave.

Tears slid down her cheeks. "Julian!" she called to him.

He turned, hope nestled in his blue eyes.

"Stay," she relented. "For dinner," she clarified as she set the box on the ground so she could swipe away her tears.

He smiled, and she could see that it was genuine.

She stretched out her hand. "Come…let me show you my rose garden," she offered.

He reached out to take her hand, and as their fingers entwined, years of pain and anger seemed to slip away.

Together, they took the first steps toward healing and forgiveness.

What Julian didn't reveal was what lay below the letters at the bottom of the hatbox.

Together, for the first time in nearly thirty years, lay the complete set of Meridian's crown jewels—the sapphire and diamond necklace, the tiara and the ring.

Along with Merrick's royal insignia ring, Rusty Broun had also delivered the necklace Julian had once given Fiona as an engagement gift. This time, Julian planned to give her the entire set. As the legend went, only once the entire set was reunited would the King of Meridian find his true love. This time, he wasn't taking any chances.

* * * * *

Set in darkness beyond the ordinary world.
Passionate tales of life and death.
With characters' lives ruled by laws the everyday world can't begin to imagine.

Introducing NOCTURNE, *a spine-tingling new line from Silhouette Books.*

The thrills and chills begin with
UNFORGIVEN by Lindsay McKenna

Plucked from the depths of hell, former military sharpshooter Reno Manchahi was hired by the government to kill a thief, but he had a mission of his own. Descended from a family of shape-shifters, Reno vowed to get the revenge he'd thirsted for all these years. But his mission went awry when his target turned out to be a powerful seductress, Magdalena Calen Hernandez, who risked everything to battle a potent evil. Suddenly, Reno had to transform himself into a true hero and fight the enemy that threatened them all. He had to become a Warrior for the Light….

Turn the page for a sneak preview of
UNFORGIVEN by Lindsay McKenna.
On sale September 26, wherever books are sold.

Chapter 1

One shot...one kill.

The sixteen-pound sledgehammer came down with such fierce power that the granite boulder shattered instantly. A spray of glittering mica exploded into the air and sparkled momentarily around the man who wielded the tool as if it were a weapon. Sweat ran in rivulets down Reno Manchahi's drawn, intense face. Naked from the waist up, the hot July sun beating down on his back, he hefted the sledgehammer skyward once more. Muscles in his thick forearms leaped and biceps bulged. Even his breath was focused on the boulder. In his mind's eye, he pictured Army General Robert Hampton's fleshy, arrogant fifty-year-old features on the rock's surface. Air exploded from between his lips as he brought the avenging hammer down. The boulder pulverized beneath his funneled hatred.

One shot...one kill...

Nostrils flaring, he inhaled the dank, humid heat and drew it deep into his massive lungs. Revenge allowed Reno to endure his imprisonment at a U.S. Navy brig near San Diego, California. Drops of sweat were flung in all directions as the crack of his sledgehammer claimed a third stone victim. Mouth taut, Reno moved to the next boulder.

The other prisoners in the stone yard gave him a wide berth. They always did. They instinctively felt his simmering hatred, the palpable revenge in his cinnamon-colored eyes, was more than skin-deep.

And they whispered he was different.

Reno enjoyed being a loner for good reason. He came from a medicine family of shape-shifters. But even this secret power had not protected him—or his family. His wife, Ilona, and his three-year-old daughter, Sarah, were dead. Murdered by Army General Hampton in their former home on USMC base in Camp Pendleton, California. Bitterness thrummed through Reno as he savagely pushed the toe of his scarred leather boot against several smaller pieces of gray granite that were in his way.

The sun beat down upon Manchahi's naked shoulders, grown dark red over time, shouting his half-Apache heritage. With his straight black hair grazing his thick shoulders, copper skin and broad face with high cheekbones, everyone knew he was Indian. When he'd first arrived at the brig, some of the prisoners taunted him and called him Geronimo. Something strange happened to Reno during his fight with the name-calling prisoners. Leaning down after he'd won the scuffle, he'd snarled into each of their bloodied faces that if they were going to call him anything, they would call him *gan,* which was the Apache word for *devil.*

His attackers had been shocked by the wounds on their faces, the deep claw marks. Reno recalled doubling his fist as they'd attacked him en masse. In that split second, he'd gone into an altered state of consciousness. In times of danger, he transformed into a jaguar. A deep, growling sound had emitted from his throat as he defended himself in the three-against-one fracas. It all happened so fast that he thought he had imagined it. He'd seen his hands morph into a forearm and paw, claws extended. The slashes left on the three men's faces after the fight told him he'd begun to shape-shift. A fist made bruises and swelling; not four perfect, deep claw marks. Stunned and anxious, he hid the knowledge of what else he was from these prisoners. Reno's only defense was to make all the prisoners so damned scared of him and remain a loner.

Alone. Yeah, he was alone, all right. The steel hammer swept downward with hellish ferocity. As the granite groaned in protest, Reno shut his eyes for just a moment. Sweat dripped off his nose and square chin.

Straightening, he wiped his furrowed, wet brow and looked into the pale blue sky. What got his attention was the startling cry of a red-tailed hawk as it flew over the brig yard. Squinting, he watched the bird. Reno could make out the rust-colored tail on the hawk. As a kid growing up on the Apache reservation in Arizona, Reno knew that all animals that appeared before him were messengers.

Brother, what message do you bring me? Reno knew one had to ask in order to receive. Allowing the sledgehammer to drop to his side, he concentrated on the hawk who wheeled in tightening circles above him.

Freedom! the hawk cried in return.

Reno shook his head, his black hair moving against

his broad, thickset shoulders. *Freedom? No way, Brother. No way.* Figuring that he was making up the hawk's shrill message, Reno turned away. Back to his rocks. Back to picturing Hampton's smug face.

Freedom!

Silhouette
Desire

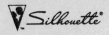